ONLY RIVALS

USA TODAY & WALL STREET JOURNAL BESTSELLING AUTHOR

CHARITY FERRELL

content warning

1

AMELIA

"WHY ARE you sleeping in your laundry room?"

I open my eyes to find my best friend, Ava, staring down at me like I'm a teenager, tardy for school.

Her question is valid, given I live alone in a two-bedroom townhome—both bedrooms fully furnished.

Alone.

That's the part I'm struggling to get past.

I managed to keep my sleeping arrangements a secret for months but should've known it wouldn't last forever.

Sunlight streams through the skylight window, and I yawn while rising. I scoot across the floor, my sleeping bag still wrapped around me, and settle my back against the dryer.

"I fell asleep," I answer around another yawn, stretching my arms.

"You fell asleep?" Ava slowly asks and gestures to the sleeping bag. "You've literally turned this into some frat-house bedroom."

I shut my eyes, remembering the first time I slept in the cramped laundry room. It was three in the morning, and sleep-deprived, I lay down on the *Alexa, Do My Laundry* rug. It worked. I finally slept longer than three hours.

Since that night's success, I've added to my makeshift bedroom—a sleeping bag, two pillows, and even a candle.

"It's comfortable," I say, staring down at the porcelain Spanish tiles and running my finger along the grout before turning my sore neck from side to side.

Porcelain tile is as comfortable as sleeping on an airplane.

"It's comfortable?" she repeats in the same tone as her last question. "Five hundred dollars that your bed is *comfier*."

Comfier? Yes.

Peaceful? No.

In need of a subject change, I ask, "What's up with the surprise visit?"

"I've been calling you for hours."

"I've been sleeping."

"Yes, sleeping with fabric softener and dirty panties." She bends down to grab a pair of black lace panties from the basket of clean clothes and holds them up. "Cute. I never took you as a bondage kind of girl."

I nearly face-plant out of the sleeping bag when I rise to snatch them from her. "Stay away from my panties, you freak."

"Get up then." She snaps her fingers. "I'm taking you to breakfast."

"I don't want breakfast."

"Well, I do, and I'm here. It's only polite for you to feed your guests."

I stay quiet and chew on my lower lip.

"Fine," she groans. "I'll order breakfast, and while we wait, you can explain why you're sleeping in here."

Oh, hell no.

I unzip my sleeping bag and roll out of it.

I'd rather suffer through sixteen breakfasts and have my fingernails removed than tell her I'm sleeping in the laundry room because being in my bed makes my skin crawl. I tried to sleep in every other room—hell, even the bathrooms—but nothing worked. Before resorting to the front porch, the laundry room was my last option. Thankfully, it worked.

It worked because there are no memories of Christopher in the laundry room. I never trusted that man to do laundry. He said separating the colors from the whites was unnecessary since they all got washed anyway.

I grab a clean change of clothes from the basket without a word, and on my way to the master bathroom, I pass my unmade bed. It's been that way since he left me. I sniffle at the faint smell of him. With each passing day, it's weakening, and I dread the day it vanishes completely.

After brushing my hair and teeth, I get dressed and meet Ava in the living room as she's looking through her phone.

She slides her phone into her crossbody bag. "We're going to Shirley's."

"We are going through a drive-through," I correct, grabbing my sneakers and slipping them on.

"When was the last time you sat down somewhere and ate?"

"Gee, I don't know. I must've forgotten to write it in my planner."

"We're going to Shirley's and having a kick-ass breakfast." She catches my hand in hers. "As your bestie, it's my job to help you. Step one is breakfast in a public place."

"We have a problem with step one. I hate public places."

I was the opposite once. No one would've labeled me a homebody. If you wanted to have dinner, see a movie, or go for drinks, I was the friend for you. Now, my stomach churns at the thought of being around any more people than necessary.

"Ah, but public places love your beautiful face, babe."

———

Shirley's Diner has the best breakfasts.

Since I moved to Blue Beech, Iowa, when I was fifteen years old, it's been my go-to. My father, Silas, brought me here every Sunday morning for strawberry pancakes and cookies-and-cream hot chocolate. As I got older, Christopher started taking me instead. Sometimes, my parents would join us. They loved Christopher.

The chime above the door announces our arrival, and people gawk at me as soon as we walk in. My eyes scan the diner, not meeting anyone else's, and I take in the crowd. Nearly every booth and table is occupied with diners.

"Hi, ladies!" Margo, Shirley's granddaughter, greets, menus clutched in her hand. "Just the two of you?"

I nod while Ava says, "Yeah."

"Ryan is cleaning a booth, and then we'll get you seated." Her smile meets her eyes before she wipes her hands on her apron and scurries away when a waiter calls her over.

"I'm going to take a restroom break," Ava says. "Be right back." She walks away, strolling through the aisle between booths, and heads toward the back of the diner.

"Motherfucker. What a way to ruin my morning."

My back straightens, and shivers run up my spine at his voice.

I'll know who that voice belongs to until the day I die.

It's distinctive—masculine and as smooth as the coffee the people around us are drinking. There's a chill to it though, a hint of calculation, as if he could ruin you with the snap of his fingers.

Jax Bridges.

My deceased fiancé's best friend and the man I've hated for over two decades.

I keep my back to him and say, "The same goes for you. I was here first, so you can see yourself out."

Jax doesn't deserve to witness the effect his words have on me. Once, so many years ago, that voice—albeit not as deep—put me at ease. Now, all it does is make my chest ache and deepen the wounds already there.

"Don't you think it's time you moved?" he continues with a hateful sneer. "No one wants your ass here."

My breathing heightens, and I clench my fists, my half-painted nails digging into my palms. "Don't you think it's time to stop fucking talking to me?" Unlike him, I keep my voice low, so only he hears me.

"Aw, listen to *sweet* Millie, throwing out the F-bomb." He releases a cruel laugh. "I'm glad you're finally showing your true colors and how much of a terrible person you are."

Terrible person?

Maybe it's the sore muscles from sleeping on the floor.

Or the headache from dodging the stares coming in our direction.

Or just the sorrow I've had in my heart for the last six months.

But the frustration finally hits me. Anger rides through my body, and I whip around to face him. I glare at his face, refusing to meet those green eyes of his. I stopped looking at him in the eyes the day of Christopher's funeral. When he stared at me with such hate and told me Christopher's death was my fault. The asshole doesn't deserve eye contact with me.

You'd think his face would match his words, his tone—conniving and cutthroat. But, no, Jax's face has never given him away. It's always been his voice that reveals his true self. Whether he wants to hurt you or make you smile, he's always been particular about how he is with his tone and words.

He's brutal with them, and I'm his latest punching bag.

Unfortunately, unlike him, you can read my face.

My pain is as clear as the Weddell Sea.

The anger as red as Hormuz Island.

I rest my hands on my hips and sneer, "And exactly what am I, Jax?"

We've caught more attention from the patrons in the diner—more eyes on me than when I walked in. They're witnessing two people who blame each other for the same thing.

"You are the reason my best friend is dead."

More cutthroat words.

The worst he's ever spoken.

His weapon to destroy me without lifting a finger.

I swallow and blink away tears.

Please don't let my face show how deep his accusation struck me.

"You are the reason my entire life has been turned upside fucking down."

Another stab. Another wound.

"Whoa, Jax," Ava says, approaching us. "Not cool."

Jax takes a step back and runs his fingers through his messy, dark hair. "Don't kill the guy who states the truth." He stops to hold up a finger. "Or wait, will you kill me too, Amelia?" He clenches his jaw as he shakes his head. "I'm out of here."

Without giving either of us a chance to reply, he turns. The door chime now announces his departure as he disappears into the parking lot.

"Your, uh … table is ready," the teenage busboy nervously says, throwing a towel over his shoulder while refusing to look at me.

"I need to go." My voice cracks as panic sets through me.

Ava stops me. "And what? Go hang out with Jax in the parking lot?" She gently smiles. "Come on, babe. Let's sit down. You need a moment anyway. If you want to leave in five minutes, we'll go."

I nod and keep my head down while doing my walk of shame before slumping down into the booth. I immediately snatch a menu and use it to shield my face from the wandering eyes. It was bad enough when I got here. Jax's behavior only elevated their curiosity.

Who else here blames me for Christopher's death?

My parents don't. My friends don't. His friends—minus Jax —don't.

But Christopher's family? I have no idea.

His mom showed up to the funeral—late nonetheless. She

never called or asked me to help with his arrangements. She came, saw her son in his casket, and walked out. And just like Jax, her face gave nothing away.

"I'll talk to Easton," she says, referring to her cousin, one of Jax's friends. She rests her palm on the top of my menu and drags it down, exposing my face. "He'll tell Jax to stop with his antics."

I drop my menu. "Jax has acted like this toward me for years. He's just getting worse."

"You're both struggling with Chris's death, and you two have always lashed out at each other. He'll come around."

"I don't want him to come around. I want him to stay the hell away from me."

She sighs, her eyes meeting mine. "You two need to sit down and talk to each other."

"I need that like I need another foot." I hate the hostility in my voice, on my face, the effect Jax has on me.

"You could bond over Chris's death."

I almost laugh at the hopefulness in her voice. "There's no bonding with that man. All he wants is to argue."

Our *Jax is an asshole* talk is interrupted by Margo stopping at the table to take our order. I don't order strawberry pancakes or cookies-and-cream hot chocolate. I order chocolate chip waffles and black coffee—both were Christopher's go-to breakfast choices.

"I'll put that in for you." Margo clicks her pen shut, collects our menus, and hurries away.

I sigh and pay a glance out the window next to me. Chills crawl up my spine when I see Jax leaning against his black truck. His muscular arms are crossed, and his glare is pinned straight on me. He's watching me from the outside. And for what seems like forever and even though it's through glass, our eyes meet.

It's only for a moment.

Not long because Jax flips me off, circles his truck, and leaves.

I change the subject and ask Ava for an update on her residency at the hospital.

Margo delivers our breakfast, and unlike Ava, I don't take a bite. I stare down at my plate. It's not only food in front of me; it's another memory of the man I lost.

I don't eat the waffles or drink the coffee. Ava says nothing and allows me to ignore my food and sip on my water. A few times, I can tell she's ready to question me about it but changes her mind.

When she's finished, I ask Margo for a to-go box, taking the waffles home with me, unsure if keeping them will help or be more of a punishment.

2

JAX

ALL I WANTED WAS a goddamn Western omelet.

Can't a guy get breakfast without seeing the woman he despises?

It'd been a minute since I'd had one of Shirley's breakfasts, but I woke up with an omelet craving. When I walked in, I didn't need the woman in front of me to turn around. No, I know Amelia Malone so well that I could pick her out of a crowd anywhere.

I might hate her, but I know more about her than some of her closest friends—what her favorite meal is, her biggest fear, and how her mind works. Everything I wish I could forget.

I flexed my jaw to hold myself back from engaging with her, but there was no stopping myself.

When I saw Amelia, when I thought of her, it was a reminder of what I'd lost. I saw someone to point the finger at, to blame, so I wouldn't have to look at myself. My wicked words won't bring Christopher back, but in the back of my mind, it makes me feel better to take my grievances out on someone else.

Do I feel good about doing it?

Sometimes, yes.

Sometimes, no.

After storming out of the diner, I stood in the parking lot, wondering if I'd gone too far. To which the answer was yes. Neighbors who'd watched me grow up, friends of my parents, and even brewery customers observed my spite. It was wrong, bad for business, but my pain had clouded my thoughts from those consequences.

But it's not like Amelia and I have ever been nice to each other. Everyone knows we competed against each other on everything and have for years. We hated each other, then lusted after the other, and it might've turned into love, but we circled back to hate. The difference now though is, our hatred for each other has moved into darker territory.

———

Don't go into business with your best friend.

Because what the fuck do you do when they die too young?

You want to tear the place apart since it's a daily reminder of him. That's what you want to do. You want to walk away because the other player on your team is gone. But you can't.

Chris was only twenty-six. He hadn't even hit thirty, had children, or witnessed our business thrive.

I sit at a table in the back of our brewery and take in all we put together in the last two years. We'd been at the top of the world when we opened Down Home Brewery in Blue Beech, Iowa—our hometown.

So many times, I do this.

Look around and wonder what I am going to do without him.

We'd already started discussing opening a second location. The brewery became our baby, our life, but Chris asked me to wait a year before taking that step. He planned to marry Amelia and wanted to focus on the wedding. I reluctantly agreed and planned his bachelor party, but then he came in and broke the news six months ago.

Amelia had called off the wedding.

I'd never witnessed a man so heartbroken.

In that moment, I was happy I'd never had a serious relationship.

That I hadn't been stupid enough to give someone else that much power over me.

Hell, sometimes, I wondered how much of a heart I had inside.

The only person I'd ever had any thoughts of affection for was the woman who had broken off their wedding.

But I'd suppressed that years ago, let it go, and moved on. So had she.

I grab my phone when it rings, interrupting my thoughts, and see *Unknown Number*.

Fuck that.

Not in the mood for a spam call.

I blankly stare at my phone, watching it vibrate against the table while ignoring it. When it stops, a voice mail notification pops up on the screen. Solicitors don't typically leave voice mails, so I listen to the message.

"This message is for Jax Bridges. This is Marshall Haney from Haney and Burnett at Law. I'm calling regarding your business partner, Christopher Simpson. I'd like to set up an appointment at my office to talk. Please get back with me at …"

I don't listen to him recite his number. Instead, I immediately call him back. His secretary answers, and within minutes, I'm on the phone with Marshall Haney.

"Mr. Bridges," Marshall greets from the other end. His voice is businesslike, like the men speaking in those litigation commercials that tell you you're able to sue everyone in the goddamn world. "Thank you for returning my call."

"You're welcome," I reply, unsure of where this conversation will lead.

Chris had an attorney?

For what?

He was a great business partner, but he wasn't the best man about paperwork and appointments. We each had our own roles, and dealing with contracts wasn't Chris's.

"Christopher left a will, and I'd like to go over it with you."

"A will? What would Chris need a will for?"

"His assets, among other things."

I scratch my head. "All right."

We schedule our meeting for tomorrow.

What assets did Chris have?

The brewery. I guess my dumbass didn't consider that he owned half the business and, unless he had it set up otherwise, the bar would go to his family.

Shit.

My stomach turns, a headache forming, and I scrub a hand over my forehead.

Chris's family are the last people who deserve anything from him. They abused and neglected him in so many ways. I couldn't see him leaving his share to them. Fingers crossed Marshall tells me that I'm now the sole owner of Down Home Brewery.

If his side of the business did get left to his family, I'd pay anything to buy those assholes out. No way would they ever be my business partners.

And if he didn't leave his share to them, who the fuck else would he have left it to?

I nearly drop my phone at the thought of him having left it to the one woman I hate.

No fucking way.

3

AMELIA

OTHER THAN MY friends and family, no one has contacted me about Christopher's death. Not his mother, distant relatives, no one from that part of his life.

No one's offered condolences.

Or asked questions about his death.

It's as if he only existed to us.

Until I receive a call.

The call from Christopher's attorney shocks me, and my hands shake as I schedule a meeting with him ... to review Christopher's *last wishes*.

Since when did Christopher have an attorney?

After hanging up the phone, I take my Chinese takeout and pop a squat in the laundry room. I open the lid, grab the chopsticks, but drop them when something hits me. Bringing my knees to my chest, I scoot across the floor to rest my back against the wall.

The call confirms everything I've been terrified of.

Christopher hadn't woken up one day and decided he wanted to die.

No, if he talked to an attorney and got his wishes in order, that means this was a well-thought-out plan.

Day after day, he knew he was leaving me.

He'd looked me in the eyes and told me he loved me while knowing he was going to break me in every way possible.

How could he do this to me?

He hadn't trusted me enough to tell me.

He hadn't loved me enough to talk to me about it.

It made sense. Christopher's father had done the same thing. When he was ten, his father purposely ran his car into a tree to kill himself. Christopher said his mother had been relieved that her abusive husband was dead—not that she was any better. That relief morphed into anger when she learned that Christopher's father set up a will and left the modest insurance policy to his son. He couldn't touch it until he was eighteen though.

It was the ultimate insult to his mother, and since his father wasn't there for her to unleash her fury on, she threw it all at Christopher. And he hadn't only gotten it from her, but his new stepfather as well. To them, Christopher was a thief, stealing the money they deserved.

I want to scream.

He'd planned to leave me.

Christopher is no longer mine.

But I still feel like I'm his.

The office of Haney and Burnett at Law is in a small brick home, converted into an office, fifteen miles outside of town.

My steps are slow as I walk toward the building. At twenty-six, never have I considered making a will, of having *last wishes*.

An older red-haired woman greets me when I walk in and then directs me to an empty room. My nose twitches. The room smells like old firewood, but there isn't a fireplace in sight. A circular table crowds most of the room, and four chairs are seated around it.

"Mr. Haney will be with you in a moment," the woman says with a sincere smile. "The other party will be in here as well."

I stiffen.

Second party?

I don't get the chance to ask who this other party is because she's already left the room. I inhale deep breaths in an attempt to not freak out.

Is it Christopher's mother?

For the love of God, please don't let it be his mother.

"Amelia, thank you for coming." A balding man enters the room. The odor of firewood is overpowered by Old Spice. "Marshall Haney."

He sticks out his hand, and it's sweaty when I shake it.

Then, the man behind Marshall is revealed.

I cringe and shuffle back a step, into the wall.

This might be worse than Christopher's mother.

Behind Marshall is Jax. His face hardens at the sight of me.

My stomach drops, and the room goes quiet for a moment, but the silence is broken when Marshall claps his hands.

"Let's get started, shall we?" Marshall's voice almost sounds as if he's making an announcement.

The room suddenly feels smaller, as if we're being sucked into a vacuum. Jax glares at me, and for the first time in a long time, I allow myself to take him in. His cologne overpowers Marshall's. Jax has grown from using cheap cologne to smelling like a man walking into a million-dollar business meeting. A man's man. His style has matured—ripped black jeans, a designer tee, and white Chucks. He went from no facial hair to ruggedness along his cheeks, under his nose, and down his chin and throat.

I struggle to keep my composure as we sit—Jax and I taking a chair on each side of Marshall. Jax stares straight at me, as if I'm something he wishes would disappear, and as much as I want to avoid eye contact with him, I feel that it'd make me look weak, make him think he has the upper hand on me.

Even while still grieving, I can't let Jax think he's won.

Ever.

Now even more so.

Now that he blames me for something I didn't do.

"Amelia, Jax, you two know each other, correct?" Marshall opens the folder that's been sitting on the table since I walked in.

I only nod.

Jax doesn't answer.

"I'll make this quick since it appears neither of you wants to be here, and I don't blame you. I'm sure you're going through a rough time," Marshall says with sympathy in his tone and on his face.

He knows what Christopher did.

And Marshall might have the answers as to why Christopher did it.

But why now?

Marshall makes it quick, just as he said he would. "Christopher left his share of the brewery to Amelia."

"What?" Jax and I say simultaneously.

Marshall apprehensively glances between Jax and me. "He wanted you to run it together."

"I'll buy you out," Jax immediately says. "Name your price."

Marshall holds out his hand to stop my response. "Now, wait. Per Christopher's will, she must wait ninety days before she can sell."

"And what about Jax?" I throw my arm out to gesture to the jerk across from me. "Does he have a stipulation on when he can sell?"

He shakes his head. "Jax is already co-owner of the brewery. You're the only one who has to wait, Miss Malone."

"What the fuck?" Jax hisses.

"Marshall slides a stack of papers to each of us. "Here are the details. If you have any questions at all, let me know."

"Is that all that's in the will?" I ask.

Marshall nods. "Yes. Those were his last wishes."

Why would he do this to me?

Was it out of love or spite?

Sensing the animosity, Marshall says, "Miss Malone, you don't have to be involved in the business. *But* you will acquire the income from Christopher's profits, as he did when he was alive."

"So, I'm supposed to just hand her money without her doing the work?" Jax hisses, gesturing toward me with disgust on his face.

"That's for you two to work out," Marshall answers, every inch of his face screaming, *Get me out of here.* "I'm only the messenger of his wishes."

"Is that even legal?" Jax asks, his strong jaw clenching. "To just hand over a portion of your business to someone?"

"It is," Marshall replies.

My head spins.

Why did Christopher throw this plot twist at me?

Did he think I'd want the brewery ... that I'd want to work with Jax?

"Christopher said his wish was for the two people he cared about more than anything to run the business together."

"How do you possibly think two people who don't like each other can do that?" I ask with a tremor in my voice.

It's a stupid question for Marshall.

How would he know this?

He doesn't have a personal history with us.

Marshall's face falls. "That isn't for me to declare. I don't ask my clients these things."

I'm not sure if he meant for that to sound heartfelt or cold.

It gave the vibe of both.

When I pay another glance to Jax, it looks as if the idea of working with me makes him sick.

Same, buddy. Same.

"Yeah, well, all wishes can't come true," Jax snarls.

Marshall ignores his comment and pulls out two envelopes

from the folder, handing one to Jax and one to me. My name is scrolled on mine in Christopher's handwriting. He had sloppy handwriting—a weird mixture of cursive and print, as if he'd quit in the middle of learning each one and kind of just morphed them together.

It hurts, seeing my name. He'd written it knowing what he'd do.

Jax has a similar envelope, but I don't know if his name is written on his. Not that I'd ask. The less conversation we have, the better. I'm still processing the whole *you two are now partners* thing.

Jax Bridges and I can't be business partners.

Hell, we can't even be friends.

Did Christopher want us to kill each other?

To join him in death?

I want to scream at Christopher for this.

"Why did you wait all this time to give us these?" Jax asks, as if Marshall had been holding on to them like a winning lottery ticket. Like he'd witnessed us in the diner and thought it was the perfect time to ruin our week further.

"That was another one of his requests," Marshall replies. "To wait until this very date to give it to you."

The room goes quiet again.

Neither one of us opens our letters.

It's funny, really. How two people who despise each other so much have so many similarities—similar actions, similar things that anger them, and similar thoughts that once brought them together before destroying them.

"If you two need anything, please let me know if I can be of any assistance." Marshall shoots us one last nervous smile and leaves the room.

Christopher obviously didn't hire him for his sympathetic personality.

"I'm going to tell Marshall he can assist in kicking your ass," I hiss to Jax, carefully sliding the envelope into my purse.

"Touching, given you just had your chance and didn't," Jax says. "You were a chickenshit when we were kids, and you're just as much of one now."

I grimace. "Piss off, Jax."

We aren't in public any longer, aren't a show for our entire town to watch, so I won't be as nice to him as I was at Shirley's. Jax knows how spiteful the real Amelia can be, and he's about to see it full force. Maybe if he sees that bad side of me, he'll sell me the brewery. It'll be tough though, given that they built it from the ground up and it's named after Jax's family's bar, but not impossible.

"Say hello to your new business partner," I say, standing. "I'll make sure it's hell, working with me."

"Oh, evil Amelia." Jax rises from his chair. "You don't need to work with me at all. Keep your ass at home, and I'll manage the brewery just fine."

"And what? Steal money from me?" I stomp over to face him with only inches separating us. We're so close that I inhale the sweet smell of wintermint gum. "I don't think so."

"We both know you don't give two fucks about a dollar that comes from the brewery. You either want it because it reminds you of Chris or to make my life a living hell, which I'm sure you'd take infinite pleasure in."

"And you don't seek pleasure in my being miserable?"

Our attention leaves each other when the secretary lightly knocks on the door and clears her throat.

"Mr. Haney has an appointment in five minutes," she says in a low voice.

She is politely kicking us out.

"Okay," I say.

As I turn to leave, I kick Jax in his shin.

Is it immature? Absolutely, but Jax brings out a side of me I've never shown to anyone else. A competitive side, a side that can get dirty, and one that likes to get back at him for everything he's ever done.

When I get back to my car, it hits me.

Marshall said Christopher requested he wait until today to give us these letters.

Today would've been our wedding day... had I not canceled it.

———

I play with the letter in my hands.

Can I do this?

Christopher left nothing but questions when he died.

Since his death, I've searched for clues, racked my mind, but I always come up empty. Maybe I'm not looking hard enough because as much as I crave those answers, the thought of knowing them terrifies me.

What if it was my fault?

What if I made him unhappy?

Closing my eyes, I inhale a calming breath that does the opposite. It's what happens almost every time I enter my bedroom. I stare at the envelope, running my finger across the curve of my name, and my throat turns dry. Then, I set the envelope on the bed and scramble out of the room.

As if I just completed the most difficult task of my day, I sigh and drag a bottle of wine out of the fridge. I don't bother with a glass before going into the laundry room and drinking straight from the bottle.

Ninety days.

Then, I can sell my share of the brewery.

Why make us wait?

Christopher knew how Jax and I felt toward each other.

I take another swig of the moscato.

Christopher hated moscato. So does Jax. Beer men, obviously.

Don't you have to be a beer man to open a brewery?

I guess it doesn't matter. My father has been sober for decades, and the man owns two bars and bartended for years.

My mind swims from thoughts of Christopher to Jax as I take another drink. He asked me to sell my share of the brewery. And even though it'd only been mine for seconds, I already felt protective of it. Possessive. Unsure if there'd be a time when I'd want to let it go.

Fuck that.

I might not have been married to Christopher, but I was there with him every step of the way. Not only that, but the brewery is also all I have left of Christopher—besides our townhome, which I'll eventually sell. I only need to find a buyer who's okay with the previous owner passing away in their new home. No biggie.

I do social media management for multiple businesses, so I can manage doing that job and working at the brewery. The brewery used to be one of my clients, but Jax fired me the day after Christopher's funeral.

I set the wine down, grab my phone, and call Ava.

"Hey, babe," she answers.

"Christopher left his share of the brewery to me."

She's quiet for a moment before saying, "Oh, wow. Does Jax know?"

I'm sure that will be everyone's first reaction upon finding out this new revelation of events.

"We found out today," I reply. *"Together."*

"Oh, man, I'm sure he's ecstatic." She lightly laughs. "So, what's your plan? Will he buy you out?"

"That's the first thing he asked when he found out."

"Do you want him to buy you out?"

I rub at my tired eyes. "I can't sell for ninety days, per Christopher's request."

She sighs. "Why would Christopher do that to you?"

"I'm just as clueless as you."

"You want to keep it, don't you?"

"I mean ..."

I might have to wait to sell, but Jax doesn't.

"If you want to keep it, keep it. Don't let Jax scare you away from it. But if you think it'll be too hard, let it go. Sell to Jax the earliest you can."

"I wish Jax weren't such an asshole," I moan, throwing my head back.

"He's an asshole who loved Chris like a brother."

Ava is right. Jax and his family took Christopher in and saved him from his horrible life.

I yawn as my neck tenses. "I need to get some sleep."

"In a bed?"

"None of your business."

"If you can't sleep at your place, come to mine. Don't keep sleeping in your damn laundry room, Amelia."

"It's fine. I like it here. It's close enough to the memories, but not too close."

We hang up, and right before I finish off the bottle of wine, my phone beeps with a text.

Jax: I'll figure out a way to buy you out.

I curse him while replying.

Me: Good luck.

4

JAX

"MOTHERFUCKER," I hiss before downing a shot of whiskey.

I'm sitting at Down Home Pub. Not as a bartender, but as a patron.

I need to clear my mind, and what better way than at my father's bar?

That he also co-owns with Amelia's father, Silas.

I just can't get rid of the thorn in my side.

Down Home is exactly what its name implies—down-home. Here, you feel like you're sitting with friends, having a drink, not in a noisy bar with drunk assholes surrounding you. Other than the brewery, it's one of my favorite places and where I go anytime I need to clear my head.

I assumed I'd no longer have to deal with the pain in the ass after I fired her. Sure, we see each other in passing since we live in the same town and have the same circle of friends, but putting that professional distance between us was one more step in getting rid of her.

"Hey, son," my dad, Maliki, says, stopping in front of me from across the bar. "Everything okay?"

"Chris left his share of the brewery to Amelia." I lean back in my stool and scrub a hand across my face.

"Ah," is all he says for a moment, as if he's searching for the right two cents to give to his son. "You and Chris never discussed what would happen if something were to happen to one of you?"

I shake my head. "I guess I thought I was invincible at this age."

"I won't lie and say I was any different."

Everyone says I remind them of my father. Which is a damn good compliment. He's the best man I know. And I see the similarities. We tend to be distant, quiet—a trait my mother said she wished I hadn't inherited from him. We're not called the nice guys, yet we're also not referred to as cruel. We smile, but it's rare for us to sport cheesy-ass grins.

Then, there are the physical similarities. Our six-foot frames. Our dark hair. The permanent black five o'clock shadows, but his is now peppered with gray.

He releases a heavy sigh. "You're my son, and I love you, but I'm about to play devil's advocate."

My shoulders slump. "I wouldn't expect it any other way."

"Did you ask her to sell?" He stops, shaking his head. "You don't even need to answer that. I know you did. And from the pissed off look on your face, I'm assuming she said no."

"She did. Not only that, but she can't sell for ninety days."

"Did you ever think just as much as the brewery is all you have left of Chris, it's also all she has left of the man she loved?" He grabs a glass and fills it with soda water before sliding it to me. "Try to work together."

I scoff. "She and I working together will be a nightmare."

"You don't have to like each other to run a business together."

"That's easier said than done." I shake my head. "Could you run the bar with Silas if you didn't like him?"

"I never take my own advice." He slaps his hand onto the bar. "I just give it out. I listen to shit your mom says and repeat it."

I scoff again because that's the only reply I have.

He chuckles. "Now, onto *my* personal advice."

"I knew this was coming." I grab the glass and take a long drink.

"Get over it. There's nothing you can change."

I hold up my glass in a cheers motion. "There's the dad I know."

"Hey." He raises his hands in an *I'm innocent* gesture. "I tried playing your mom, but that shit is hard."

"I'd rather hear your honesty than some *positive quote* bullshit."

"And that's why your mom says you're just like me." He reaches over the bar to clap me on the shoulder. "You don't have a choice in working with her, but you do have a choice in how miserable you'll be while working together."

"I need to sleep this day off."

Scratch that.

I need to pay a visit to Little Miss Amelia.

5

AMELIA

I'M WRINGING out my freshly showered hair when someone knocks on my door. Even though I told Ava that I needed sleep, Jax's text overpowered that sleepiness. I tried for twenty minutes, tossing and turning, before giving up and stomping to the guest bathroom to shower.

My thoughts raced as I showered.

Was Christopher messing with me?

With us?

He knew Jax and I hated each other. He witnessed it first-hand anytime the three of us were together. When he asked us to play nice for his sake, Jax and I then pretended like the other didn't even exist. When we walked into a room, we'd say hi to everyone, except each other. I'd offer everyone but him a beer when the guys were over for football games.

So, why in the world would Christopher think we could work together?

As much as it frustrates me that he stuck me with Jax, it's also consoling to know that Christopher thought about me, wanted me involved in the business he loved so much. Now, if only I could find a way to kick Jax out, all would be well in my new business world. That sounds selfish, I know, since they built the business together, but what else can I hope for?

Barefoot, I walk through the townhome to the front door and peek through the peephole to find the last person I expected to see. My head pounds, and I stare at him for a moment, taking in how he shifts from one foot to the other and how he runs his hand through his thick, wet hair in frustration.

He's standing in the rain, and I contemplate how long I should leave him out in the cold before answering.

Hell, should I even answer?

Since I'm not as evil as he claims I am, I swing open the door and immediately set my glare on him. "What the hell are you doing here?"

Jax rubs his hands together in an attempt to warm himself and blows out a ragged breath. "We need to talk."

"About what? I can't sell my portion of the business anyway, so why are you here, looking like a miserable, wet goat?" I smirk. "A little cold out there, jackass?"

"Shut up and let me in," he grumbles.

"Eh, we can save this talk for tomorrow. Thanks though."

He shoots his hand out when I go to shut the door in his face and stops it. "Don't." He inches a step closer, and his firm chest heaves in and out from his heavy breathing. "Don't slam the door in my goddamn face."

We stand there, staring each other down, and he ignores the rain pelting him from all angles. Our eyes meet, the porch light putting his face on display, and the hurt and frustration are clear in his eyes. I'm sure he finds the same in mine—pain and loss, mixed with confusion and anger.

A combination of every emotion that passes through me daily.

He nearly has me in a trance, so I stumble back when he pushes the door open farther, wide enough to allow him entrance, and he slides past me into my home.

"What the hell?" I shriek, scooting away from him. "You

know I can, like, beat you with a baseball bat until you can't walk, take out a kneecap for breaking and entering?"

He shakes his head to remove the water droplets from his hair before running a hand through it. "Break them then." He gestures to his knees. "I don't think you have the balls to do that, but go ahead, Millie."

Rain drifts through the doorway as we stare at each other in agony. Both of us with dripping wet hair, sorrow in our eyes, and hate toward each other in our hearts.

He stands there almost tauntingly.

I point to the door. "Get the fuck out."

"We have to talk."

"We have nothing to talk about, Jax. All you do when we talk is throw Christopher's death in my face and find some ridiculous way to blame me for it. So, the less you're around, the better for my goddamn mental health and sanity. You're like a leech, sucking any small bit of happiness out of my soul."

His voice is icy when he says, "You can't get pissed at someone for speaking the truth."

"How dare you come to my home and talk to me this way! I am done being your punching bag."

He throws out his arms and raises his voice. "He was my best friend. I'm allowed to be fucking angry."

"And he was the goddamn love of my life," I scream.

Jax's mouth snaps closed, his eyes widening. We've never spoken about my feelings toward Christopher. That's something I left between Christopher and me or my friends. Never Jax.

"I wish I'd never introduced you two," he snarls.

His words are a slap in the face. Tears well in my eyes, and I close them to gain my composure. "Of course you do. You had it out for our relationship the moment we started dating, like some jealous toddler forced to share his toys. You acted as if Christopher couldn't be close with anyone but you!"

We're in the small space of my entryway, our faces merely inches apart, screaming our hurt and anger out toward the other.

This seems like it's the closest we've been in years—the closest we've allowed ourselves to be.

"That's such bullshit. You know that's not the reason." Spit flies from his mouth. "You meeting him would've been inevitable, but ..." He trails off, his words ending, and pulls at the roots of his hair. "Fuck!"

I cross my arms. "Exactly. You're the reason we met, but it would've been inevitable, no matter what."

Jax tilts his head down. And for what seems like the first time in a long time, he looks at me. Yes, we've glared at each other, shot looks of disgust toward each other, but we've never locked eyes long enough to truly understand one another.

There's a sadness in his eyes that matches mine.

There's also fear.

It's as if releasing our anger and hate toward each other has made us lighter for only a few stolen seconds. I gasp when his cold finger swipes over my cheek, wiping away a tear. I slightly open my mouth. It's wrong—I know it's wrong—but I haven't been touched by a masculine hand in so long. Even just a simple wipe of a tear feels like something I've been longing for.

His finger slides from my cheek to my lips, and he runs the tip of it along my bottom lip. A light moan escapes me, and it's exactly what we needed for him to pull away. It's the reality check we needed to tell us whatever emotion flooding through us is wrong.

He reverses a step, his back hitting the wall. "Go put on some goddamn clothes." He gestures to my towel, and his shoulder brushes against mine as he spins on his heels and walks farther into the townhome.

Shit.

It's this moment that I realize I'm wearing a towel. I'm surprised Jax didn't comment on my lack of clothing before.

I tighten the fabric around me before stomping into the living room, where he's standing. "In case you've forgotten, this is my home, and you showed up in the middle of the night. Don't come in here, barking demands."

I planned to change out of the towel, and I will, but I don't like him telling me what to do. I'll stand here all damn night in this towel to go against what he wants. His back is to me, and he's frozen in place, standing next to the couch, as if he were surveying a crime scene.

Jax hasn't been here since Christopher's death, but his friend is everywhere. There are endless framed pictures of Christopher and me, Christopher and Jax, and some with our friends and Jax's family. My therapist suggested I take them down for a month to see if that would help with my grieving, but I can't bring myself to do it.

Minutes pass as silence fills the room, and when I take a step forward, the floor creaks, causing him to peer back at me.

"We can't work together," he says, almost pained.

"We have no choice but to do it," I reply, sniffling. "At least give Christopher what he wanted for ninety days. Then, we'll go our separate ways."

I'm unsure of what I'll do with the brewery, but for now, I want to grant Christopher his last wish. I'll give him what he wanted because it is the only thing he ever asked of me, and as far as I know, we're the only people he asked anything of.

"We can't work together, Amelia, and you fucking know why," Jax yells.

The pain is clear in his eyes.

The guilt.

Something he's carried—*we've* carried—for years.

At times, I wonder if it's something we should feel guilty about.

But do we feel guilty about our actions or for keeping them a secret?

Our hatred for each other aided in us not telling Christopher —or anyone really—the truth. If we hated each other, we didn't have to think about it. People wouldn't suspect us to have the history we have. And Christopher would definitely never suspect what happened.

Jax and I have always been toxic.

Even when we tried not to be.

At one point, I thought it might be love, but we were stupid kids.

"You can sell me your share," I finally say. "Then, it's done."

He smacks his hand across his chest and takes two steps toward me. "Over my dead body will I sell you what Chris and I worked our asses off for."

I cross my arms. "Then, that means we're partners."

"I won't make this easy on you," he snarls.

"And I won't make it easy on you."

"I'm going to make your life hell until you sell."

"Samesies."

"I always win, Amelia. Always."

"We'll see about that."

6

JAX

"THEN, THAT MEANS WE'RE PARTNERS."

Amelia's words are on repeat in my head on the drive back to my apartment. When I park in the lot—the one behind Down Home Pub—I slam my hand against the steering wheel in frustration.

Who does she think she is?

Amelia wasn't there, working day in and out, like Chris and I were.

Sure, she made appearances, helped some, and dropped off food. I'll give her that. But she didn't put her blood, sweat, and tears into it. It was never her dream. All that woman did was cause me to lose my best friend. She's done enough damage here, so why can't she just stay the hell away?

All I've ever needed from Amelia Malone for years is distance.

It's what keeps me sane.

What keeps me out of the past.

What doesn't make me remember so many things.

And that's what I need to convince her to do. She needs to be a silent partner, and then when the time comes, I'll convince her to walk away. I'll convince her to keep that distance we've fought like hell to maintain all these years.

Today, Amelia and I became business partners.

Tomorrow, we go to war.

———

My body and my mouth are dry when I wake up. A strand of sunlight creeps through the curtains, and while on my back, I rub the spot between my eyes and groan.

I'm blind on what today will bring.

My life, my business, changed the moment I got the call about Chris's death. He'd already left me with enough on my shoulders, so why would he do this to me—throw Amelia in the mix of the chaos that is now my life?

I was finally getting in the routine of tackling every job of the business head-on. It was a struggle, learning Chris's jobs since we'd split responsibilities. But I've managed without any additional help.

Amelia can't wake up this morning and suddenly know how to run a brewery. She doesn't know the equipment, the drinks, or about fractional distillation. And I don't plan on teaching her this shit either. Just because she manages social media for bars and companies that sell booze doesn't mean she'll know what she's doing here.

Chris and I performed so much research to get the business started. It was risky to putting our life savings and the money I'd borrowed from my parents, into it, knowing the possibility that we could lose it.

I drag my tired ass out of bed and trek to the shower, and as I wash my face, I pray to the good Lord above that Amelia doesn't show up at the brewery today. And if she does, I'll be more than happy to prove why she doesn't belong there.

———

The brewery is silent when I walk in.

It's my favorite part of the workday.

That enjoyable moment of uninterrupted silence, where I take everything in and make sure it's running okay.

When Chris and I announced our plans to open the brewery, some thought our business would be in competition with my father's. The fact that anyone would ever assume I'd do that to my family over money is dumb as shit. We aren't a bar. We brew and distribute craft beer. We do have a small tasting area in the front, where we sometimes hold events, but it's nothing fancy.

Down Home Brewery creates craft beer. Good beer. No chemicals, preservatives, or any of that gross shit in it. We focus heavily on perfecting our malts.

Starting the brewery was a process but well worth it. Since Amelia's mom, Lola, is the VP of 21st Amendment, one of the largest liquor distributors in the Midwest, I showed up at her office and pitched the idea of them investing with us. She took it to the board, and boom, we had another investor.

We purchased a chunk of land outside of Blue Beech, construction began, and everything took off from there. I hired a guy at the equipment company to guide us through everything we needed and the best way to run the business. When I asked him for his best advice, he told me to have fun cleaning. When I asked why, he said owning a brewery was ninety-percent cleaning and ten percent paperwork.

The dude wasn't lying.

I've never been so OCD about cleaning in my life.

No bullshit, the first batch of beer we brewed was what I'd imagine sewer water tasted like. I couldn't even swallow it. It took us another three months of tweaking recipes to fine-tune our beers. It was long hours and stressful but fun as hell, especially experiencing it with my best friend.

The next plan was to expand it and make another Down Home Pub location, but that was a few years out.

After checking that everything is in order, I head to the office.

Leaving the door open, I set my coffee down and take a seat in the rolling chair behind the desk.

The office isn't anything special. Our time and energy were spent on the brewery and the front of the building. We only threw the basics of what was needed in here, and then we were done with it. The large desk is minimal with only a computer and the absolute office essentials. The stack of papers on the edge of the desk typically isn't there, but I've been playing catch-up.

I spend the next thirty minutes answering emails and going through the nightmare of paperwork Chris left behind, but the sound of a door slamming interrupts me.

The fuck?

Our day employees don't come in for another hour. I turned the security system off but locked the door, so whoever it is either broke in or has a key. I stand, venture out of the office, and take a sharp left into the brewery room—the largest part of the building, where the majority of our equipment is.

Amelia's back is to me as she stands there, her head moving from side to side as she takes in the room. She hasn't been here since Chris's death. When she came with Ava and my cousin, Essie, to collect Chris's personal things, I told her she wasn't welcome here again. She called me an asshole, Ava kicked me in the shin, and Essie flipped me off.

But she did as I'd said. She took Chris's stuff, clearing him from the place we'd built together, and hasn't looked back.

Until today.

Until Chris handed her everything I don't want her to have.

Everything she doesn't deserve.

She could've at least given me a few hours to enjoy the day before ruining it.

"What are you doing here?" My question is said sternly, and my tone is cold, startling her.

She groans before turning around to face me. I'm standing in the doorway, keeping my distance, and she narrows her eyes at me.

Her dark hair—on the edge of a deep brown and black—is pulled back into a sleek ponytail, displaying every inch of her face. I might not be an Amelia fan, but there's no denying she's breathtaking.

I've thought that for as long as I've thought girls were pretty, and my attraction to her grew when I hit my teens. Her thick hair, plump pink lips, and the dimples that pop out when she smiles are perfection in my eyes. Our friend and my cousin, River, once made fun of her dimples, and I elbowed him in the stomach.

My eyes travel from her face down the rest of her body. Black leggings hug her curves, showing off her tight waist, and she's wearing a black zip-up jacket. Half of her legs are covered by her Hunter rain boots.

At least she was smart and wore decent shoes. The brewery floors are always wet. She will need to get a better pair though, so she doesn't end up slipping and busting her ass.

"I work here now." Amelia shrugs and walks toward me.

There's no smug expression on her face. It's blank, expressionless. A rarity because I can typically read her so well.

I cross my arms. "How'd you get a key?"

She's quiet, and I step to the side, allowing her space to go into the front of the building, where the office and tasting area are. There's a temperature increase from the brewery room to the front, so she unzips her jacket and shrugs out of it, displaying a black tank that shows off her cleavage—which she has plenty of. I gulp, hating myself when my cock stirs.

Hating myself for finding my dead best-friend's girl so damn attractive.

She folds the jacket over her arm and simply answers, "Christopher."

I scoff. "Of course he gave you one."

He was so pussy-whipped. He would've given her anything she asked for.

Except a future.

"I'm his fiancée, so yes, of course he did." She uses the present tense, as if he were still here, as if he'd be the next one to walk through that door.

"Wrong, Millie," I bite out. "You *were* his fiancée, and then you turned into his ex-fiancée."

She shuts her eyes in pain before slowly opening them and almost looking at me in desperation. "Don't say it like that."

"Truth hurts, doesn't it?"

She shakes her head, as if attempting to knock away her emotions, to rid herself of my hurtful words. "Are we going to talk about the same stuff repeatedly?" She takes a step closer to me, the scent of her sweet perfume—the same one she's worn for years—taking over my space. "You not liking me and blaming me for his death?"

I wince when she reaches forward and stabs her fingernail into my chest.

"But you know what?"

"What, Amelia?" Those two words are strained as they leave my lips, and she pulls away from me, but not as far as I'd like.

"At times, I blame *you* for his death."

Her words are a sucker-punch to the gut, and it's as if all the air in the room left.

I reel in my pain, gain control of myself, and then place a hand over my heart. "That's real rich, coming from you."

I don't need her coming in here, trying to manipulate me. I was nothing but a good friend to Chris for years. I almost ask her why, to hear her bullshit reasons for how she could even try to point the finger at me, but I don't. I don't because what if she knows something I don't?

What if she says something about Chris that would consume me with guilt?

She juts her chin out and focuses on me. "I'm not arguing with you. I'm here. Get over it. We have a business to run now."

I recoil at her words. "I've been running it just fine without you, sweetheart."

"Really?" She snorts. "Let's start off with whoever you hired for social media marketing after firing me. It's terrible, and I'm taking that job back over."

I slip my hands into my jeans pockets. "I didn't hire anyone."

"Wait." She holds up a finger. "You've been doing it yourself?"

I scratch my head. "Well … yeah."

"That makes sense why it sucks then."

"Whoa. My apologies for not being someone who spends all day tweeting and posting bullshit." I quit being a social media fan after my mom saw a picture of me doing a belly shot off my high school teacher on my twenty-first birthday.

"Which is why you hire someone who does."

"Whatever." I dismissively wave. "Consider that one of your new responsibilities as an employee then, but I'm not sending money to your company for it."

"As a *partner*, not an employee."

"As an *employee*." I curl up my lip. "You can't be a partner in a business you don't know shit about."

She raises a brow. "Haven't you seen *Shark Tank*, dumbass? Sure you can."

I ignore her point-making response.

"And who's to say I *don't know shit* about this brewery, huh?" Her tone is challenging. It's a tone I recognize since she had it every time we argued when we were kids.

"Have you ever worked here before?" I rub the spot between my eyebrows. It's not even eight in the morning, and I'm already getting a headache.

"Sure did. I helped Christopher sometimes."

Christopher. She always calls him by his full name for some reason. Everyone else, including me, called him Chris.

I offer her a fake smile. "Bringing him coffee and lunch can't be defined as helping."

"I know more than that."

"Prove it then." I jerk my head toward the doorway we just walked through and motion for her to return to the brewery room.

She places her jacket on one of the barstools in our tasting area and slowly grins before walking away from me. I follow her.

"I probably know just as much as you, if not more," she says.

I smirk. "You wish, sweetheart."

Those are the only words I can form because I'm fighting to keep my eyes from focusing on Amelia's chest, where the cold has hit. Her nipples are peeking through her thin tank top, and it's hard to focus on being an asshole to someone when you can't stop staring at them.

I turn and signal toward the first thing I see. "What are those?"

She gives me a *really* look. "I've known what kegs are since freshman year of high school."

Good job, asshole. Help her out by choosing something a damn teenager knows about.

"And this?" I nod toward another large kettle.

Another *really* expression. "A brew kettle. Are you going to make all these that easy?"

I point to the malt mill. "Why do we need this?"

She rolls her eyes. "You can't brew beer without milling grains, obviously."

"And this?"

"The fermenter."

"And why do we need a fermenter?" I feel like Bill Nye the fucking Science Guy, asking her all these damn questions about this shit.

"To *ferment* the brew, so there's actually alcohol in it."

As we walk through the brewery and into different rooms,

she answers most of my questions correctly. It half-pisses me off and half-impresses me. Her tone turns professional, as if she's pitching a life-changing deal.

She gives me a smug smile when I've run out of questions. "Now that we know I *do know shit* about this business, you can listen to me and my suggestions."

"I don't need your suggestions. You get an A-plus for your brewery knowledge. For that, you can clean the brewery room, stock the bottles, and help load the trucks."

"Sorry, but I am spending the day going to local bars and stores to convince them to carry our product." She taps me on the shoulder. "Like it or not, I'm an asset to this brewery. And I will do right by it because it's all I have left of Christopher and it was one of the most important things in his life."

7

JAX

NINE YEARS OLD

I HATE AMELIA MALONE.

More than I hate letting my younger sister, Keelie, watch her stupid cartoons.

More than when I get grounded from my PlayStation.

She wears annoying clothes. What girl wears leather jackets?

And the brat has thrown rocks at my head too many times.

Everyone says we'll get married one day, but that's disgusting.

Who'd want to marry a girl who drives you bonkers?

Not me. That's for sure.

Let some other stupid boy have the lunatic girl.

But somehow, no matter how much we hate each other, we always end up in the same place. Even when I try to stay away, to not tease her, those are the days she decides to become my worst nightmare.

If I don't push, then Amelia pulls. If she doesn't pull, then I push.

"I can run faster than you," I say, standing next to Amelia, a mischievous smile on my face. "If I win, you have to give me your ice cream later."

Amelia snorts, giving me a dirty look before sticking her tongue out at me. "You wish, Jaxson."

"What did I tell you about calling me that?" I nudge her side. "My name is Jax, *Millie*."

"And my name is *Amelia*." She rests her hands on her hips, kicking out her foot and showing off her black Converse with pink laces.

I had my Converse sneakers first.

Amelia made fun of them and said my green laces were stupid.

But now, she's wearing them with ridiculous pink laces.

"I'll call you Gross Girl or Millie," I say. "Take your pick."

She swats her dark hair out of her eyes. "My pick is you losing to a girl … again."

"I wouldn't have lost last time if you hadn't cheated."

"I don't cheat. I just …"

"You what?"

Instead of answering, she shoves me onto the grass and takes off running. Taken off guard, I fall backward, and she laughs while sprinting toward the large tree we deemed the finish line to our race. The same tree I'd snuck behind and put gum in her hair last week.

"That's the only way you can win, cheater!" I shout while standing.

I go to chase after her, but Ava's voice stops me.

"Don't you think it's time to stop bullying her?"

"I'm not bullying her," I reply with a frown.

"What do you call it then?"

I tap my chin, struggling to recall what my mother called us the other day.

It hits me.

"They're like little rivals. It's cute," was what she said.

"We're rivals," I state.

"Rivals?" Easton, my friend, repeats. "What are rivals?"

I laugh. "If you don't know what it means, then you're dumb."

Joke's on me because I don't know what it means either, but, hey, if my mom says we're rivals, then we're rivals. My mom tells the truth. Like last week, she said I was the best son ever. The woman never lies.

I dash toward the tree where Amelia is hunched over, trying to catch her breath.

"Cheater." I push her side.

She picks up a wad of grass and throws it at me. "You're such a jerk."

"No, I'm your rival." I smirk.

TWELVE YEARS OLD

I hate Amelia Malone more than I hated her years ago.

She frustrates me.

She makes me want to pull my hair out.

Like just now, when we're at my house at a birthday party for my older sister, Molly, Amelia looks right at me and says, "My dad's bar is better than yours," out of nowhere.

We weren't even talking about our dads' bars, but of course, she finds another reason to think she's better, another reason for us to argue.

"You're dumb," I reply as we sit by the pool, our feet dangling in the water. "My dad has had his bar *way* longer. My grandpa and great-grandpa worked there too. I win."

"No, *you're* stupid, Jaxson." She kicks her feet so that water splashes in my face. "My dad's bar is bigger."

"I'm not stupid," I argue. "I got all *A*s and *B*s on my report card." I make a *take that* face.

I'm proud of my grades. I did overhear a teacher say I was

pretty smart for being a little asshole though. I probably shouldn't have taken that as a compliment and could've tattled —or threatened to tattle—for a better grade, but I'm really not a little asshole.

"I got all *As*," she says smugly, playing with her long braid.

"My teacher said I'm a smart asshole, so that means I'm smart."

She gasps and points at me. "You just said *asshole*. I could tell on you."

"I heard you say *bitch* with Ava earlier. I'll tattle on you too."

"No one would believe you." She laughs. "Besides, aren't you the one who got soap in his mouth last time?"

That incident was all Amelia's fault. She told my parents I'd told her to *fuck off*. My mom threatened if I said the F-word again, I was getting soap in my mouth.

I got cocky because I wanted to look cool in front of Amelia and said, "I don't want that shit in my goddamn mouth."

And then I really did get soap in my mouth.

So, the next day, when Amelia and I were together and alone, she looked straight at me and said, "Shut your goddamn mouth."

I told on her, but she called me a liar.

She didn't get soap in her mouth, but she did get grounded and missed a ski trip she had been looking forward to. That was when she wrote me a letter, threatening to put spiders in my mouth and saying she hoped I coughed them up for days. She also called me a jackass and drew a lame excuse for a donkey.

I wrote her back. My note had a better donkey drawing, and I pointed out that she couldn't draw worth a crap. Then, I actually did put spiders in her bed. I got grounded for that one, too, and I had to miss a birthday party, which sucked because it was at an amusement park.

The next time Amelia came over, she left pictures on my bed —pictures of her and our friends at the amusement park. On the back, she wrote, *Didn't wish you were there.*

"You've never even been in your dad's bar before," I say. "I've been in mine."

That's somewhat of a lie. My parents have never allowed me to go into the bar, but there's an apartment above the bar, where my mother and father once lived. If they have to work and don't have a babysitter, then I stay in the apartment. One night, my sister was stuck babysitting, so she and her friends were hanging out at the apartment. I got bored and snuck downstairs to the bar.

It was crazy, but I liked it. I knew from that moment that, someday, I was going to be like my dad and work in a bar. Hopefully his bar.

There was a guy at the front of the bar, singing into a microphone and playing music while people—some I recognized, even the teacher who'd called me a little asshole—were dancing to the music.

I walked around for a bit, seeing the shocked stares when I passed people. A guy spilled a beer, and his friends called him a "fucking douchebag." I made a mental note to call Amelia that the next time I saw her. I didn't make it long until one of my dad's waitresses spotted me and ratted me out.

I got grounded for that too.

Man, do my parents love to ground me.

Amelia crosses her arms. "I don't believe you. It's against the law for you to go into a bar, and if you had, you'd have gone to jail."

"That's for those who get caught." I wink at her.

Her expression changes. "Truth or dare?"

"Dare."

"I dare you to sneak me into the bar with you next time."

8

AMELIA

TOBY, a man in his fifties and an employee Christopher had deemed their right-hand man, shuffles in not too long after I make Jax listen to my ideas to improve the brewery. Which is fine with me. The less time I spend alone with Jaxson Bridges, the better. I've scheduled two appointments with prospective retailers to stock our beer, thanks to my mother.

Toby side-eyes me when he sees us in the office together. I'm sure it does look weird. Your deceased boss's girl in the office with his best friend–slash–business partner. So we won't look suspicious, I introduce myself to him and tell him I'm now the new partner.

Toby looks to Jax for confirmation. It annoys me, but I also understand. You can't randomly stomp into a business and tell employees you're the new boss without them questioning it. Jax reluctantly nods, most likely not wanting to look like a toddler in front of his employees, and Toby shakes my hand. We'd met before, shaken hands before, but it seems to be more of a respect thing to Toby.

Nolan, the next employee to come in, is a new face. Jax must've hired him after Christopher's death. He's on the younger side, and he shoots me a flirtatious smile when I introduce myself. That smile drops when Jax smacks the back of his head and says to keep his eyes to himself.

I'm not a hundred percent on what their jobs are, but I put it on my list to discuss it with Jax. I'd come here to show him I was serious. Even though I hate it when it happens, Jax is right. If I want to be taken seriously, I have to prove myself.

Which is why I spent all of last night researching brewery information, and I hoped to God I sounded like I knew what I was talking about.

Christopher's dream won't be in my past. I might be afraid of letting him go because I'm still healing. I'm unsure if I'll ever really be healed. One thing I do know is, I'll never be the same, never love the same, and never have as much hope in life as I once did.

As I leave the brewery and get into my car, my mind drifts to his letter.

The letter I can't open.

It probably has answers to so many questions.

But it also has the potential to destroy me.

So, I decide to give myself another day of not finding out what it says.

9

JAX

"YOU SHOULD BE HERE," I mutter.

Chris should be here.

It's a thought that repeats in my head as I pour a beer—Razzle Dazzle from our brewery—and slide it across the bar to a waiting Darcy.

I'm bartending at Down Home Pub tonight.

The pub has been in my family for generations. My great-grandfather passed it down to my grandfather, and then when my grandfather almost lost it, my dad returned to Blue Beech to prevent it from going bankrupt. He had planned to help him get back on his feet and then leave, but then my grandfather moved to Florida, and my father stayed. So, he took over the pub and then never left after falling in love with my mother.

Before there were ever even thoughts of a brewery, Chris and I bartended at Down Home. We talked about so many plans—having a business together, and when my father stepped down, we'd merge the brewery and the bar into one.

Now, I have to accomplish that dream solo.

Because over my dead body will Little Miss Amelia Malone share this with me.

I won't let her fuck more shit up.

I'll push her out if it's the last thing I do.

I don't bartend as much as I used to, but I've been asking my father for shifts.

Bartending helps clear my mind of business problems, losing my best friend, and how I'm feeling about the woman he left behind ... and practically dumped right into my lap.

"Thanks, Jax," Darcy says, winking at me.

I like Darcy. We dated for a few weeks in high school, but it never went anywhere. She ended up marrying a guy from our high school, who then cheated with their daughter's dance coach. Said dance coach is across the room, dancing with her friends to the live band's music. Thank fuck Darcy's ex-husband is nowhere to be seen. My hopes are that Darcy doesn't notice the mistress. After dealing with Amelia these past few days, breaking up a girl fight sounds like a goddamn headache.

I jerk my head in her direction. "Welcome."

"You doing okay?" She reaches out to brush her hand along mine.

I shut my eyes, hating this part—this constant question after losing someone you were close with.

Are you doing okay?

How are you holding up?

I don't mind as much when it's coming from Darcy though. She's been good to me. She found me, drunk and sitting on the curb of the funeral home, the night after Chris's wake. She grabbed the bourbon from my hand, brought me home, and took care of my wasted ass. She asked if I wanted to get a drink sometime, but I asked for a rain check. That rain check hasn't come, and she hasn't brought it up.

I've been so damn busy that I don't have time to date. My head needs to stay on the brewery. I saw what being in a relationship, being *in love*, did to Chris. And like hell will I let a girl destroy my heart as much as Amelia did his.

Darcy shifts in her chair, almost as if she's scanning the bar, and she briefly focuses on something before turning back around and saying, "Your girl is here."

My girl?

Since when the fuck do I have a girl?

I glance over her shoulder in the direction she was looking, and my gaze focuses on Amelia, who's headed our way. She appears uncomfortable, her purse pressed tight against her stomach, and her eyes don't meet any other customers'. Or mine. No doubt she wants to dodge anyone asking how she's been.

She probably gets that more than I do.

I hope so.

She deserves it.

Let them rip her apart.

"My girl?" I snort and pull her drink from her hand. "You're drunk and therefore cut off."

Darcy snatches back the glass. "Not everyone is blind in this town, Jax." She rolls her eyes before giving me a cheers motion and downs her drink. "Have a good night. I promise to make it easier by holding myself back from pulling the homewrecking whore out the bar by her hair."

I throw my head back. "Jesus, fuck, please don't."

Amelia has never been my girl.

She was Chris's girl.

Even though I had known her first.

Even though I had touched her first.

In the end, she became his.

And now, she's no one's.

"You were so much more fun in high school," Darcy says around a groan. "If you need someone to clear your mind after seeing your first love in here, you have my number." She slides off her stool, shoots me a flirty smile, and walks away.

I gape at Amelia with each step she takes toward me. She changed out of the clothes she had on earlier today at the brewery and is wearing a pair of tight jeans and a tank top that shows a hint of her cleavage. Unless she's wearing a turtleneck, I don't think there will ever be a time she doesn't have cleavage.

She was once so comfortable at the pub—a regular with Chris and our friends—and always visited him while he bartended here. I once told her if she was going to be here so much, she needed to get a towel and start cleaning. She then took that towel, poured someone's leftover beer onto it, and threw it at me.

Darcy stops to talk to Amelia on her way out, and Amelia gives her a timid smile before saying good-bye.

Amelia, timid?

That's a new one.

I've been around Amelia more in the past few days than I have in months. I kept as much distance between us as I could after Chris's funeral. I was doing well until the whole partner situation. One thing I've noticed is, she's definitely different. There's a deep brokenness to her. It's explainable, obviously, but so unlike her.

She's not the same Amelia—bright, bubbly, outspoken, and someone who always had the right thing to say on the tip of her tongue. Amelia was almost … perfect. I'd never say that shit out loud because I loathe her.

Surprisingly, Amelia strolls to my side of the bar. She pulls out a stool and plops down on it without looking up at me.

When she does peek up, she blows out a breath at the sight of me. "You've got to be kidding me. Why can't I seem to get rid of you lately? You still bartend here?"

I guess she didn't realize she was coming to my end of the bar.

"My bad." I scowl at her. "I forgot to sync my schedule with you."

"Funny." She pinches her plump lips together. "You might want to start doing that, so we can schedule the day you sell me your half of the brewery."

Even though Amelia is talking shit, there's no doubt she's had a rough day.

I know she's had a rough day because since she walked into the brewery, it was my goal to make it rough on her.

The rougher, the better. Just like sex.

I click my tongue against the roof of my mouth. "Millie, one thing you need to get through your mind is, that will never—and I repeat, never—fucking happen. *My* brewery shares the same name as my family's business. You honestly can't think I'd ever give that to someone, especially *you*. I thought you were smarter than that."

Her head jerks back. "Screw you."

Resting my elbows on the bar, one on each side of her, I lean into her space. "Why are you here, Amelia?"

Her breathing hitches at our proximity. I'm practically whispering into her ear. I suck in a breath when I see goose bumps form along her bare arms. I start to comment on them but decide against it. This isn't the time to point out shit like that. It's the time to continue being an asshole, getting out the worst jabs that I can.

There's so much commotion surrounding us in the bar, but it's as if we were in our own little world. Gone from my mind are people screaming out drink orders or people yelling *cheers* too damn loud.

Amelia doesn't pull away. "I needed a drink, and sometimes, I don't like doing it alone."

"Your dad co-owns another bar." My face and voice harden. "Go there."

"He's working there tonight. Last thing I want is for him to see his daughter in the corner of the bar, drinking away her sorrows."

"And being a dead guy's ex-fiancée, drinking away her sorrows at his old workplace, is any better?"

She flinches.

My words hit her exactly as I'd intended them to.

It was mean. I know. And I'm typically not a mean person, but the chick needs to stay away from the brewery and let me run my business in peace. If her not wanting to be around me because I say asshole shit assists me in getting my way, well, even better.

"Don't you dare say it like that, Jaxson."

Her face reddens in fury, and I push myself off the bar, certain she's contemplating punching me in the face.

I tilt my head mockingly. "Don't say it like what, Amelia?"

"Don't you dare call me the *dead guy's ex-fiancée*." She curls her upper lip. "Not only are those words incredibly insulting, but Chris and I were much more than that, nor were we ever ex-anything."

"What do you call someone who calls off their wedding?"

I'm ignoring customers right and left, not giving one fuck because I know my father will take care of them for me.

Amelia is stating the truth.

She and Chris were a lot more than that.

A hell of a lot more.

But she broke his fucking heart, so I don't mind breaking hers.

She slams her hand down onto the bar. "If we're going to play it that way, then I'll refer to you as the dead guy's best friend. How does that feel?"

"Don't you dare do that shit," I snarl.

"Do what? Play your game back on you?" She raises a brow. "You love judging me for decisions I made, which I don't have to explain to you. What about you, Jax? What about the bad decisions you made with Chris?"

My blood boils.

If she wants to go there, we'll go there.

"Millie Monster, are you referring to when we fucked one night and hid it from our dead friend?" I tsk her and advance a step, not caring if we catch bystanders' attention. "Don't forget you failed to tell him as well. So, that's an *us* decision."

She grimaces. "Why are you so cruel?"

"When have I ever been nice?"

She stays quiet a moment before saying, "If I had a drink, I'd throw it in your face right now."

"I'll help you out with that then." I turn, snatch a glass from the rack, scoop ice into it, and make her favorite drink without paying her another glance.

Why I'm making her favorite drink, I don't know.

I should be giving her something she hates.

When I'm finished, I slam the drink down in front of her, and sprinkles of cranberry juice hit the bar. "Throw away." I reverse a step, holding my arms out, emphasizing that I'm her target.

Her gaze slides from me to my father. "I won't make a scene at *our fathers'* business. I have too much respect for them, unlike you."

"All right then." I gesture to her drink. "Drink that guilt up."

Without waiting for a response from her, I walk away, pretending I don't care. My brain goes to all the times I've drunk away my guilt.

I was twenty the first time it happened. Young, dumb, and spiteful. I'd texted Amelia, suggesting we tell Chris because it was the right thing to do. Even though I knew it wasn't. She told me I'd lost my mind, to which I told her that the only time I'd ever lost my mind was when I had sex with her.

We never told Chris.

It remained a secret between us.

To everyone.

And it always will.

———

Not too long after our conversation, Amelia stands from her stool. I watch her, assuming she's leaving, but she only moves to the other side of the bar, where my father is working. He kindly smiles at her as she slumps into a leather barstool in the corner, slightly turning toward the wall. Her body language screams, *Leave me the hell alone.*

Throughout the night, I drop two glasses and spill a beer. All of which are unlike me. Hell, I haven't broken anything at the bar in years. Some of them are because of my wandering mind, and the others are because I keep sneaking glances at Amelia.

Why is she still here?

After the shit we said to each other, she should have realized she wasn't welcome here.

For the next hour, my father serves her. He also adds less alcohol to her drinks than normal—most likely not wanting her to get completely shitfaced. He understands her hurt since he suffered a loss along with us. He'd taken Chris in, raised him for years, and treated him like a son.

The first and only time I've ever seen my father cry was at Chris's funeral. The sadness in his eyes matched mine whenever his name was brought up.

One night, I overheard him telling my mother he felt as if he'd failed Chris and not been a good enough role model for him. That he was scared he wasn't a good enough father for us. My mother assured him he was, which is the truth. I have damn good parents. And though it wasn't for a long time, I'm happy that Chris was able to experience that too.

It's around midnight when my father approaches me and says, "I'm heading out. Frankie is taking over for me, but keep an eye on Amelia. I haven't made her drinks strong, but I don't want her driving home. Call her parents or a friend at the end of the night to take her home. Do not leave until she's safely on her way."

I salute him. "I'll make sure she gets home safe."

My father slaps my back. "I know you will."

There's no doubt on his face that I won't do what I said. Amelia and I have our differences, but I'd never leave her somewhere drunk. Hell, I wouldn't do that to any female. I don't know how many times women have handed me their phones and asked me to call someone from their Contacts for a ride.

Another hour passes, and people start clearing out of the bar. When I glance at Amelia, she's yawning, and her eyes are glossy as she talks to Frankie.

"She's cut off," I tell Frankie, my voice demanding, as I walk to them.

I couldn't care less if she's hungover tomorrow.

Let her feel miserable.

What I don't want is her sitting alone, vulnerable, in a bar.

Amelia glares at me. "You're not my boss." Her attention pings to Frankie. "Pour me another one, babe."

"Pour her a water or soda," I correct, my tone serious.

Frankie glances back and forth between us, as if attempting to put two and two together, and then nods. "Okay." She briefly smiles at Amelia. "Sorry, babe, but it's for the best. You'll thank us when you don't feel like crap tomorrow."

Frankie only started working at the bar a few months ago, so she doesn't know my history with Amelia. She also sees me as the boss's son, and most likely, she doesn't want to argue with me. We also made it clear upon hiring every employee that we have no problem with cutting customers off or refusing service.

I point my chin at Amelia. "Call Ava, Essie, or your parents—someone to pick you up. I'm not babysitting you."

"Did you forget everyone is in Vegas?" She rolls her eyes. "And I'd rather walk home than have you help me."

"Then, find a ride."

She snatches her phone from her purse and waves me away.

———

Forty-five minutes later, Amelia hasn't moved her ass from the other side of the bar.

The fuck?

I told her to leave.

I don't want her here.

There are enough reminders of Chris here.

And she's the worst of them.

When I see her, a combination of shame and anger rises through me.

I see Chris, our past, what we did, and how I once fell for her. I don't need to feel that shit right now.

I charge over to her. "Where's your ride?"

"Don't have one," she replies, playing with the straw in her water glass.

"I told you to *find one*."

"And I couldn't." She shrugs. "Our friends are out of town. I'm not calling my mother and telling her I'm alone in a bar. I can already hear her *staying safe* speech—"

"You're at Down Home," I interrupt. "She knows you're safe."

"Exactly. I talked to Frankie, and she suggested you give me a ride."

I cup my hand around my mouth and yell for Frankie. She skips over to us.

"Did you suggest I take her home?" I ask, tipping my chin toward Amelia.

Frankie bites into her lower lip and nods. "Kinda, sorta."

My attention snaps back to Amelia. "What happened to you'd *rather walk*?"

"I don't think you'd let her walk even if she tried," Frankie says, flipping her brown hair over her shoulder. "Now, either I can leave and make you serve everyone or I can tend the bar and you can take this sweet girl home."

"See," Amelia says with a smug, inebriated smile. "She said I'm sweet, asshole."

"She's young, and she isn't mature enough to know who Satan is," I reply.

Frankie throws her head back and laughs. "I've got this. Take the girl home."

I shake my head. "Frankie, I know you're new here, but I don't play babysitter."

"You're not a *babysitter*," Amelia says with a smirk. "You're my Uber."

I run a hand over my face. "I'm not your goddamn Uber either."

"It's a ten-minute drive. You can take me home."

Amelia hates me.

I hate her.

Why would she want me to take her home?

Because she's tipsy and not thinking clearly—that's why.

I narrow my eyes at her. "You'd better not try to kill me on the way home, so you can have the entire brewery to yourself."

"You're not worth the prison time, Bridges."

———

I clean up my side of the bar and double-check with Frankie that she's good to handle things on her own. Then, I point to Amelia's drunk ass and say, "Let's go."

There's no missing the curious glances we receive when I assist her off the stool, hold her elbow, and lead her toward the employee door at the back of the bar. Thank fuck my Land Rover is parked in the back lot. It's less steps, which means less people claiming we left the bar together. Just that sentence alone sounds bad.

No one knows details, so all they'll relay to their friends is, *Did you see Jax and Amelia leave Down Home together?*

While I love living in a small town, I hate that it's big on gossip. And a guy leaving the bar with his deceased best-friend's girl is grade-A gossip and shameful. And no one would bother to question if that was really the case.

Us walking through the employee hall doesn't exactly mean we've dodged all questioning looks in our direction. It might be worse. Most people in the back kitchen know Amelia. They'll either see me as a jackass for being with Chris's girl or the good guy for making sure she gets home safely after having one too many.

One too many at a bar I didn't want her at.

One too many at the last place she should have been.

I push the back door open, and we walk out into the night. She groans when we reach my truck, and I open the passenger door. Grabbing her elbow, I help her inside. When her ass hits the seat, she turns her head, her eyes meeting mine. Our only sources of light are the overhead parking lot lights and the faint glow from my car. Her brown eyes soften, and for a second, I'm transported to a time when we were two kids who loved picking on each other.

She relaxes into the seat, as if she feels safe and content for the first time in a while.

Without thinking, I reach out and slowly push a fallen strand of hair away from her face before running my knuckle against the soft skin of her cheek. She shudders. I'm not sure if it's a result of my touch or the chilliness of my hand. She briefly shuts her eyes, as if my touching her is a stress reliever, but I instantly pull away at the sound of a door slamming.

Our eye contact drops as I look past her to Cal, one of the cooks, walking out. He tosses a bag of trash into the dumpster and walks back inside without paying us a glance. Thank fuck for Cal though.

Amelia bows her head, no longer looking at me, and I slam the door. I curse myself on my walk to the driver's side. For a moment, I contemplate whether driving her home is a good idea. I could call my dad, her dad, ask Frankie to do it.

An uncomfortable silence fills the car as I shift the car into reverse and pull out of the parking lot and onto the street. One thing I at least have on my side is the drive is short since Amelia's townhome is only a few miles from the pub.

Neither one of us knows what to say.

Or how to break this stillness.

Or even if we should.

I don't say anything until we pull in front of her townhome and I put my Land Rover in park. "As payment for this ride, I'd like for you to steer clear of the brewery for at least a month."

She stares straight ahead. "Can you shut up about that for ten minutes? It's getting old, Jaxson. There shall be no business talk when alcohol is involved."

"The only thing we need to talk about is business, Amelia."

She blows out a breath and rests her head against the headrest. "Remember when we used to sneak into Down Home?"

"How could I forget?"

"Our parents wanted to kill us."

"We wouldn't have been in nearly as much trouble had you not dared me to try some beer."

My mind drifts back to that night. We were fifteen, and it was right after our parents became partners. Our dads were in the bar, working, and left Amelia and me in the apartment—which is now mine—located above the pub. Why they even thought that was a good idea is beyond me. We were bored, so Amelia came up with the bright idea to sneak into the bar.

She'd dared me to do it with her when I was twelve, but I chickened out, knowing that my dad would have my ass for it.

But I wanted to show off for Amelia, so that night, I shrugged and said, "Why not?"

A hot girl was suggesting we break the rules. I was all for it.

We didn't make it twenty minutes until someone ratted on us. Our dads dragged us back upstairs and called our mothers to snitch.

My mom laughed, which earned her a stern, "Really, Sierra?" from my father.

She mentioned some shit about *like mother, like son*.

That was how my mom and dad had first met. She'd snuck into the pub when she was only eighteen, and my dad kicked her out.

Amelia and I have changed so much since we were stupid teenagers.

"Do you honestly believe Chris's death is my fault?" Her question comes out of nowhere.

"Didn't we say there'd be no talk of business?" I ask, raising my hands to grip the steering wheel.

She plays with her hands in her lap. "That's not exactly business."

I stay quiet.

"Be honest," she whispers.

Looking away, I work my jaw before clearing my throat and saying, "Don't ask questions you don't want the answers to, Amelia."

"What have I ever done for you to hate me this much?" Her voice is despondent and riddled with pain. "You know I loved him."

I talk before she can continue her lies. "You loved him?" I scoff. "You fucking *broke* him."

As if she can't endure another word from me, she frantically unbuckles her seat belt, swings the car door open, and nearly face-plants out of it.

"Goddammit." I hurriedly step out of the car before she hurts herself and gives me an even bigger headache.

"Don't!" she screams into the night. "I don't want or need your help!"

I'm waiting for a neighbor to call the cops on us for acting like fucking lunatics.

Not wanting to deal with that possible problem, I extend my helping hand to her. "Come on. I'll get you inside and then be on my way."

Tears well in her eyes, but she blinks, attempting to keep them at bay so I'm not satisfied with her breakdown.

Lowering my voice, I say, "Amelia, come on. The more time you spend out here, giving me the death stare, the more time we spend together. Let's get you inside."

She stares at me grimly before slowly nodding and sliding her ass off half her seat. I grab her trembling hand, gently helping her out of her seat, and her elbow is shaking when I guide her onto the sidewalk and up her porch stairs. Neither of us mutters a word in the process. I keep her up with one hand, and with the other, I grab her keys from her jeans pocket to unlock the door.

She hits a light switch. The hallway illuminates, and I free her from my hold.

"Come on," I say, gripping her wrist. "I'll throw you in bed, and you can sleep off your buzz and call in to work tomorrow."

She halts, her arm reaching out for me, and shrieks, "No!" Realizing her outburst, she shuts her eyes. "I mean ... you don't have to do that. Just drop me off in the living room, and I'll take care of myself from there."

The last thing I need is her hurting herself, trying to get into bed. We've come this far, so I might as well finish the job. I'll consider it my good deed for the week.

She glares at me, not moving.

"Trust me, I won't try to touch you, if that's what you're thinking."

No one has ever referred to me as a man you need to worry about being alone with, so Amelia's behavior is strange, but so the fuck is she. So, I ignore it.

She still doesn't move.

Jesus.

"You think you're going to vomit?" I ask. "I'll dump you in the bathroom, and you can sleep it off in there."

She goes quiet.

"Oh shit, *are* you about to vomit?"

"The bathroom is fine," she mutters.

I nod, and on our trek to the bathroom for Amelia's possible upchuck, we pass her laundry room.

I stop, blinking like I had too much to drink and am seeing

shit. "Whoa, why does it look like someone is camping out in your laundry room?"

The disheveled blankets, the sleeping bag, and pillows.

"It's nothing," she quickly replies.

"What the fuck is going on, Amelia?"

"Oh, I don't sleep in my bedroom anymore." She shrugs.

"Why the hell not?"

Her eyes are vacant. "That's none of your concern."

"You're right; it's not. But it's also pretty fucking weird."

She shrugs. "People do it sometimes."

"I've never heard of anyone crashing in their laundry room, and I know damn well before Chris passed, you were sleeping in bed together." My stomach churns at those words.

"Things change," she says, using the wall as leverage to slide out of my hold and move past me.

I snatch her hand. "Tell me why you're sleeping in your laundry room."

"Go home, Jax." She jerks away from me. "You got me home. You did your good deed. Thank you."

"Why aren't you sleeping in your goddamn room, Amelia?"

"Would you be able to do it, Jax?" she cries out, the tears she's been holding back now slipping down her face freely. "Would you be able to go into that same room after you found the love of your life dead in there?"

10

AMELIA

THIS IS IT.

The moment all my hidden pain decides to reveal its ugly face.

And the worst part?

Jax has a front row seat.

"The fuck?" he asks. "Why aren't you staying with someone? Why are you here if you can't even sleep in your own bed?"

"I don't want people to know!" I scream at the top of my lungs, as if I'd been holding that in for so long and it could finally no longer sit there.

He grabs my shoulders and shifts me to face him. His deep eyes bore into mine, his face creased in concern. "Why?"

"I don't want people to worry about me. It's also embarrassing to say you can't sleep in your own bed."

Jax huffs. "It's not like you're not sleeping in there because you're scared of the dark." He grabs my chin, cupping it in his palm, forcing me to face him. "People will understand. Quit trying to act all right if you're not all right!"

I don't pull away from him or smack his hand away. Let him see the pain I'm feeling. The pain he's contributed to every time he pointed his finger at me in blame.

"Why do you care?" I ask, fixing my gaze on him. "Why do you care where I sleep?" I sneer. "And better yet, why are you still here?"

"I keep asking myself that goddamn question." In frustration, he runs a hand through his hair. "Pack a bag. You're sleeping at my place."

"The hell I am."

He pinches the bridge of his nose. "That wasn't a question, Amelia."

11

JAX

WHAT THE FUCK *is wrong with me?*

I'll regret this later.

But the pain on her face was enough to bring a man to his knees.

"Why are you doing this?" Amelia asks from the passenger seat.

"I don't know," is the honest answer I give.

"I'll end up sleeping in your living room or the kitchen, so I don't see much difference from my laundry room because no way am I sleeping in that guest room."

She's referring to the guest room that was once Chris's before they moved in together.

"You can have my bedroom." Another *what the fuck is wrong with me* moment.

"I don't want to sleep in your room either."

"What the hell is wrong with my room?"

"I'm not trying to lie in the same sheets as your random hookups," she states matter-of-factly. "Who knows how many girls have been in that bed?"

"Not as many as you'd think."

"Pfft. I've heard the stories."

"From who?"

"Christopher. Our friends. Everyone in this godforsaken town."

"Why are you talking about my sex life, Millie?" I hiss, not glancing in her direction. "Do I ask about yours?"

"I don't have one, idiot. You and Christopher are the only men I've ever been intimate with ..." She lowers her voice. "The only men who've ever touched me."

Her words send a jolt of guilt through me. Yet, for some reason, that guilt is then consumed by memories of what it was like, being with her ... touching her. I want to scream at my cock as it stirs. This conversation needs to move to something else —fast.

I shift in my seat. "I'd prefer not to hear about any of those times."

"Come on." She smacks the center console. "Don't act like Chris didn't get dumb and talk about him and me before."

"I shut him down every time." It's easier to tell her these things when the only light showing our faces is when we pass a streetlamp. It's easy to not be a dick when we're in the dark.

"Yeah, whatever," she grumbles. "Boys will be boys."

"You think I wanted to hear about the first girl I slept with sleeping with my best friend?"

She goes quiet.

I always tuned out Chris when he talked about him and Amelia being intimate. Not that he was a douchebag who bragged about it all the time.

Chris tried to get Amelia and me to get along. He'd ask me to go on double dates with them, but I always made up a bullshit excuse. I tended to steer clear of them together, but that doesn't mean it never happened.

Not another word is said until we're back at Down Home. I park in the back, kill the engine, and unbuckle my seat belt. Amelia doesn't. She's frozen in place, staring ahead, as if her mind is on something but nothing at the same time. I'm not sure if it's because she isn't confident if she can walk or if she isn't comfortable with going into my apartment.

"Do you want to get out of the truck or sleep in it?" And for the first time since the entire ride, I pay her a glance.

Her head is lowered, and she's biting her nails.

"It might not be as comfortable as your laundry room though," I add.

She shoots me a look of annoyance before rubbing her tired eyes. "Yes, but more annoying since you'll be there."

"For someone helping you out, I'd think you'd be more appreciative."

"I never asked for your help, nor did I ask to be dragged out of my home."

"Whoa. You willingly walked to my car and didn't fight me once on coming here, sweetheart."

"I'm tired." She takes a deep breath. "Let's continue this argument tomorrow."

Same. Fucking same.

"Let's go inside then."

I climb out of my truck, and this time, she doesn't fight me when I help her out of the vehicle. There's no struggle or conversation as we walk through the parking lot, up the stairs, and into my apartment. I grip her shoulders, ensuring she's level, before hitting the lights.

She leans against the wall, and her voice is monotone as she says, "Wow. It's been forever since I've been here." Her gaze is straight forward, and she doesn't look around the room.

"It has." I cup her elbow and walk her to my bedroom. "Here you go, princess."

She turns to stare at me, wide-eyed. "What?"

I scratch my jaw. "Did you think I lied about offering you my room?"

"Uh ... actually ... maybe ... yes." A blush spreads along her cheeks.

"We'd better get you in there before I change my mind and make you sleep in my closet or fridge."

She shuffles into the room and mutters, "A made bed ... shocker."

I move past her to grab two shirts and two pairs of sweats, and I toss her one of each before taking my toothbrush and toothpaste from the bathroom.

She hugs the shirt to her stomach. "Where will you sleep?"

I turn on the bedside lamp. "Why do you care?"

"Um ... maybe because I'm taking your bed."

"Go to sleep, Amelia." I walk to the door. "I'm fucking exhausted."

I hit the light switch, the room dimming, and as I go to shut the door, she speaks.

"Hey, Jax?"

"Yeah?" I keep my back to her.

"Have you read your letter yet?"

My shoulders tense. "Nope. Have you?"

She sighs. "No."

"Why not?"

"I'm afraid of what it says."

"Me too."

Not wanting to continue this conversation, I shut the door and walk away before she tries to ask any more questions. My chest is tight as I stalk to the guest bathroom, drop my toiletries on the counter with more force than necessary, and then place both palms on each side of the sink. I bow my head, and for what seems like the first time tonight, I really absorb everything that happened.

Today felt like one of the longest days of my life.

Tears prick at my eyes, and I violently shake my head to get rid of them. I drag my arms up, glance at my reflection in the mirror, and then quickly look away. Amelia and I hurled one too many insults and too many truths at each other tonight.

"Would you be able to do it, Jax? Would you be able to go into that same room after you found the love of your life dead in there?"

I shut my eyes. "Goddamn it."

Then, I splash water onto my face, brush my teeth, and head into the living room. I shrug out of my shirt, throwing it onto a chair, dump my shit from my pockets onto the coffee table, and then change my pants. I snag a blanket and my phone before collapsing on the couch. When I check my phone, I find a text from my dad.

> Dad: Frankie said you took Amelia home?

Not exactly *home*, but he doesn't need to know all the details.

> Me: I did.

> Dad: Thank you.

My head pounds as I toss my phone on the coffee table.

After making myself comfortable on the couch, I throw my arm over my face and groan.

My thoughts drift to the letter.

The one I'm too terrified to open.

And I sure as hell can't open it while Amelia is in my bed.

12

AMELIA

WHAT'S WORSE than waking up on your laundry room floor?

Waking up hungover in Jax Bridges's bedroom.

I hate admitting Jax was right, but his bed was definitely more comfortable than my laundry room.

His bedroom smells fresh, like clean linen, and I'm impressed with how tidy it is. I don't know why I assumed it'd be messy. Probably because I was constantly picking up after Christopher. I assumed that was how guys lived until they either got whipped into shape or stayed that way.

Jax has the basics of a bedroom with only a few small touches. His mom, one of the best interior designers in our state, most likely did the majority of the work.

I sluggishly slip out of his bed, a rush of nausea hitting me, and I bow my head.

Please, for the love of God, do not let me vomit on this man's floor.

I can't imagine the shit he'd give me for that.

Or even the embarrassment from it.

Not that the asshole doesn't deserve to clean up some vomit.

I sigh on my way to use the bathroom, and it's not until I glance at my reflection in the mirror that I remember I traded my shirt out for Jax's last night and kicked my pants off. My only thought before doing so was that it smelled good and that the soft cotton would be ten times more comfortable.

In need of a drink of water and planning to change back into my clothes after, I walk into the kitchen. Shutting my eyes, I mutter, "I'm never drinking again."

When I open them, Jax's mom, Sierra, is standing across from me.

I freeze.

This looks bad.

Real bad.

Panic sets in. I'm wearing Jax's shirt and leaving his bedroom early in the morning. My hair looks like a rat's nest, and I didn't bother wiping the streaked mascara from underneath my eyes.

The kitchen is silent for a moment as we stare at each other.

"Good morning, Amelia," she finally says, her lips forming a warm smile, no doubt to mask her confusion. "I'm sorry. I had no idea Jax had a guest over."

"Oh, no," I rush out. "I drank a little too much at the pub last night, so he let me sleep it off here."

She motions toward the grocery bags on the kitchen island. "I figured Jax would be at work."

I look around the kitchen, wondering where Jax is. "I was about to head home." My voice turns hesitant.

"Sit down." She points to a barstool. "We haven't seen each other in a while."

"Mom."

My back straightens at Jax's voice behind me, but I don't turn to look at him.

"I didn't know you were coming this morning," he adds.

Sierra whispers, "I bet you didn't," while reaching down to open a bottom cabinet. "I grabbed you a few things from the store."

Sierra is gorgeous. She's tall, all hair, and outgoing. She

reminds me of my mom. Maybe that's why they're such close friends.

My breath catches in my throat when Jax enters the kitchen, barefoot, shirtless, with loose cotton sweats hanging low on his waist. My heart lurches, and I quickly look away.

Then, as discreetly as possible, I slowly return my gaze to him. He towers over his mom and me. His body is athletic, but not too brawny—all the right muscles in all the right places. Dark stubble is dusted over his lower cheeks, chin, and neck. His thick brown hair is a tousled mess at the top of his head. Sierra once referred to his hair as unruly, and Jax always refused to shave it. His hair was always long enough for me to pull when I wanted to torture him. Now, my stupid hungover mind ventures to different ways I could pull his hair … more intimate ways.

I had no idea the man was still sporting a six-pack.

Ugh.

It's not fair that I'm fighting to not eye-fuck him.

"I called but got no answer," Sierra says, opening the fridge. "I assumed you were at work." She turns back, gripping two water bottles, and hands one to each of us.

Jax runs his hand through his hair. "I'll be headed that way in a sec."

She nods. "How are you two doing, working together at the brewery?"

"It's not going well," I answer at the same time Jax says, "Let's not ruin my morning."

Sierra glances back and forth between us before giving her son a stern look—most likely knowing he's giving me a hard time.

"Jax," she says in warning.

"Not talking about this with you." He opens his water, takes a long drink, and sets it on the counter. "I need to shower."

My gaze levels on him as he kisses his mother's cheek and leaves the room, not shooting one glance or word in my direction. I open the bottle and gulp down as much water as I can, choking on some, and it takes a moment for me to regain my composure. All the while, Sierra quietly observes me.

"Is your car out front?" she asks when I settle the water bottle on the counter.

I nod.

"Come on." She waves me in her direction. "I'll walk you to it."

I return to his bedroom, collect my clothes and slide into my pants, but I leave Jax's shirt on. When I come back out from his bedroom, Sierra eyes me, noticing I didn't change out of her son's clothing, but she doesn't comment on it.

We leave the apartment, the morning sun smacking us in the face, and walk side by side around the building and to the nearly empty front parking lot.

"How have you been?" she asks.

"Good." I don't meet her eyes. "Getting by, I guess."

I used to see Sierra a lot, not only because our families were close, but also because Christopher lived with Jax and his family. She became the mother that Christopher had always wanted.

"As much as Jax is being a pain in the ass, I think you two working together at the brewery will help you both heal."

"If we don't stop arguing with each other about quitting."

"You're both strongheaded. Jax won't sell, and I've known you long enough to assume you won't either."

We stop at my car, and she reaches out to gently squeeze my hand.

"My son won't be happy with me saying this, but he'll get over it. I think it'll be good for the both of you."

Then, she embraces me in a tight hug.

———

I toss Jax's shirt on the laundry room floor when I get home.

What was I thinking, going to Jax's house and sleeping in his bed?

I get in the shower. My body not as sore as it tends to be in the morning. My head pounds, the hangover reminding me of how much I drank last night. Getting wasted hadn't been my plan.

But I'd needed something to clear my mind of Jax and the brewery. And my dumbass hadn't thought to check if he still worked at the pub.

As I tip my head back in the shower, warm water hitting me, my shoulders relax.

I'm not giving up on the brewery. I'll prove myself to be an asset there and show the employees that I'm a much better boss than Jax.

Jax and I have called ourselves rivals for years.

We can either stay that way or learn to work together.

13

JAX

"HOW AM I going to get rid of her?" I ask my mom as I walk out of the bathroom, my hair still wet from my shower.

She's standing in my kitchen, coffee in her hand, and she stares at me with gentle eyes. "You're not. And, honey, I don't think you want to."

I grab a mug from the cabinet and fill it with much-needed coffee. "She won't let me buy her out."

"Does that surprise you?" she asks. When I only give her silence, she continues with, "It's all she has left."

"It's all I have left of him too."

"Maybe you two can help each other heal."

"I don't want to be near her."

"Is that why she slept over last night?"

"That's different."

"How so?" She wrinkles her nose. "You refuse to work with her but will have a sleepover?"

My shoulders fall slack. "I took her home, discovered she'd been sleeping in her damn laundry room, and stupidly brought her back here."

My mother's brows furrow. "Why is she sleeping in her laundry room?"

"She doesn't like sleeping in her bedroom because of ..." My voice trails off, as I'm unable to say the words out loud.

She puts me out of the misery of having to finish my sentence. "I can understand that." Her voice is soft and comforting. "Why isn't she staying with someone? If Lola knew about this, she'd be at Amelia's right now, packing her stuff up."

"Which is why you won't say anything to Lola—to *anyone*." I stress my last two words, as if they were my last wish.

"You sure have me keep a lot of secrets between you and Amelia."

I rub the back of my neck. "I don't know what you're talking about."

She gives me a *really* look. She's the only person—other than Amelia and me, obviously—who knows about Amelia and me having sex.

She came in when I went to the bathroom to toss the condom, but not wanting to embarrass Amelia, she told me, "We'll talk about this later," and left.

Amelia never found out, and my mother never told anyone.

"We were sixteen. Stupid teenagers. That's all it was."

She nods but doesn't believe me.

"She probably wouldn't have come here had I not practically forced her or she wasn't exhausted or tipsy."

"I appreciate you doing that, but maybe you should talk her into staying with someone else."

I scratch my cheek. "Nah. Knowing Amelia, she'll keep crashing in that laundry room before she lets anyone do anything about it."

"You have an extra room here. See if she wants it."

I give her a stern look. "No."

"Oh, come on." She laughs. "Your father and I were roommates here."

I wiggle my finger at her. "Yes, and now, you are also married with kids."

She grabs her coffee and wraps both hands around the mug.

"Sometimes, happiness comes along when you think it's the last thing you'll ever get back."

———

"I like the new boss." Toby says when I walk into work late—thanks to Little Miss Amelia.

Toby was the first employee Chris and I hired when opening the brewery. Chris was skeptical of hiring an older guy, but I could tell Toby wasn't about the bullshit. Yeah, sometimes, younger guys have a little more kick to them, but they can also come with problems too. Toby doesn't sit around and complain about relationship issues, nor does he come in hungover. He's one of the most responsible men I've ever known. His parents owned a winery and brewery before closing it when he was fifteen, so he's knowledgeable and helpful as fuck. He doesn't mind hard work and long hours.

"Not a new boss," I reply sternly, crossing my arms. This feels like the first time I've ever spoken in an *I'm the boss* tone.

He follows me into the office. "Did you hire her? Why is she here?"

"Chris left her his share of the brewery."

At this point, everyone will find out anyway. Might as well be honest about it. I don't want anyone to think I hired Amelia out of the kindness of my heart. They need to be made aware that her being here is against my will.

Toby chuckles. Yes, the dude fucking chuckles. "This will be interesting."

"No, it won't." I collapse into the chair behind the desk and level my palms on it. "I need you to be a dick to her, make her not want to work here."

It's an asshole thing to do—ask someone to be mean to Amelia. But a business owner has to do what a business owner has to do.

Toby shoves his wrinkled hands into his more wrinkled

slacks. "I will not be impolite to a woman who recently lost the man she loved." He shakes his head in disappointment, the way a man would to a child throwing a tantrum. "A man who was my friend and boss. Find someone else to do your dirty work."

I glare at him. As much as I want to argue, I respect Toby. I admire the respect he has for Chris.

"May I speak freely?" he asks.

I make a *have at it* motion.

"I'd do the same thing for the woman I loved. I'd leave her the one other thing that I cared about." He walks deeper into the office, standing only inches from the desk, and I've never seen him so solemn. "Who would you leave your half to?"

I frown. "I'm going to pass on giving hypotheticals if I die, man."

He pushes his thin-framed glasses up his nose. "It's good to know these things, Jax. If you died right now, who knows if Amelia would become the sole owner of this place?"

My eyes harden at him and the idea of that.

"But right now, she seems like a better boss than your grumpy ass."

My mouth drops open. I've never heard Toby mutter a profanity before.

"I'm not grumpy," I argue.

"You are grumpy."

I lean back in the chair. "I lost my best friend and business partner."

"True, but you were—"

"Were what?"

"You're a great guy—a playboy, as one might say—but Jax, there has always been an emptiness inside you." His attention stays fixed on me. "That's the reason you overwork yourself. You don't want to face whatever that emptiness is."

"What are you now"—I rest my elbow on the arm of the chair—"a profiler?"

"You've never asked what I did in the military, now have

you?" He arches a brow. He takes a seat in the chair and keeps his shoulders straight as he continues to analyze me.

I should stop him, but I'm interested in his words.

"I always thought Chris was blind," he states. "To not see that something had happened between you and Amelia. The two of you played it off well. The more you pretended to hate each other, the more animosity there was between you."

"I don't like the chick," I interrupt, no longer wanting to hear him spit facts.

"You have feelings for her."

My head spins, like I drank as much as Amelia last night, and I avert my eyes away from Toby. Whatever reaction I'm giving, I don't want him to witness it.

I swat my hand through the air and hate myself for glaring at an old-timer. "You're fired. I can't have an employee this batshit crazy."

My warning doesn't faze him, and he continues, "You mean, you don't want an employee who points out the obvious?"

Did hating each other look worse than us being friends?

Would it have been easier if we'd gone the opposite route?

In the back of my mind, I figured no one could ever suspect something had happened between two people who despised each other so much. No one would question if I'd been intimate with a girl I ridiculed all the time.

"Think about it," Toby says, proceeding to beat up my emotions. "Why do you hate each other? With how much you tried to push her away from Chris, it was obvious. Either you were in love with him or with her. And seeing you two yesterday, I'm guessing it's most likely the latter." He runs his hand through his gray beard. "Amelia doesn't hide it as well as she thinks either, you know."

"Amelia loved Chris," I bite out, wanting to throw something.

To get up and leave.

To pull myself out of this conversation.

He nods in full agreement. "She did love him. There's no denying that. But no matter what people say, you can love more than one person. Whether it be at different times in your life or at the same time, you can. I've seen her interact with Chris's other friends, and trust me, boy, she's never looked at them like she does you."

"I need a drink," I say, blowing out a stressed breath and wishing I'd never entertained this conversation with Toby in the first place.

"It's nine in the morning." He huffs before dragging himself to his feet.

"Exactly. You come in first thing in the morning, spitting out nonsense that Amelia and I have feelings for each other." I stand from the chair and tighten my jacket around my chest. "Get back to work before I fire you."

"Fine by me. I'll just ask Amelia to rehire me."

"My decisions outweigh Amelia's."

Toby turns and is staring at the open doorway, shaking his head. "No, I think Amelia has just as much say." A smile takes over his face.

I stiffen when I look past Toby to find Amelia standing in the doorway. Her arms are crossed, a bag is slung over her shoulder, and she's scowling at me.

"Yeah, Jaxson," she says, "I have just as much say."

An adrenaline rush shoots through me, and I ignore her. "How long has she been standing there, Toby?"

My ears ring as I await his answer, as if he were taking a year to reply.

"Not long," Toby replies. "Just right after I said she'd rehire me." He beams with pride.

I grind my teeth, seriously considering firing him. That thought doesn't last long since it'd be almost impossible to run the brewery without him.

Toby tips his head toward Amelia, wishing her good morning, and disappears out of the office.

"You can have the day off," I immediately tell her. Long breaths release from my chest when she comes closer.

"Toby is right, you know." She drops her bag to the floor.

What exactly does she think he's right about?

Was Toby lying when he said how long she'd been there?

My stomach churns, and my mouth turns dry. I don't mutter a word.

"I have just as much say as you," she finishes.

My heart slows, no longer thudding harshly against my chest at her having overheard our conversation.

I mimic her arm crossing and sit on the edge of the desk. "Toby said that to fuck with me. Don't worry; he'll be fired."

"The last person you're firing here is Toby."

"True, and the first person is you." I slide off the end of the desk and inch toward her. "You look like hell. Hungover. Like I said, take the day off." I stand tall, and even though Amelia is on the taller side, she still has to look up to see me. "Or the week. Hell, take the entire fucking year off."

Tension bleeds through the room. For so long, we've avoided being this close, and now, it's becoming a daily occurrence.

Can we prevent it?

Yes.

We could do so much to avoid it, but for some reason, anytime we're in the same place at the same time, we're drawn to each other.

And the closer we are to each other, the heavier our breathing grows. The more she releases light whimpers. Whimpers I don't think she realizes are coming from her full lips.

We're so competitive with each other, neither of us wanting to be the first to pull away. But we don't look at each other. My eyes are on the top of her head, and hers are on the tiled floor. When we speak, it's like we're talking to nobody but ourselves.

"I'm here to stay, Jaxson," she hisses.

"No, you're not."

"Don't make this difficult."

"I will."

"Act like I'm a normal partner. Someone you hardly know."

"I can't."

"There was a time you didn't hate me. Go back to that."

"Briefly." I clench my fist. "It's hard to hate someone when they're letting you stick your fingers inside them."

I let out a grunt when an elbow plows into my stomach, and she pushes me away.

I expected her reaction, but damn, I didn't think she had that much strength in her.

I right my balance, and my breathing is ragged when I adjust my gaze back on her. Her brown eyes stare at me with a mixture of pain and anger.

Am I proud of my response?

Not exactly.

But it caused her to back off.

To create the distance that we need.

She swats her hair away from her face and runs her hands over her cheeks. "Make a list of Christopher's job responsibilities." Her voice starts shaky, but she quickly gains control of it.

"Online marketing. You can do that from your laundry room." I stalk to the doorway and motion for her to leave. "Good-bye."

She shakes her head, nearly staring at me with repulsion. "I'm here, and if you don't like it, that's your problem. Not mine." She strolls over to the desk. "I survived losing Chris. I think I can survive handling you."

"If only he could've survived you."

I hear a loud gasp, and I should've known not to let my guard down and look away. I fall back a step when something hits the side of my head, and a deep pain rumbles through my skull. It happened so fast that I don't even know what was thrown at me. I don't get the answer until I nearly trip over the stapler that fell at my feet.

I rub my head, searching for the right words to scream at her, while she acts indifferent. She snatches her bag, pulls out her laptop, and circles the desk. I blink, processing what the hell happened as she takes my abandoned seat. She props the laptop onto the desk and makes herself comfortable.

Ignoring the throbbing in my head, I ask, "What the fuck? You just assaulted me."

"I need to work." She signals toward the doorway. "You should go home and ice that. I'll take over from here."

"No, I need you to move out of my seat, so *I* can work."

"Too bad. You move your feet, you lose your seat."

"What are you, five?"

"Don't insult me. My aim is more of a ten-year-old, thank you."

"Oh, I'm not insulting you. I'm calling the cops on you."

14

AMELIA

JAX STARES at me like he wants to rip my head off.

Good. Because right now, I want to rip his dick off.

For years, we never muttered a word about what we'd done.

Now, it seems to be half of what we talk about.

The brewery.

Our secret.

The brewery.

Our secret.

Like a science rat on a wheel, circling repeatedly.

My heart races, and I'm sweating.

He won't really call the cops on me, right?

But the man does claim to hate me.

I'll deny it. Say the bump forming on his forehead was from a quick slip when he hit the wall.

Please don't have cameras in here.

It's not like I meant for the stapler to hit him. My target was the wall, but apparently, my aim decided to do the right thing and hit Jax.

"Call the cops and say what?" I ask in regard to his threat. "Do you want people to know you can't dodge a simple stapler? You were the kid picked last for dodgeball, weren't you?"

Jax narrows his eyes at me. "Amelia, get up."

I ignore him and pretend to focus on my blank laptop screen. "No."

Call it childish, but the only way I'm moving from his seat is if he physically removes me. Let him sit in a different chair, pop a squat on the floor, or work outside for all I care. If he'd kept his mouth shut, he'd still have his precious spot behind the desk.

Prepare to deal with the repercussions of your actions, Jaxson.

"Amelia, I will pick you up and toss you outside this room," he warns, his nostrils flaring.

"I dare you." I pick up the scissors and dangle them in the air, as if I might throw them next.

He shakes his head. "I should've let your ass sleep on the floor last night. Maybe you wouldn't have been rested enough to come in here and think you can throw shit at me. But, sweetheart, reality check. Just because I don't throw shit at you doesn't mean I can't hurt your feelings."

"Okay, Mr. Bully on the Playground." I drop the scissors and pretend type on my keyboard.

"You don't even know what you're doing," he points out.

"I'm answering emails," I lie, puffing out my chest and straightening my posture. "Pretty sure I know what I'm doing."

"Do you even know how to work the software we use?" He widens his stance and taps his chin. "What about balancing the books?"

I stay quiet since I most definitely do not know, but a girl can learn. "That's your job—always has been. Therefore, it's not a job requirement for me at the moment. Shall you decide to leave, then I will take on that responsibility. I'll finish my email and work. If you then decide to work on your attitude, I'll give you your seat back."

Jax opens his mouth to continue our petty argument, but he's interrupted.

"Boss, we have a problem," Nolan calls out before he barrels into the office.

He comes to a halt when he sees me sitting behind the desk and not Jax. He backtracks a step, as if he has the wrong room, but pauses when he spots Jax standing in the corner, looking all sorts of pissed off.

"Do you, uh …" Nolan signals between Jax and me. "Should I come back?"

"Yes," Jax replies at the same time I say, "No."

"What's the problem, Nolan?" Jax asks, rubbing the sore spot on his head.

"The heat exchanger is fucked up again—" Nolan stops himself again. "Sorry, ma'am. I mean, messed up."

I grab a pen and write *heat exchanger* on the notepad sitting to the side, right underneath Jax's scribbles and random notes.

I don't know much about Nolan, other than he's young—my guess, early twenties—and he's Toby's assistant.

Jax gives him a curt nod. "Thank you, Nolan."

"I'd start searching for another one." Nolan shoves his hands into the pockets of his ripped jeans. "I'm not sure if it's fixable."

"I'll get it taken care of," Jax replies.

Nolan salutes Jax, does some weird curtsy-bow to me, and leaves the office.

Jax takes the few steps until he's standing on the other side of the desk, facing me. "Unless you know how to fix a heat exchanger, get out of my chair."

I rip off the page from the notepad, not caring if he'll need whatever he wrote down, and hop out of the chair. "You're lucky I have an appointment with a possible client, or I'd keep my ass there all day. Business first, of course." I smirk. "That's how a *real* owner thinks."

"All you've *owned* is a social media business with an employee count of one—Y-O-U. That's not saying much."

I carefully slide my laptop back into my bag. "Wrong. I own a home. Unlike *Y-O-U*, who still stays at his mommy and daddy's old apartment."

"Screw off. I pay rent."

"That's so precious of the big boy to finally pay his own bills."

———

"I have to say," Suzanne LaPorta practically squeals, "this is absolutely delicious, and I'm typically not a beer fan."

Before leaving, I asked two of our distribution loaders to put sample boxes in the back of my car. I had six meetings scheduled for the day, and my goal was to get at least half to carry Down Home Beer. Not to sound cocky, but my sales skills are legit. I interned for my mother at 21st Amendment for a year before starting my business. She's asked me to come work for her countless times, but I like being my own boss.

My mom sent me Suzanne's contact information yesterday, and she was excited to schedule an appointment. She and my mother are friends, and my mom has tried to sell her on our beers, but she's always been hesitant to bring them into her high-end country clubs.

I convince her to give us a trial run in three of her clubs, and then we will take it from there. I also offer to dog-sit sometime, but, hey, I love pups and making money. Win-win for me.

We finish our business, and somehow, along with the dog-sitting, I also agree to sign up for her daughter's cookie subscription service.

I smile for what seems like the first time in a very long time and practically skip to my car.

Five out of the six deals were made.

Maybe this is exactly what I needed.

———

Jax is still in the office, his elbow resting on the desk, and he's so deeply focused on his work that he doesn't realize I'm there until I knock on the door.

"Fuck," he groans, shutting his eyes. "I thought you'd be out of my way the rest of the day."

"You thought wrong." I march into the room and toss the stack of paper-clipped contracts in front of him. "Here you go."

He scoops the papers up and flips through the pages. "What's this?"

"The deals I signed today."

His eyes widen. "You snagged LaPorta Country Club?" He whistles. "We've tried to land them several times."

I drop into one of the chairs to the side of the desk, making a mental note to get nicer, less scratchy chairs than these ugly tweed ones. "You haven't signed a new contract since Chris's death." I wasn't sure if I'd broach this subject yet. I planned to see how big of a knot was on the side of Jax's head before deciding to play nice or piss him off further.

It's only a little red, so I choose to bring up the sensitive topic.

"Bullshit," Jax bites out.

"You haven't, so don't lie to your business partner."

"Don't pretend to know shit."

"I have access to the software, Jaxson."

He winces. "How?"

"I kept Christopher's passwords because he constantly forgot them. He also used my laptop from time to time or had me do things for him." I cross my legs. "During my lunch break, I logged in to the software and skimmed some reports. Jax, what the hell have you been doing?"

He drops the papers. "I've been doing everything I can to keep this place running."

"To run a business like this, you have to acquire new clients."

"I am!" he roars, causing me to jump at his sudden change. "I've gone from having a partner to split responsibilities with to taking them all on my own. It's hard, finding employees who know what they're doing, and that's also adding to payroll." His eyes grow colder. "And news flash, Amelia: this isn't 21st Amendment. We're a new business with a new business budget, so we're not raking in cash. So, don't expect to become rich."

"I wasn't expecting to," I whisper.

Christopher drained his savings into the brewery, and he didn't take a large salary. I didn't mind paying most of the bills while he got his career together, but that didn't mean Christopher didn't struggle with it.

Jax stares at me in torment and doesn't stop talking. "I'm keeping this business running because it's the only thing I have, and the person who swore to do it with me backed out."

"Christopher didn't back out," I yell, swallowing thickly. "Don't you dare say it like that."

"How am I supposed to say it then?" He levels his palms on the desk, and I watch the muscles in his arms as he tenses before bringing himself to his feet. "Tell me, Amelia."

I hold in a breath as he starts pacing the room.

"He fucked us both with this little partner bullshit." It's as if Jax is rambling off every thought he's had for months, like these words can't be held in any longer. He stops in front of me and drops down to one knee, so we're eye-level. "Would he have done that if he had known what we did?" His breath smells like fresh mint and coffee. "If he'd known we were goddamn liars?"

I slowly release that breath as he reaches out and cups my chin.

"Do you think he'd want us to be good ole partners if he knew our history?"

My jaw trembles in his hold. "Does it matter now?"

His eyes meet mine.

Gone is the animosity.

Now replaced with sorrow. Hurt. So many emotions I connect with.

I shiver when his chilly finger runs along my skin.

I feel his brokenness in my blood. In my heart. In my soul.

I've experienced it so many times. I've lashed out. I've cried. I've wanted to throw every item in every room.

I want to comfort Jax, to tell him that I understand, but I do something else instead. Something dumb.

Without thinking, without hesitation, I lean forward, erasing the few inches separating our faces, and press my lips to his. He sucks in a breath, pulls back, and stands. Refusing to look at him and see the horror on his face, I scramble out of the chair, needing to get out of here.

"Don't." Jax grabs the back of my neck, turns me, and kisses me.

He doesn't kiss me how young girls dream about their first kiss or how you see in Hallmark movies—all cute and sweet. No, he devours me, kissing me like I'll provide his last breath and he'll die if his lips break from mine.

It's rough and aching with desperation.

With need.

I whimper into his mouth, and our lips don't separate as he walks me backward. He grips the back of my head, his hands in my hair, until my back is shoved against the wall.

"Millie," he groans into my mouth.

I shiver as his hand leaves my hair to travel down my shoulder and my arm before settling on my hip. His free hand drifts to the other hip, and he cups my waist, holding me in place. He holds me tight as if we were in a storm and I'd drift away if he released me.

Or in our case, reality will sink back in the second we pull apart.

Right now, Jax and I are in a different world as our tongues brush together. It's Jax and Amelia, no problems, no thinking.

It's a kiss so deep that it buries our thoughts of the consequences.

But those will be dug up later.

They will eat us alive.

We gasp for air when we separate, and he rains kisses along my jawline before licking the lobe of my ear.

"I want you," he groans into it. "So bad."

I hitch my leg up, wrapping it around his waist, and he grips my ass.

When he shifts himself, his hard erection brushes between my legs.

Then, everything crumbles at the sound of my ringtone.

He jumps back, as if he'd just stuck his hand on the stove.

"Goddamn it," he yells.

My shoulders slump against the wall, my brain moving a thousand miles per minute, and Jax storms out of the room. I recoil when I hear a door slam.

I stand there, unmoving, until I regain my composure. There's no Jax when I grab my bag and walk out of the office. His truck is gone when I leave the building, and I sag into the seat of my car.

What have I done?

I shuffle through my bag for my phone.

I grab it, then drop it, then grab it, then drop it again.

I scream into the silence of my car and manage to keep hold of it on the next try.

A call from Ava.

Then a text from her.

> Ava: Don't ignore my call. Girls' night. You need this.

I start my Jeep and swerve out of the parking lot.

I've passed on every girls' night invite since my life went up in flames.

But if I go home, all I'll think about is Jax as I sit in my laundry room, consumed with guilt.

I guess I can consume liquor alongside that guilt.

A guilt cocktail, coming my way.

———

Even though, I swore I was never drinking again, there is a myriad of reasons why I'm attending girls' night tonight.

- Sleeping at Jax's and his mom catching me coming out of his room this morning.
- Overhearing him and Toby talk in the office. I pretended I hadn't—like I'd arrived at the end of the conversation. I acted like I hadn't stood against the wall, my chest heaving in and out as Toby said things neither of us wanted to hear. Jax and I have a past, yes. But that's it. Nothing happened beyond that … until earlier today.
- And the topmost reason: the mistake of kissing him. Not only did I drop my walls and press my lips to his, but we also didn't stop there. No, we consumed each other, as if that thought had been sitting dormant in us for years.

And because of that, I park on the side of the road in front of Callie's Bake Shop. It's a dainty place, resembling something you'd see in a fairy tale. My friend and Jax's cousin, Callie, opened the restaurant last year. Her parents purchased the building and helped her remodel it into the place it is today with its hanging chandelier, French doors, and pink walls.

I draw in steady breaths before stepping out of my car. A sense of relief hits me that girls' night is here and not in some bar or club. I'll take mimosas, sandwiches, and cupcakes over dudes hitting on me any day of the week.

The hostess greets me by name and points me in the direction of the corner table, crowded by my friends.

"Amelia," Ava calls out, waving me over, a grin taking over her red lips.

Everyone's attention swings to me as I grow closer. Also at the table are Jax's cousins, Callie and Essie, and Mia.

Every girl at this table and I have been friends since childhood.

Callie smiles at me, her blue eyes wide. "You came."

Essie pushes her black glasses up her nose. "I honestly didn't think you would." She opens her bag, pulls out a twenty, and slides it to Ava.

Ava rubs her hands together. "I love it when I win bets."

"And I hate it when you wager if I'll go somewhere or not," I say, drawing out the chair next to Callie and sitting down.

Callie leans in and gives me a side hug.

Callie is the sweetest of the group, the positive one who never has anything negative to say about anyone. Ava and Essie are the loudest of the group, and Mia is the most closed off.

Not that I blame Mia. She's been called a rich bitch her entire life due to her mother being a wealthy celebrity, and she's always worried she's being used.

Frankie—the same bartender from Down Home—stops at our table to take our drink order. She splits her time between here and the pub. I order a mimosa—something that'll give me a little kick, but not strong enough for me to end up in someone else's bed again.

We go back and forth on what to order, and when Frankie returns with our drinks, Essie asks, "Amelia, have you and Jax talked since the whole *Chris leaving you part of the brewery* situation?"

Frankie shoots me a quick glance, most likely because she knows Jax and I left the pub together, but doesn't mutter a word.

I wait until she leaves before answering. I don't know Frankie well, and though she's always been nice to me, she still sometimes works with Jax. I'll steer clear of mentioning his name around anyone who can report back to him.

"We have," I mutter, taking a sip of my mimosa.

"And?" she stresses, pointing her glass at me.

"We're attempting to co-work," is the best response I can muster.

"Co-work?" Callie repeats.

"Is that even possible between you two?" Mia asks, leaning toward me.

"I don't know." I collect fake lint from my shirt, looking away from them. "I guess we'll see."

So far, it's not working out well.

I've slept in his bed, thrown a stapler at his head, and made out with him as he practically dry-humped me against a wall.

I'm not sure how much of that could be considered co-working.

Essie perks up in her seat. "I have a great idea."

"That's scary," Ava says, bumping her shoulder against Essie's.

Essie's attention stays pinned on me. "Maybe you two should finally admit that you like each other."

"Essie!" Callie hisses, slapping Essie's arm.

"What?" Essie asks, leaning back in her chair. "We've kept our mouths shut for years, but come on. She needs to know we're not blind."

A cold tremor runs through my body.

Is today everyone bring up Jax and Amelia together day?

I should've stayed in my laundry room.

Stuff like this doesn't happen there.

I open my mouth to say something, but no words come.

All I have in me is denial, but I'm not sure if I can look my friends in the eyes when I had my tongue down Jax's throat earlier. I'm easy to read and not a good liar. That's why I'm shocked that I've been able to keep my secret with Jax.

"Don't you think it'd be weird?" Mia asks Essie. "Telling them to get together is easy for you because you wouldn't be the one gossiped about."

"I mean, I've heard worse situations," Essie says. "It's not like it's immoral."

"You're right," Mia says. "But Blue Beech would rip her apart for it." She shoots me a sympathetic look.

I give her a thankful nod.

Mia doesn't speak much, but when she does, it's always facts. If anyone knows how harsh the Blue Beech critics can be, it's her.

My heart flutters wildly, and I'm racking my brain for ways to move this conversation away from me.

"How's working at the new firm?" Mia asks Essie, changing the subject for me.

"Stressful," Essie says. "Thank God for coffee, energy drinks, and Mario Kart–themed music."

"Mario Kart–themed music?" Callie asks.

Essie nods. "If you need to stay awake, blast it. I promise you, no sleeping will occur."

The conversation then moves to Callie telling her that lack of sleep is unhealthy, to Ava saying she chugs more coffee than she breathes to stay awake for doubles, until we're discussing the pros and cons of getting a good night's sleep.

I don't bother adding that I had the best sleep than I'd had in months in Jax Bridges's bed.

15

JAX

I'VE NEVER DREADED a birthday party so damn much.

And that makes me feel like a complete asshole since it's Easton's daughter, Jasmine's, party. Easton is the only parent in our circle of friends—unsurprisingly. It seems our group has failed to become the *fall in love with your high school sweetheart and live together forever* trend that's the norm in most small towns.

Easton became a teen dad and then a single father since he doesn't know where his baby mama is half the time. He doesn't let that bother him though. Hell, sometimes, I think he finds it easier to do it without her because she's a shit person.

I got here at the ass crack of dawn to help Easton set up for the party and held in the urge to ask if Amelia was coming.

I get my answer when Amelia walks in, looking every bit of gorgeous I wish she didn't. And I'm using all my strength to not stare at her the entire time.

When I shut my eyes, I relive what happened with us in the office. It's consumed my every thought. Her soft lips against mine. The way she whimpered into my mouth, as if I was exactly what she needed. How her body melted into mine. She tasted like butterscotch, like the candies my grandma used to give me.

It was wrong. So wrong.

But I can't stop thinking about it.

We haven't seen or talked to each other since.

For the last few days, she told Toby to tell me that she was meeting with clients, like we were playing telephone on the damn playground. Toby warned that it was the only time he'd do that for her, and going forward, he wouldn't be our proxy for when things got awkward.

"Dude, could you make it any more obvious?"

My attention breaks away from Amelia as I turn and look at my cousin River, sitting next to me. "What?"

River sends me a pointed look. "You're watching Amelia like you'll never see her again."

"Whatever, man." I frown. My not-so-genius plan to keep my Ray-Bans on today just in case I glance in her direction isn't working. "I was zoning out."

"Dude," River scoffs. "Don't act like it's the first time."

I massage my temples and grumble, "Don't talk shit."

My nonstop thoughts of Amelia are causing me lack of sleep.

When I do fall asleep, I dream of her.

So, either way, Amelia Malone is keeping me up all night.

"Seriously." River's smile widens, flashing his white teeth. "I had a 4.0 GPA. Don't act like you can outsmart me."

Other than Chris, River and Easton are my closest friends. River liked Chris, but they weren't buddy-buddy. They didn't hang out by themselves without Amelia or me. Chris didn't click with many people because he was standoffish. I was shocked with how close he'd allowed Amelia to get with him.

River runs his hand through his brown hair and throws his head back. "Do you ever regret letting Chris have her?" When he looks back at me, there's nothing but seriousness on his face.

"I didn't let anyone *have her*," I say harshly. "She's not Park Place on a damn Monopoly board." Even though I can't stand Amelia, she's no one's *property*.

"Screw you, dude." He grabs the cap from his water bottle and pings it at my head. "You know that's not what I meant."

"You out of all people should know Amelia and I have hated each other for years." I scowl but am also thankful he waited to bring this up until it was only the two of us at the table.

Just ten minutes ago, Essie, River's twin, and Mia were sitting with us. I was shocked neither of them had muttered a word about Amelia or the brewery, but my guess is, they've already had their chats with Amelia. I'd also bet my last dollar that Amelia never told them about our little office mistake. Otherwise, knowing Essie, no way would she have been able to stop grinning at me, suggesting Amelia and I get married or some shit.

I clear my throat, looking at each side of the yard, and then lower my voice. "Did you forget she was *in love* with Chris?"

"Yes." River clicks his tongue against the roof of his mouth before pointing at me and saying, "But she loved you before him."

Why has everyone been up my ass about this lately?

It's as if Chris giving Amelia his half of the brewery meant Amelia and I would become more than business partners.

I rub my forehead and move my neck from side to side. "Why don't we pay attention to the Aladdin birthday party happening here? Not my goddamn love life." Or lack thereof.

"Yes, because you're very interested in princess ponies or tiaras painted on your face." His voice is thick with sarcasm. "Speaking of which, how did Easton get a pony here? My mom is about to have a bad day when I ask why I had to not only share birthday parties with Essie, but why I also only had a bounce house. I would've at least settled for some goats."

I shake my head. "Sometimes, I want to punch you in the face."

He gestures to his face. "And fuck up this prettiness?"

I swing my scowl from him to Amelia, watching her paint a poor girl's face. The little one has no idea what she got herself into. I had better art skills in the womb than Amelia does. Give that girl a paintbrush, and you'll be guessing what the picture is until the day you die.

"Uncle Jax and Uncle River!"

I hear Jasmine's voice before seeing her come barreling in our direction. Her brown pigtails swing in the air, and as she comes closer, I make out the tiara on her cheek. She was smart enough to choose Ava as her face artist. She comes to a stop, nearly falling into the table, while grinning at us with her gap-toothed smile.

"Grandma said you're hard of hearing because I've been yelling at you about what cake flavor you want." She bounces on her toes. "I told them I'd come over and ask and tell you thank you again for my gifts."

You've got to give it to Easton.

His daughter has better manners than River.

I hunch forward in my chair, so I'm eye-level with her. "I'm okay on cake, sweetie."

My stomach has been uneasy as I contemplate my emotions toward Amelia.

And I don't want to waste the poor kid's cake,

Jasmine plays with her *Birthday Girl* sash and frowns.

Oh hell. I've never felt like such a jerk.

"I'll take chocolate—"

"He's on a diet," River says at the same time. "You can give me his slice. Strawberry." He playfully shoos her away. "And make sure it's a super-duper big piece."

Jasmine's frown turns upside down, and she squeals, "I'll get you the biggest piece ever!" Turning around, she dashes back across the lawn, where Willow is cutting slices of the three-tiered purple cake.

"It's decided," River says. "All your ass is getting on your birthday is a bounce house and a heart. No ponies for you, asshole."

I flip him off.

———

An hour later, the crowd of children start clearing out, and River ditches me to talk to one of Essie's friends.

Groaning, I bring myself to my feet and stroll through the grass toward my mother, who's deep in conversation with the women at her table. Their conversation ceases, and everyone's eyes turn to me as I pull out the chair between my mother and Amelia.

I shift my back toward Amelia, refusing to look at her. "Willow, as always, you threw an amazing party."

Willow nods. "Thank you, and we appreciate your help this morning." Her attention swings from me when Jasmine calls her name and asks for help opening a jewelry kit. She tells us good night, blows Amelia a kiss, and jogs over to her granddaughter.

"How's the brewery—" Lola starts to ask before she stops herself, her eyes flashing to Amelia's in apology.

There's never been a silence so loud between four people.

Amelia and me.

Both our mothers.

All at the same table and lost for words.

I tap my fingers along the table before plastering a smile and looking at Amelia. "Can we talk for a minute?"

The color draining from her face confirms she wants to tell me no, but knowing Amelia, I know she won't refuse me in front of my mother. She might be rude to me, but she's never been disrespectful to my parents.

"Yeah." She straightens her shoulders. "Of course."

"We'll leave you to it," my mother says.

Lola glances to her daughter in reassurance. Lola gives her a single nod, and she brushes her hand along Amelia's back before she and my mom walk into Easton's home.

"I see you're still a terrible artist," is what I say to lessen the tension.

I didn't plan on talking to her today. I was prepared to do the opposite.

She dips her hand into her drink, grabs an ice cube, and flicks it at me. "Shut up. I don't think knowing how to paint Bambi on the side of a face will hold me back from living my best life."

"Are you sleeping in your laundry room tonight?"

It's a question I shouldn't care at all about the answer.

But it's one of those questions you feel like you need to know —like who decided Earth's name, or who smoked the first cigarette, or why your best friend died. Alongside that list now is where Amelia will lay her head down tonight.

She looks from side to side, as if she's worried someone over-heard me. "No."

"Liar."

"I don't care if you believe me. Just like you shouldn't care where I'm sleeping. It could be another man's bed for all you know." She smiles, proud of her taunt.

My heart lurches in my chest at the thought of her doing that.

It's for my friend's memory, of course.

I don't want her doing that to him so early. It's too soon.

But can I say that? I'd be a hypocrite because she already crossed that line with me.

I change topics. "Why did you kiss me?"

Yet another question I should have kept to myself.

She holds her hand up in front of my face. "Don't."

"Why did you kiss me, Amelia?" My voice is low and plead-ing, and it shouldn't be.

"I'm not doing this with you," she hisses.

Her face reddens, her cheeks a rosy pink, and I can't help but fight back a smile.

She pulls her chair out and starts to stand, but I grab her elbow and pull her back down.

"Why?" If I need to sound like a broken record all night, I will.

"I was bored," she grits out, dodging eye contact.

"Bullshit." Spit flies out of my mouth with that one word.

"I thought it'd make you leave me alone."

"Liar."

She peels my hand off her, finger by finger. "It doesn't matter because it won't happen again." She's on her feet faster than I can stop her this time, and she dashes into the house, as if I told her a storm was coming through.

I almost repeat, *Liar*, but stop myself. I shouldn't challenge her like that because, like she said, it'll never happen again.

———

Easton cups my shoulder as he comes up behind me. "Thanks for coming today and for all your help. I couldn't have done it without you guys."

Like Amelia, I haven't spent as much time with our friends as I once did. When they call and invite me to hang out, I decline, blaming it on work. Work is such a convenient scapegoat when you can use it. No one told me it'd be one of the biggest perks of owning your own business.

"Sorry, man. Some equipment broke down at the brewery. I can't make it."

"An employee didn't show up for their shift. I have to cancel."

No doubt, most were shocked I showed up today. But I couldn't bail on Jasmine.

Amelia left after our talk, but I stayed and helped Easton clean up. It helped pass the time because I'd already told Toby I'd be gone for the day and there were no shifts for me to pick up at the pub.

So, it was either me, my thoughts, and lying in sheets that smelled like Amelia or cleaning up frosting fingerprints, taking out trash, and helping to load up the pony.

The pony's name is Tigger.

Tigger is an asshole who bucked at everyone the entire time

we tried to load him up. I'll stick with the bounce house in the future.

Easton collapses onto his leather recliner next to me and hands over a beer—a Down Home brewski, of course. "How have you been holding up?"

"Same shit, different day," I answer, my mouth dry. I pop open the beer and chug down half of it.

"I hope that's not the case," he says, staring straight ahead at the TV playing some ridiculous cartoon. "I hope each day is a better one for you."

My mother has referred to Easton as the emotional guy of the bunch. He's not a crier or someone who wears his heart on his sleeve. He's the guy you go to when you have a problem, when you need advice, or when you just need an ear. The dude gives better advice than half these shrinks on TV.

That's the great thing about Easton.

But it can also be the pain-in-the-ass thing about him.

He isn't afraid to dive into the awkward questions.

My dad told me Dallas, Easton's father, was the same way. He was the responsible one, the one who did marry his high school sweetheart and then who became a widower later. That was before Easton's mother came along and helped his father heal.

Easton kicks his feet onto the coffee table. "Want to get anything off your chest? It's been a while since we caught up."

"I'm good."

I chug my beer, shutting my eyes and relishing the taste. It's the first beer flavor Chris and I mastered. We called it the Brother Brew. We swore we'd never stop carrying it even if only we bought it. It became our best seller.

I stand, walk to the kitchen, and snag two more beers. Then, I slide them back into the fridge and stand on my tiptoes to reach the cabinet above the fridge to find something that'll hit me harder. That will erase my mind faster. That will numb me better.

When I return to the living room, I hold up the bottle of whiskey and two shot glasses I snagged from the cabinet.

Easton shakes his head violently. "The whiskey only comes out on nights I don't have Jasmine, but you have at it. Out of the two of us, you're the only one who seems like he needs it."

I shrug. A dude can't argue with that.

Put your kids first. It's what Easton does. What my dad did.

If only Chris's parents had done that.

My stomach tightens at the thought of him. I twist the cap off the whiskey and weirdly shove the cap into my pocket—as if I plan to drink the half that's left tonight.

Easton doesn't say anything as I rudely take a swig straight from the bottle.

I hold the bottle toward him. "I'll buy you another one of these."

He nods. "And add a twelve-pack of that new beer you have."

"I got you, bro. I got you."

I settle back down on the seat, holding the neck of the bottle between two fingers, and relax my neck. For the first time in a long time, it feels like I'm getting a second without having my mind race. Maybe it's because I'm so damn tired and I haven't had more than two hours of sleep, but it's not like I get much anyway. I average four, and that's on a good night.

It's hitting my body harder and harder each day. And I'm not the only one noticing. Just last week, my mom showed up with a *sleepy-time* tea and asked me to watch some awards show while my father worked.

It knocked my ass out. I woke up on the couch with a blanket wrapped around me, the apartment dark and empty. The next morning, I sluggishly walked into my kitchen to find a box of the tea in my cabinet.

Turns out, her *sleepy-time tea* was laced with melatonin. I haven't trusted my mother with a tea since. Hell, I won't even touch one of her smoothies. That was a lesson learned when she threw some weird-ass vitamins into one because I wasn't *eating healthy* enough, according to her.

"I heard you and Amelia are working with each other at the brewery."

Easton's comment snaps me out of my zone.

I don't raise my head when I answer, "I'm trying to figure a way to get out of that."

He snorts. "I wish you all the luck, trying to change Amelia's mind on something she's already decided on."

"She doesn't deserve it." I tilt my head up slightly to take a drink.

"You spill that, and I'm kicking your ass," Easton says in his best dad voice. "Drink it right, or I'm taking it."

"Jesus Christ," I groan, bringing my head upright. "I'm not Jasmine."

"Then, drink like a grown-up, and I won't treat you like a kid." He gestures to the couch. "I just bought this last week because Jasmine spilled fingernail polish all over the last one. I'm not about to replace it because you don't know how to drink whiskey correctly."

I set the whiskey down on the coffee table, pour a shot, and then drain it.

Then, I pour another.

And another.

After the fifth, Easton adds, "And don't puke on it either."

I cast a glance to him. "I think we both know I handle my alcohol well."

"Eh, true." He reaches forward to grab the remote and turns the channel to some health documentary on Netflix.

I stay rooted in my spot, back hunched forward over the coffee table, and drink until my head turns dizzy.

"You're obviously not driving home," Easton says when the documentary ends, and he stands. "You can crash on the couch."

No way in hell would Easton wake his daughter up to give

his drunk friend a ride home. Not that I'd ask. It's either sleep on his couch or phone a friend.

I decide to *phone a River.*

That'd make a good country song.

Jesus Christ. What is wrong with me?

I need to focus on finding River's name first, and then when I'm sober, I'll be changing his Contact name to *Phone A River.* I laugh at my internal joke.

Easton only stares at me like I've lost my mind and snatches the whiskey from my hold.

I hold my phone up. "Nah, River can get me. He stays up all night."

River answers on the third ring.

———

"Damn, man. Did you get ahold of Jasmine's apple juice again?" River asks when I slide into his car. "I told you that organic shit Easton buys gives you a deeper sugar high."

"Take me to Amelia's," is all I say.

He rears back and looks at me from the driver's side. "I'm sorry, what?"

"Drop me off at Amelia's."

"Do you want her to kick your ass?"

I stay quiet.

"Do you want her to kick *my* ass?"

I don't say anything.

"Maybe you should wait until you don't smell like you've bathed in liquor."

"I won't tell her you were my ride."

"Damn straight you won't. I'm dropping you off three houses down, so you'd better be okay to walk in a straight line."

16

AMELIA

IT'S after midnight when there's a knock on my door.

I spent the last two hours cleaning glitter off my face and hands and out of my hair.

Wearing an old pair of pajamas, I set my glass of wine down on the floor and trek down the hallway. I freeze inches from the door.

Who would be at my door this late?

It's either a serial killer or Jaxson Bridges.

I'm almost hoping it's a serial killer.

It's not like I'd answer the door for a serial killer.

I'd call the cops. The murderer would be caught. Amelia for president.

That'd be better than Jax.

When I look through the peephole, I loudly groan.

His eyes are red. He's somewhat wobbling in place. And his hand almost falls limp after he gives another weak knock to my door.

"Amelia!" he yells. "Open this damn door, you laundry room sleeper!"

I take the two steps and swing the door open, every bit of pissed off.

"Shut up," I hiss, grabbing the collar of his shirt and jerking him inside. "What the hell is wrong with you? Do you want to go to jail for drunk and stupid conduct?"

The corner of his mouth tips up. "I am here to check on your sleeping arrangements. Call me the sleep police."

I cover my face with my hands. "I can't deal with a sober Jax. You can bet your ass my patience doesn't have room for drunk and annoying Jax."

He rests his back against a wall, his shoulders hitting a picture frame, and his eyes are glossy and on their way to being bloodshot.

As much as I want to knee him in the balls, the memories of a wasted Jax sweep through my mind. When he and I stole his dad's liquor from the apartment and drank it. When he teased me for being a lightweight but then vomited five minutes later. When I kissed him once and it was the first time I ever tasted whiskey.

"What are you thinking about?" His voice is hoarse and thick.

I cross my arms. "For someone who hates me so much, you sure seem to like showing up at my doorstep an awful lot."

He chuckles. It's not a nice chuckle.

It's more of an ... edgy one?

"I told you, sweet Millie, I'm here to see where you're sleeping."

"I'm calling River to come get you."

When I turn to walk away for my phone, his hand captures mine. As much as I shouldn't, I allow him to lace our fingers together. He drags me toward him, turning me, and my back is now the one against the wall. The whiskey on his breath reminds me of the first time he touched me in places I'd never been touched.

My mouth waters, urging me to get just one more taste, to see if it's changed any. To know if it's gotten smoother, finer, and more delectable with age.

Something that sounds like my name leaves his drunken lips in a whisper, and he cradles my chin in his strong hand. His breath brushes against my cheek, and I inhale, taking it in.

I don't say a word.

I *can't* say a word.

It's as if any verbal communication will tear us apart.

Jax and I don't do well with words.

We don't say nice things to each other.

The only time there's peace between us is when our mouths or hands are on each other.

He moves my chin, exposing my neck, and brushes three light kisses along my jawline, whispering my name between each one. My heart shakes at his touch, at the feel of his lips against my bare skin.

"Amelia," he whispers into my ear, and I shiver. "What's going through your mind right now?"

I don't mutter a word.

His fingers dig into my waist through the thin fabric of my pants. "Tell me."

When I open my mouth, he draws back and presses a finger on my lips.

"And don't lie to me either."

Our eyes meet. His full of despair and turmoil and need.

Reality hits me.

He's drunk.

We're both vulnerable.

This can't happen.

I say his name through my closed mouth, and he slides his finger off my lips. "We can't do this."

I see the moment the truth of my words hits him. His head tips forward, his forehead against mine, and he rests it there for a moment. He plants a quick peck to the top of my hair.

"All you have to do is tell me," he whispers.

"Why do you care?" I return his whisper.

"I told you not to ask questions you don't want the answers to."

"What if I want this one?"

"You don't."

"Why are you here?"

"I ... I don't know."

"Then, you need to leave. I'll call you a ride."

"Please"—his voice turns begging—"don't kick me out."

"Jax, we can't do this."

He withdraws his hand from my waist and backs away at my words. I open my mouth, positive he's leaving, and I'm ready to stop him. But he doesn't open the door. Instead, he slides down the wall until he's sitting on the floor with his knees up.

Resting his elbows on his knees, he lowers his head. "I don't know why I'm here."

My breathing is shallow as I stare down at him.

My heart is breaking in so many ways, and I don't know if there will ever be something to fix it. To heal it from two men who can no longer be a part of my life like I once wanted them to be.

"I don't know why I care," he goes on, his voice strangled yet loud enough for me to hear. "It's fucking killing me that I don't have that answer for you. All these years, I've been a good man and kept my distance from you. Made sure we were never alone together again or put in any compromising situations." He lifts his head, his eyes meeting mine, but neither of us moves. "I knew at times, what happened between us would slip through the cracks, and I'd remember that I once had feelings for you, that I once craved every inch of you every single second of every single day."

"Why didn't you tell Christopher then?" I shiver, a cold chill hitting me, as if Christopher's ghost were here at the mention of his name. I retreat a step—the thought of him a reminder that this is such a bad idea.

"For the same reason you didn't tell him."

I stiffen.

"Don't you remember when you met him, Amelia?" He rises to his feet, using the wall for leverage, but still, he stumbles some. "He hated life. But then he saw you ... and I don't know. For the first time, he seemed to have found happiness. I hated to take that away from him."

I shut my eyes, remembering every detail.

"And I thought ..." Jax stops and shakes his head. "I thought that it'd be a little crush he'd get over. You two could flirt some, but never, never did I think you'd fall in love with him."

My heart matches the hurt clear on Jax's face.

"I didn't intervene because my best friend was hurting, and I knew you were the only one who made him feel better."

I'm shaking. I can't pinpoint exactly where I'm shaking. Maybe because it's everywhere. My hands. My voice. My arms. My thoughts. I hug myself, wishing that I could do the same to Jax, but I'm terrified that if I did, I might do more than hug. I might press my lips to his. Pour my heart out to him. Ask him not to leave. I'm struggling to stay on my feet, to not collapse onto the floor in the same position Jax was just in.

As if he senses I'm growing weak, as if he sees the tears welling in my eyes, he steps to me.

"I knew you could make him feel better because you always made me feel better." His voice rises, and he sticks his fist to his heart. "You weren't supposed to fall in love with him because I wanted you to fall in love with me."

17

JAX

FIFTEEN YEARS OLD

"OKAY! LISTEN UP!" River calls out. He reminds me of a teacher trying to get the class's attention. "The game is Seven Minutes in Heaven. Two people go into the closet for seven minutes."

"And do what?" Essie asks, looking up at her brother from the floor.

"Talk. Make out—" Easton says.

"Whoa, whoa," River says, stopping Easton. "No one is making out with my sister."

Essie throws a pillow at him, and River steps to the side to dodge it.

"You can do whatever you want—even nothing," River says.

I've already played Seven Minutes in Heaven twice before. To be honest, it's nothing special. The last time I played, River was with me. Peyton Moore had snuck us into her sleepover, and we played. Mia and Callie were there too. Callie kissed a boy. Mia said if any boy touched her, she was slicing off their balls with a steak knife.

I'm fine with playing it again because there's someone I actually want to make out with here. Amelia. We haven't seen each other in a few weeks since we go to different schools, but we've texted a few times. Mainly talking shit, but a text is a text. I at least have her attention.

"Looks like I'll have to sit this one out," Essie says, shooting River a dirty look. She crosses her arms and falls back against the ratty couch. "I never get to do anything."

We're in Ava, Mia, and Easton's grandparent's basement. The three of them are cousins.

"How do we know who goes in with who?" Ava asks.

"Well ..." River holds his hands in front of his face and wiggles his fingers, all *villain from TV* style. "Who are two people you think should be in a closet together?"

The *dude* expression he gives me is a clue for me to say him and Ava. He's been crushing on her for a minute.

"Better yet," Easton says, his voice threading with excitement, "who are two people we know who wouldn't want to be in the closet together?"

They all say their form of, "Jax and Amelia."

"Whoa," Amelia says, holding her hand up and giving us all dirty looks. "You can't just nominate people. Aren't you supposed to spin the bottle?"

I narrow my gaze at her. "Have you played this game before, Amelia?"

Call me a hypocrite, but the thought of her being in the closet with another douchebag sends my heart racing. And it's not like I enjoyed either time I had *my time* in the closet. One girl made out with my ear, and another one just moaned out my name because she wanted people to think we were banging. I made sure to correct everyone when I stepped out.

Just because Amelia and I attend two different schools doesn't mean word doesn't travel between them. Anchor Ridge, her school, is our rival team in every sport. There's also the internet, and then loudmouth Ava would definitely say something.

"We can do it by vote," Easton says. "And everyone votes on you two."

Essie laughs. Ava rolls her eyes. Mia is on her phone, acting like she doesn't care. Callie doesn't know what the hell is going on because she hasn't looked up from her book all night.

I stroke my jaw and look to Amelia. "Are you too chicken?"

She scoffs and jumps off the couch. "None of you will be invited to my birthday party." She turns in a circle. "Not a single one of you assholes."

River is nearly jumping in excitement, but he groans when Ava smacks the back of his head. I hear her say he'd better not try to get her in that closet or she's kneeing him in the balls. Everyone follows us to the closet. It's a small room, and only inches separate us.

Easton opens the door, and Amelia turns to me.

"You touch me, you die," she warns, flipping her long hair over her shoulder.

"Who says I even want to touch you?" I snort, and River smacks my stomach. "You'd better keep as much distance between us as you can."

She walks in behind me, and my heart feels like it's going to burst out of my chest. The closet smells like old lady and moth-balls, and as soon as the door slams shut, it's pitch-black. I reach up and pull the string attached to the light.

Click.

Darkness.

Click.

Nothing.

"It's out, of course," I grumble.

"On the plus side," Amelia says, "I don't have to see you."

"I was thinking the same thing." I scratch my head, my cheek, shift from foot to foot. This is the creepiest and weirdest Seven Minutes in Heaven I've had.

Seconds of silence pass.

Amelia's sweet-smelling strawberry-mango perfume and the

whiskey on her breath—whiskey that we stole from upstairs—starts overpowering the mothball smell.

"I wonder if their ears are against the wall," I whisper, making sure to keep my voice down, just in case. It's what everyone did at the last party.

"Probably."

I can picture her rolling her eyes.

I cringe when some type of old coat rubs against my shoulder. "And could they have picked a smaller closet? Jesus. I can hardly move in here."

"Pretty sure that's the whole point, genius."

"Want to get them back?"

"Definitely. Who should we vote for?"

"I'm going to vote for you and someone else. In fact, I'm voting for you every single time."

Lies.

And my friends know I'll punch them in the face if they try to go in with her.

"Yeah, well, same," she mutters. "Ugh, this is going to be the longest seven minutes of my life."

I lower my voice even more. "Have you ever kissed anyone before?"

"That's none of your business," she hisses.

"I think it is since we're Seven Minutes in Heaven partners."

Please say no. Please say no.

She blows out a long breath. "You know, we don't have to make out in here. I can kick your ass, and that'd be fine."

"Do you want to kick my ass though?"

"Sometimes, yes."

I chuckle. "Just answer my question."

"Of course I've kissed someone," she says around a groan.

"How many people?"

"None of your business."

"You're probably a terrible kisser." I crack a smile at my lame, juvenile joke.

"Excuse me?" She reaches out and nudges my shoulder. "Have you ever kissed anyone?"

"Hell yeah. Plenty of girls."

"Right," she says sarcastically. "I'm sure you're a crappy kisser, if that's even true. What girl would ever let you kiss her?"

"Would you let me kiss you?"

"Absolutely not."

I take a step closer. "Not even to prove to you that I'm a good kisser … and to prove you're not?"

She doesn't push me away, doesn't try to move away. Instead, she only stays in place.

"Let's see then." I reach out and sink my fingers into her hair and lower my mouth to hers, but I don't touch her lips yet. I just linger there, waiting for when the moment happens.

"You'd better not tell anyone about this," she says against my mouth.

"You think I want someone to know we were in here, swapping spit? I'll tell them you wanted to kiss, but I declined—"

"No, I'm telling them I forehead-slapped you to keep your distance."

I drag my hand from her hair and down to her chin, cupping it. "This is only for testing purposes."

"Only for testing purposes."

"To prove you wrong."

"To prove *you* wrong."

And I press my lips against hers, wondering how long this will last.

A second?

A minute?

But we don't stop.

I'm not sure when it happens or who started it, but our tongues slide into each other's mouths. I've made out with other girls before, but it was nothing like this. With teenage-boy hesitation, I lower my hand down to her waist and press her into me. She pulls away, and I'm waiting for her to slap me, but she only catches a breath of air before kissing me again.

Holy shit.

This is amazing.

I can feel a hard-on coming. I beg the guy downstairs to calm down, so I don't embarrass myself.

Him making an appearance in this closet might freak her out.

Last month, I took a girl to homecoming. We made out. It was almost boring. With her, it was like we were following some direction book. Kissing Amelia seems like the most natural thing I've ever done.

Will she be mad if I try more?

If I inch her shirt up?

I just want to feel how soft her skin is.

I play with the hem of her tank before slowly dragging it up and wait for her reaction. I hate that I can't see her face, but she whispers that I can keep going.

I keep lifting it, my thumb moving circles along her bare stomach, and she shivers. I feel grown up when I drag my lips away from hers, brush her hair off her shoulder, and drop soft kisses down her neck.

I might be a teenage boy, but I've watched my fair share of online porn.

But what teenage boy doesn't watch porn?

I consider it research for when I get to the point of touching a girl like this.

And if there's one thing I've learned, it's that kissing a girl's neck turns her on.

Just as I'm pushing her shirt up more and just as her hand slides up the bare skin of my back, there's a bang on the door.

"All right, time is up!" River yells.

We jump apart, our backs pressed against the walls, and we're catching our breaths when the door swings open. Everyone stands in the doorway with their eyes on us.

"Did you two really kiss?" Callie asks.

"Of course not," Amelia says.

Wow, that sure makes a guy feel good.

"They for sure kissed," Easton says. "Look at her hair. That's making-out hair."

Amelia rolls her eyes. "You said Seven Minutes in Heaven, so we said, why not?"

Callie gasps.

Ava high-fives her.

Essie yells, "When do I get to make out with someone?"

"Looks like you two don't hate each other after all," Mia says.

"It was a game more than anything," Amelia goes on, refusing to look at me. "We wanted to see who would pull away first."

"Yeah." I make a show of wiping spit off my face. "A game."

As we all walk away, I step next to Amelia and whisper, "I've got to say, you're actually a pretty good kisser."

She grins. "Told you so."

And I think that's the moment I start falling in love with her.

SIXTEEN YEARS OLD

"Our friends are boring as fuck," I tell Amelia, tossing the remote up in the air and catching it.

We're hanging out in the *kids' quarters* of the beach house our parents rented. Their group of friends, along with us kids, rent three houses on the same street. Ours is the biggest and has a separate wing, so we've deemed it our spot.

Essie, Easton, and Callie are sleeping on the floor. River, Ava, and Mia are crashed out on the couch across from us. Amelia and I are on the other sofa, one on each side. We're the only ones who stayed awake during the horror movie we insisted the girls watch with us.

I watched Amelia more than I did the movie tonight. She's still wearing her bikini top, showing off her full breasts, and a pair of short-shorts that are only a little longer than her bikini bottoms. Her hair isn't straight, as she normally wears it, because it got wet. And when it gets wet, it gets curly and a bit frizzy. And she still looks hot.

"It's late," Amelia says, shrugging. "We were at the beach all day. They're exhausted."

The beach was fun.

Watching Amelia in her bikini was even better.

The more we grow up, the less I see her as an annoying girl I teased and more the one I'm lusting over. Not that I was the only one staring. Guys of all ages turned their heads when she walked by, and I wanted to kick all their asses.

Since our Seven Minutes in Heaven night a whole year ago, thoughts of our kiss have taken over my brain. I want to do it again and again and again. I could spend the rest of my life kissing and touching her, and I'd never grow bored.

Sure, there are hot girls at school, but no one catches my attention like she does. No one pushes my buttons, making me want her more, the way Amelia does. When girls hit on me at school, I sometimes entertain it, but my mind is always on Amelia. She attends a different school, so I don't see her as much as I want. But anytime I know there's a chance to, I never miss it.

"We were at the beach all day too," I point out. "It's our last night here. We should be having fun."

Amelia taps her fingers against her chin. "What should we be doing instead then?"

Good question.

Our options are limited, but we can sneak out, or steal some alcohol, or play a damn game. Not catch some z's.

"Not sleeping. Not being boring."

And my response is boring.

She drops her hand from her chin and chews on one of her purple fingernails. "What do you do when you're bored?"

I level my gaze on her, and it takes everything I have not to smirk. "Amelia, I'm a sixteen-year-old. What do you think I do when I'm bored?" I gesture to my crotch with my hand.

"Oh my God, ew." She leans down to snatch a pillow from the floor and throws it at me. "What's wrong with you?"

"Are you saying you've never ..." The smirk I've been hiding makes an appearance as my words trail off.

She scoots in closer and lowers her voice. "I'm not talking to you about *that*."

"Then, that means you have." My cock twitches in my shorts, and I grab the pillow she threw at me, covering it up. "Probably to thoughts of me."

"Pfft, you wish." She rolls her eyes. "I'm sure it's the other way around."

I tip my head forward and scratch my neck.

"Oh my God," she shrieks before putting her hand over her mouth, as if she were too loud. She slaps my chest. "Please say you don't jerk your chicken to me."

"I mean ..." I run my hand through my unbrushed hair. "I might hate you, but that doesn't mean you're not hot."

The more we talk, the closer we scoot toward each other. Her legs are crossed, and mine hang off the side of the couch.

"You insult me all the time."

I wiggle my finger at her. "But do I ever tell you you're ugly? No. You're hot. I'm not a liar."

She does a scan of the room, making sure no one is awake. "I guess I'll admit that you're hot too."

I take back all my earlier complaints.

My friends had better keep their asses asleep.

Time with just Amelia is better than doing non-boring stuff with them.

I rub my hands together. "Let's play Truth or Dare."

"No way." She shakes her head repeatedly. "You have the worst dares."

"I suggest you choose truth then."

"If I pick truth, then you'll ask me personal and most likely embarrassing questions."

"Your choice, Millie."

"Fine." She throws her head back, strands of her hair falling from her ponytail. "Truth."

"Hmm ..." I chew on my lower lip. "Have you ever snuck out of your house before?" It's a weak question, but if I jump straight into too personal, she might quit on me.

She eyes me suspiciously. "Are you going to snitch on me?"

"Hell no. I'm not twelve anymore."

"Yep." She sighs and hooks a finger toward me. "Your turn."

"Dare."

"I dare you to sneak out with me and hang out on the beach."

———

Our parents will definitely kick our asses if we get caught.

I wait for Amelia to burst out in laughter, to tell me she's joking, but she doesn't.

I stand, hold my hand out, and tell her, "Come on."

I drop her hand briefly to steal the blanket off a snoring River and wrap it around my arm, and then our fingers are interlaced again.

The summer chill hits my shoulders when we walk out, and I drag Amelia in closer to me, throwing my arm over her shoulders. I keep walking until I find what feels like a safe space with a dim light overhead. It's in front of River and Essie's parents' place. My biggest goal is for us not to be in sight of Amelia's parents. Her dad would probably drown my ass in the ocean and leave me dead for the sharks.

I spread the blanket out and signal for her to sit down. Amelia slips off her sandals and crawls onto the blanket, sand following alongside her. I do the same, joining her, and we make ourselves comfortable. Amelia sits up straight with her legs brought up to her chest, and we face each other. I stretch my legs out, spreading them so she's between them. I've never felt so content and happy in my life.

She stares up at me and smiles before hugging herself.

"You cold?" I ask, reaching forward and running my hands up and down her arms.

"A little," she mutters.

I drag my shirt off and hand it to her. "Here."

"Won't you be cold then?"

"I'm good. I'm warm-blooded." I smile and twirl one of her curls around my finger. "My turn. Truth or dare, Millie?"

She hesitates before saying, "Truth," and then slips my shirt on.

I chuckle. "You're really afraid of those dares, aren't you?"

"Who knows what you'd have me do out here?" She does a sweeping gesture toward the ocean, the waves a relaxing noise around us. "The last thing I need is you daring me to swim to an island or to sleep out here alone for the rest of the night."

"I'd never do either one of those."

Her face softens.

"How far have you gone with someone?" My question is risky and could result in a punch to the face.

She stares at me with intent. "How far have *you* gone?"

I shake my head and tighten my legs around her, hardly leaving any space between us. "This isn't my truth."

"I've done ... *stuff.*"

"*Stuff* isn't an answer, Millie, babe."

She fixes her gaze on me, as if she can't wait for my reaction to whatever her answer is. "Kissed ... made out."

"Girl or guy?"

"Guy."

"Anything else?"

"Hand stuff ..."

Swear to God, my heart stops for a moment.

"Who the fuck did you do hand stuff with?" I sound almost angry.

"You only get one question, Jaxson." She runs her hand down my chest. "Now, you answer the same question."

I wiggle my fingers.

She rests her chin against her knuckle. "You've stuck your fingers inside a girl's vagina?"

I nod and grind my teeth. "And someone has stuck their fingers inside you?" I need to do some research and kick the guy's ass.

"Pretty much."

I feel so adult, talking about this. "Have you ever touched a guy's penis?"

"Have you?"

"If we're counting my own, then yes. If not, then no."

"I have."

"Hand job?"

She shyly bites into her lip.

"Who the fuck did you give a hand job to?" I point toward the house. "Is it one of our friends?"

"Oh my God," she shrieks. "No! It was some stupid guy at school."

"Boyfriend?"

"He was for a month, but then he kept asking other girls on the cheer team for nudes, so I broke up with him."

Good girl.

Leave his ass.

Leave them all for me.

"What about you?" she asks. "Was yours with a girlfriend?"

"Not really. We went out a few times months ago. One time, after a movie double date, she asked if I wanted to go into the backseat of my new car before taking her home."

"Ew." She scrunches that cute face of hers up. "I'm never getting in your backseat."

"Her parents started blowing her phone up, so we stopped."

"Would you have gone further if they hadn't?"

I shrug. "I don't know."

"Are you saving yourself for marriage?"

I snort. "I doubt I'll make it that long, to be honest. You?"

"Same." She covers her face with her hand and shakes her head. "I can't believe I told you that."

I slide my hand along her wrist, slowly dragging her hand away from that gorgeous face of hers. "Don't be embarrassed to tell me anything."

She licks her lips. "You know, none of the guys I've kissed have been as good as you."

I run my hand up and down her arm before taking her hand in mine. "That might be the first compliment you've given me." I smile and interlace our fingers the same way I did when we left the house. "The same with you. You can kiss."

"I know." She smiles when I lift our interconnected hands into the air before saying her name in a hushed whisper.

We focus on each other, our bodies relaxing, and I'm not sure who starts it, but not even a minute passes before our mouths touch. Her lips are soft, so damn soft, and she tastes like strawberries. Our hands release, and I slip my hand through her hair, dragging her closer to me. She slides across the blanket on her knees and straddles my lap.

Our tongues dance together, and I drop my hand to the hem of my shirt that she's wearing.

"Can I?" I whisper against her lips.

Instead of answering, she takes my shirt off, tosses it to the side, and unties the bottom of her bikini top.

"And this?" I skim my finger across the sequined top still hiding what I so desperately want to see.

My dick gets harder and harder.

She nods.

I caress her back before untying the strings around her neck. She shivers, goose bumps hitting her skin, and I pull back.

"Shit, you're cold." I reach around her to grab my shirt again, but she stops me.

"You're supposed to keep me warm." Her tone sounds almost like a dare.

"I can do that." I lay her onto her back, my heart slamming against my chest as I stare hers down, and hover over her.

Our lips meet again, and I play with her breast. She grinds against my leg, over and over, and when I inch closer, she gasps at the feel of my erection. I freeze, waiting for her to pull away, but she only drags me on top of her. We situate ourselves so my cock hits between her legs, and we dry-hump each other.

Adrenaline and need spread through me as I lower my head and suck one of her nipples in my mouth.

"Oh my God, Jax," she hisses. "Keep doing that."

I suck on it again, swirling my tongue around it before moving my attention to her other breast; at the same time, I lower my hand to the waistband of her shorts.

She shifts, somewhat moving away from me, and I hold myself up on my elbow, my eyes trained on her. She slowly unbuttons her shorts, and our breathing is loud as I help slide them down her legs.

My eyes roam over her perfect body, and I wonder how I got this lucky.

I must've done something for God to like me enough to give me the sight of Amelia underneath me, topless and only wearing her bikini bottoms.

She spreads her legs and wickedly smiles at me. "Do it, Jax."

Her hand circles around my wrist, and she uses it to guide my finger under her bottoms. I groan, begging my dick not to bust, and slide a finger through her warmth. She's as wet as the ocean around us.

"Stick it inside me," she whispers.

I'm shocked at how vocal and comfortable she is with me.

I slide a finger inside her, moving it in and out, and play with her clit with my thumb. She moves her hips to my speed, and her hands go to the blanket, gripping it.

I grab her hand with my free hand. "Stick your nails into my arm, not the blanket. I want to feel how good I'm making you feel."

And that's what she does.

I add another finger, and when she asks me to go faster, it's what I do. Her nails dig into my skin, and I love that, later, I'll see where she marked me. I'm sweaty, but I don't stop until she cries out my name and her back arches.

"Holy crap," she says, her legs shaking, her chest heaving in and out. "The last time I did this, it didn't feel like that."

I stare down at her, hating the mention of any *last time*. "Is that a good or bad *that*?"

"Good. Definitely good." She rises to her knees and reaches for my shorts.

I stop her. "You don't have to do that if you don't want to."

Would I love it if she did? Hell yes.

But I don't want her to feel like it's expected.

"I want to." She grins. "I really want to. Can I see it?"

I tilt my head to the side. "I thought you said you've done this before?"

"I didn't … see it. It was under the covers and weird and only lasted, like, three seconds."

Pride shoots through me that my cock will be the only one she's seen.

"He sounds lame." I sit back and push down my shorts and boxers, and my cock springs forth. I've never been so turned on in my life that it's practically aching.

She goes quiet for a moment before saying, "It's bigger than I thought it'd be."

"I think that's a compliment, so thank you." It's taking everything in my power not to stroke myself, but I don't want to scare her off.

"It's a compliment. Definitely a compliment."

My hips jerk forward when she wraps her hand around my dick with no warning. She doesn't start slow, no. Amelia gets right to it, and my eyes nearly bulge out of my head. I watch her purple fingernails as she makes my dick feel the best it ever has.

I'm close.

So close.

My breathing is so ragged that I'm waiting for my lungs to fall out of my body.

My chest heaves forward when she drops my cock and pulls away.

"Your turn to lie down. I want to try something."

She pushes my shoulders so I'm on my back, and she straddles my waist. My cock rubs against her thigh, but it doesn't faze her.

"Kiss me, Amelia," I plead. "Kiss me while you stroke me."

I don't want to sound too demanding, and I hope it doesn't turn her off. But my dick is begging for her touch.

"I have a better idea." She moves my cock so it's between her legs, and she slides her covered pussy along it.

"Jesus, fuck," I groan, tightening my hands on her hips as she grinds against me.

She stares down at me, our eyes not leaving each other as we move our bodies in sync. I'm gasping for air when she reaches down and pushes her bikini bottoms to the side.

I grip her wrist to stop her. "You have to keep your bottoms on, Amelia."

"Why?"

"I don't have a condom." I'm not sure how I can form words at this point, nor can I believe that I'm stopping her from putting her bare pussy against my dick.

"Can't you just stop before … you know?"

"I don't know." I grunt when she shifts on my lap and my dick rubs against her wetness. My voice is strained. "So, I don't want to say yes."

My dad had the sex talk with me. He basically said he hoped I kept my dick in my pants, but he doubted it, so I should make sure I always condomed up. Even if I liked the girl, I needed to wrap it up, or I'd be raising a baby instead of going to keggers with my friends. He bought me a box and told me not to tell my mom.

I didn't bring the box with me because we flew, and the last thing I needed was for my mom to find them.

"What if you don't stick it inside?" Amelia asks, biting into her lower lip—one that I've been sucking on. "We can just rub against each other." She keeps her eyes on me as she carefully slips her bottoms over. "Like this."

My hips buck forward, and she rocks against me.

My cock slides so easily through her juices.

My cock against her bikini bottoms was amazing.

But this, against her bare pussy, is heaven.

Seeing and feeling Amelia grind on me, having us touch like this, feels like everything I've ever wanted.

We don't stop.

And when I'm close, I play with her clit, hoping like hell she's right there with me.

She whimpers my name at the same time I say, "Off, off, off."

Amelia hurriedly slides off me and falls to her back. Seconds later, I come.

We lie on our backs, catching our breaths, our bodies slick with sweat.

"Next time, we can do more?"

I nod, laughing at Amelia's question. "We can definitely do more."

Note to self: bring a condom next time you see Amelia.

Second note to self: always keep a condom with you, dumbass.

I help her up, and as we're slipping our clothes back on, my phone beeps with a text.

Mom: Where the hell are you?

18

AMELIA

IT'S EARLIER than usual when I wake up on my laundry room floor with Jax snuggled behind me.

And for whatever reason, I don't freak out.

Sometime during the night, he muttered he was cold and that I needed to stop hogging the blanket. Then, he dragged me toward him, settling me so that my back was against his chest, and fell asleep. I should've stopped him, pulled away, but I didn't.

I was tired, and it felt good to be held by someone.

It'd been so long.

Lonely nights.

Cold nights.

With no one.

So, I let Jax hold me.

And even though I don't want to admit it, I liked it.

Who lets their deceased fiancé's *best friend hold you, as if you're their most prized possession in the world, while you sleep?*

It's wrong. So wrong.

I should've stopped it from the very start.

I should've told him to leave, and when he poured his heart

out to me, I should've called one of our friends to take him home. But I didn't.

After his confession, I couldn't move.

It was a confession he should've kept to himself.

One that he should've told a priest and not me.

His breathing was ragged as he waited for my reaction, but there were no words. My head was throbbing, my body sore, and all I wanted to do was go to sleep. I needed the rest before dealing with the stress.

Finally, I told him, "We can't do this right now."

And I nearly broke when he lowered his voice and said, "Don't make me leave. If I leave, you're leaving with me because I refuse to let you sleep on that floor alone. Just tonight, let me stay."

I didn't argue.

I said, "All right, Jax."

He silently followed me into the laundry room. I grabbed my sleeping bag, unzipped it, and opened it wide—something I don't normally do. I typically cocoon myself into that thing. Jax stood in the corner, his hands shoved into his pockets, his eyes bloodshot and empty. He watched me, as if he'd have to recite my moves later, until I turned off the light and made myself comfortable. His only light source then was the night-light on my essential oil diffuser plugged into the wall.

I threw him a pillow and told him to sleep off the liquor.

My thoughts of last night are interrupted when Jax stirs behind me.

I shut my eyes when his erection rubs against my ass.

He groans, and my shoulders tense.

If I roll away, will it make things weird?

"Shit," he hisses into my ear.

I shiver and immediately miss his heat when he pulls away. I watch him over my shoulder. He doesn't stand. Instead, he slides backward and slumps against the wall.

I turn on my side to see him rubbing at his eyes with the

bottom of his palms. He's wearing the same shorts and tee he had on at Jasmine's party yesterday.

"Amelia, I'm sorry," he mutters, combing his fingers through his bedhead hair.

Sorry for what exactly?

That's what I want to ask but don't.

Instead, I sit up, crossing my legs, and wave my hand through the air. "It's fine."

His eyes are red and sleepy. "I had too much to drink."

"I figured that one out really quick."

"Did I do anything stupid?" He scans the room. "Or did I come in here and crash?"

I wince and stay quiet.

Was he that shitfaced, or is he saying he doesn't remember to save from explaining himself?

"I don't see how you do it."

I tilt my head to the side. "Do what?"

He smacks his hand against the floor. "Sleep in here. It's uncomfortable as fuck."

I shrug. "You get used to it."

"Why in here though? Why not the guest room or couch?"

"There are too many memories of him in those spots." I look away from him and blink back tears.

"Get a new bed. A new couch."

"Those aren't …" I pause, biting into my lower lip, and my gaze returns to him. "The furniture isn't the problem."

He stares at me blankly, waiting for an explanation.

"Christopher and I have … memories in all those places."

His eyes widen in understanding. "No laundry room sex?"

I slowly shake my head.

He gives nothing away on his face.

Not on his feelings toward everything he said last night, or waking up in my laundry room, or hearing about his best friend and me being intimate.

The room is quiet for a beat until he clears his throat. "Gotcha. So, you two really went at it then, huh?"

"Says the guy with his fair share of random girls."

"Says the girl who said she's had sex on every inch of this place."

"It was with my *fiancé*, not rando one-night stands."

"Some were more than one night, thank you."

I scoff.

"And there hasn't been that many. I've been so busy with work that I've hardly had time to do anything."

"How many girls?"

He scratches his head. "Huh?"

"How many girls have you been with?"

"Why would you ask me that question?"

"Just curious."

"Keep being curious then."

"Why won't you tell me?"

"Why do you want to know, Amelia?"

I stay quiet, searching for the right lie to tell him.

"The only girls who want to know the answer to that question are typically ones who plan to sleep with me," he adds at my lack of answer, and his eyes darken. "Do you plan to sleep with me?"

My heart constricts, as if tightening in my chest. "Given that I have, I think I qualify for the answer."

"Ah." He snaps his fingers. "She finally admits it."

I scrunch my face. "Admits what?"

"That we've slept together."

My cheeks flush. "When have I ever denied it?"

He shoots me a *really* look.

"You never told Chris either."

He looks away, as if in shame. "I didn't."

"Did he ever ask you?"

This time, it's him turning quiet, most likely contemplating on whether to lie.

"Did he?" I push.

He grimaces. "Once." His voice cracks with guilt in just that one word. "And I said no."

I inhale a shaky breath. "What made him ask you?"

"I have no idea." He stares down at the floor. "It was out of the blue." His gaze flashes back to mine, revealing so much more guilt than his voice did. "Did he ever ask you?"

"Twice." My mind trails back to the two most awkward times in our relationship. The two times I ever looked Christopher in his eyes and lied straight to him, acting like he was out of his mind.

"Twice?" His face turns pained. "Why so many?"

"I don't know." My mouth turns dry. "The first time was when we first started dating. The second when he was drinking." I swallow, hoping it'll help. "It was like he knew … but he didn't want to believe it."

I thought I had him fooled.

He said he believed me when I acted defensive. When I looked at him in shock and asked why he'd ever think such a crazy thing.

I was not only afraid of hurting him, of losing him, but I was also scared he'd lose Jax. If Christopher didn't have Jax or me, he'd feel as if he had no one.

"If he hadn't wanted to know, he wouldn't have asked," Jax states matter-of-factly. "And maybe we should've been honest with him. You two weren't together when we slept together."

"But he would've felt betrayed by the two people he loved the most."

His jaw is set when he says, "It doesn't matter now."

I nod in agreement, my voice a half-whisper. "It doesn't."

But it does.

It does because we're the ones who have to live with it.

We stare at each other, both of us uncomfortable but at ease simultaneously. There's so much to say, but we're too afraid to dive into our true feelings.

Momentarily, I wonder what I'd be doing right now if things had gone differently between Jax and me.

What if I'd never met Christopher?

Or if Jax and I had started dating before Christopher came into my life?

Jax was a kid, having fun back then. No way did he want a serious girlfriend like Christopher did.

But I never doubted Christopher when he told me I was the only girl he'd ever be with. When he told me he loved me, when he told me he'd never cared about any other girls and not touched anyone else, I knew it was the truth. He was always my safe place.

I felt content. But I also never asked Jax those things.

I was afraid to ask, and Jax wasn't as giving with his feelings as Christopher.

Could Jax and I have been more?

I shake my head to rid myself of those thoughts.

No. It could and would never happen.

Christopher will always be a ghost, haunting us.

Even if I wanted to touch Jax, it's like we have some barrier between us, a *this isn't right* boundary line.

"Maybe you should move," Jax suggests, and I give him back my attention.

I scrunch my face. "What do you mean?"

"You can't sleep in your own fucking bed, Amelia. Maybe you should move."

"I … I want to move, but I don't want to move. Just like with the brewery, it's almost like this home is all I have left of him."

"Because of all the good memories of him here?"

I shut my eyes. "Yes … but then my worst memory of him is here too."

I've never seen Jax's face turn so compassionate, so caring, so raw with his emotions when he says, "I'm sorry you had to see that," in a low whisper.

19

AMELIA

SIX MONTHS AGO

I'VE BEEN EXHAUSTED for weeks, and the past few have been harder on me than any other time in my life.

They've been even harder on Christopher.

We're engaged, but I told him I want to wait to get married.

And that's been hard on both of us.

It broke his heart, but there's no way I can go through with it, feeling like it isn't the right time. We aren't ready, so even though I hated every minute of it, I told him that.

The longer Christopher and I live together, the more I am learning about him—grasping who exactly he is and seeing parts of him I never knew existed. I've educated myself, researched for hours, and studied the medication he takes. Pills I only discovered because I was putting his laundry away and found a bag of some prescription bottles hidden in his sock drawer.

I asked him to talk about it, but he said it was nothing.

It worsened a month ago when Christopher found out his younger brother, Corey, had died from a heroin overdose. He was only twenty-one, and Christopher hadn't seen him in years. Once Christopher had moved out of his mom's house and to

Jax's, he hardly spoke to his family. Christopher blamed himself for Corey's death, believing that maybe Corey wouldn't have turned to drugs if Christopher had stayed, taken him with him, or reached out.

Last night, I sat on the edge of the bed, tears in my eyes, begging Christopher to talk to me.

But he only said, "Everything is good, babe. I need to shower."

When I tried to join him, he gave me a kiss, washed himself off, and said it was all mine. He was sleeping when I returned to our bedroom.

When I try to wake him up this morning, he waves me away and says he's sleeping in. I have a meeting scheduled with 21st Amendment. They want to go over their marketing materials, so I tell him I'll be back in a few hours.

Christopher needs sleep since he's hardly been getting any.

He works nonstop. Which I understand.

New businesses required long hours.

The meeting is a few towns over, and I text him before it.

No response.

My mom asks me to have lunch with her. She knows something is wrong and wants me to talk about it. I tell her the same thing I've been telling others—he's working long hours, and it's taking a toll on him.

I text him again during lunch, but no answer.

Finally, on my way home, I call him two more times.

Nothing.

My next call is to the last person I want to speak to, but the only other person who might know where Christopher is.

"What?" Jax says when he answers because he greets me so well.

"Is Christopher with you?" I ask through my car's Bluetooth.

"No."

"Do you know where he is?" My heart speeds, and my voice turns frantic.

There's never a time when Christopher isn't with one of us.

"No."

"Jesus," I shriek, almost running a red light, and I slam on my brakes, jerking me forward and hitting my chest on the steering wheel. "Can you say anything else?"

"What do you want, Amelia?" He speaks as if he's annoyed. "I'm busy."

"I'm trying to get ahold of Christopher."

"Then, you'd better get off the phone with me and call him."

Over his bullshit, I hang up on him and mutter, "Asshole," as I speed through the streets until I make it home.

Christopher's car is parked along the road, in his usual spot, and I park behind it.

Then, I run up the stairs and into the house.

"Christopher!" I yell.

Nothing.

"Christopher!"

There's no sign of him.

Until I step into our bedroom.

My entire life comes crashing down on me.

And life as I knew it will never be the same.

20

JAX

THIS IS the first time I've acknowledged the pain I know is carved deep inside Amelia. From the moment I saw her at the funeral, hysterically crying in her mother's arms, I knew she was broken.

I also knew I was too.

We were two people who loved the same person in different ways.

Two people who didn't know why that person had done what he did, so we pointed fingers at the other one. We played the blame game, and we played it so well.

I stare at her, taking in the short distance separating us in her laundry room. When I woke up this morning, my arm slung over her waist like I didn't want her to leave me, I was confused. But as I forced my eyes open, it all came crashing down on me.

Showing up here, drunk.

Admitting that I'd wanted her to love me instead of my best friend.

And then pleading with her to let me stay.

I broke bro code.

I'd been breaking it for years, I guess.

I don't know how much she cares about me saying, "I'm so sorry." Or if she even believes me, but it's the truth.

I am fucking sorry because had I been the one to find him, I don't think I could even sleep on this damn street without wanting to run away. Chris and I had a close friendship, but he and Amelia had something deeper.

She doesn't reply to what I said.

I smack my palms on the floor. "I'd better get home." I look at her and put all my strength into exposing the truth in my eyes. "I really am sorry."

It's as if her brain went into a different world at my apology earlier, so she nods, not meeting my eyes. Instead, she stares at the wall over my head. Groaning, I bring myself up, shoot her one last glance, and leave the room.

As I make my way outside, I'm reminded of how much I drank last night. The sun hurts my eyes, and my head spins with each step I take. I don't make it past the sidewalk when I realize I didn't drive here.

Shit.

I turn around, grateful she didn't get up and lock the door behind me, and head back into Amelia's. I hear the faint sniffle as I grow closer to the laundry room, and when I walk in, I find Amelia still on the floor. She scooted to the wall, taking the spot where I was, and her head is bowed. Her body is shaking in a clear sign that she's distraught.

"Amelia," I whisper, but she doesn't look up.

I drop to one knee in front of her and whisper her name again, and she raises her head in what feels like slow motion. She releases a whimper as our eyes meet. Her face is blotchy, her cheeks wet from tears, and she stares at me in agony.

Not even a few minutes have passed since I walked out, and it's as if she's an entirely different person.

Was she waiting until I left to break down?

"Come on," I say. "Let's go."

"What?" she stutters.

"I can't have my business partner crying on the floor." It's the best response I could come up with fast.

"I'm fine."

"You're not."

"It's not like this is the first time this has happened. I'm used to it. You can go."

I gently grab her wrist. "Come on."

She doesn't give me trouble as I help her to her feet.

"Grab some shit."

"What?"

"Where are your keys?"

"Jax, you—"

"We can talk later."

"They're in my car."

I snatch an armful of folded clothes from a laundry basket and tuck them under my arm, and somehow, someway, my hand finds the small of her back. It's a silent walk into the garage, and I toss her clothes into her Jeep before helping her into the passenger seat.

Another bro code violation.

But I don't care anymore.

All I can think about is seeing her on the floor, crying and needing someone to take care of her. Even if for a minute.

I'm no knight in shining armor, so don't get it wrong.

But I'm here, and he's not, so I have to be the one to take care of her.

I ignore thoughts of Chris as I drive us to my apartment.

To the apartment I once shared with him.

My mind is only on Amelia as I lead her to my bed, lift the blanket, and motion for her to get in. She sniffles, wipes her cheeks, and does what I silently said. And this time, I feel no regret when I slide into bed with her.

We deserve some decent sleep for the rest of the morning.

Even if it means being in bed with the wrong person.

God, I need to stop this.

To stop caring.

I need to hate Amelia Malone, so I don't love her.

21

AMELIA

I WAKE up in Jax's bedroom *again*.

That guilt creeps in *again*.

Jesus. What's happening?

We went from trying to avoid one another to hating each other to sleeping in the same bed. He saw me cry, heard me tell him why I didn't want to sleep in my bedroom, and instead of giving me hell like I'd thought he would, he helped me.

But it's a bad idea.

We can't continue this.

Can't get any closer.

What Jax said to me repeats in my head as I lie in his bed, looking around his room. I inhale the scent of his sheets—a signature smell of his lingering cologne, my perfume, and the scent of whiskey.

How would people react if they found out where I was right now?

I have to get out of here.

I slowly slide off the bed, and he groans, sleepily grabbing for me.

I hold my breath, waiting to see if he wakes up, but his eyes don't open.

Then, I find my keys and leave.

———

"You're scared to read the letter."

I stare at Cindy, my therapist, sitting across from me, and chew on my inner lip while struggling with the best response.

When my mother first suggested therapy, I told her she was crazy. I couldn't talk about my loss with my family, so there was no way I could do it with a stranger. I also thought people doubted my pain, that they didn't think it was real or that it was deserved.

When you think of a grieving woman, you think gray hair and wrinkles, someone with grandchildren, a woman who spent decades with a man and then lost him.

That isn't me.

I'm a twenty-six-year-old woman.

People don't see my loss as painful.

Then, there's that *oh, she'll easily find another love* mentality.

Don't believe me?

Watch romance movies.

Read romance novels.

There's always that second love after your first.

But when you're eighty and grieving, people's automatic thought is, *You'll live alone for the rest of your years because too much time has passed to find someone else. Your heart is too old for you to hand over to another.*

Christopher and I weren't married, hadn't spent decades together, but that doesn't mean the hurt didn't shatter as hard. Losing someone young might be harder because it's the only love you've ever known. You haven't experienced the love of children, of grandchildren, of seeing friends and family grow old. I was only learning how to love and share a life with someone. We were merging into the real world together, leaning on each other as we matured, and then in the blink of an eye, it was all gone.

When you're old and in love, you know your time will eventually run out.

When you're naive, young, and in love, you believe you have all the time in the world.

What idiots.

It was a reality check I hadn't been prepared for.

I loved Christopher, and maybe I wasn't as experienced in love, but that didn't make the hurt any less devastating. Just like who and how we love, grief is always different for everyone.

"I am," I croak out, playing with my hands in my lap. "Is that wrong of me ... to not want to open it?"

"If you're not ready, then don't." Cindy crosses her legs in her black pencil skirt, and her tone is soothing. "Maybe you should write him your own letter. Write what you'd say to him if you were to have one last conversation. What do you think you'd ask him?"

"I'd ..." I try—and fail—to keep my voice strong and steady. "I'd ask him why he didn't come to me." I peer up at Cindy, my eyes filled with unshed tears. "If he had come to me, I could've helped him. I could've saved him." I use the backs of my palms to wipe my eyes. "Then, I'd ask myself how I could've been so blind."

Depression is an easy disease to hide. One that can be masked with as little as a forced smile and a simple lie. To know Christopher was silently struggling kills me the most.

"Amelia," Cindy says, handing me a box of tissues, "his death wasn't your fault."

I nod, snag a tissue from the box, and tightly grip it. People tell me that all the time, but sometimes, guilt is harder to beat than reality. Than the truth.

"You and Chris, you grew up differently, right?" Cindy asks.

I nod, my shoulders sagging.

"You came from a loving home with caring parents. Chris grew up in an abusive one," Cindy continues. "You said he never discussed his childhood, but most children who grow up in dysfunctional homes have trauma—most times, suppressed trauma. If they don't get help for it, it gets worse over time and follows them into adulthood. And you and your friends were happy most of the time. Sometimes, it can become difficult for sad people to relay their feelings to those they think might not understand their pain—like you couldn't relate and would see him differently. And at times, it can be even harder for them to be around happy people they see as stable. He could've felt as if he didn't belong."

He didn't belong?

Sadness clutches at my heart as if it were in Christopher's fist, and my throat throbs, making my words come out scratchy. "He belonged with me," I cry out. "My family and our friends never made him feel as if he were the odd one out. He was one of us." I stab my finger into my chest as my voice shakes. "Jax's parents took him in as their own. He was my family. My partner. My parents, they loved him. I loved him."

Heartbreak claws through me, and my shoulders move as tears—tears I wanted to hide—slide down my cheeks.

I want to heal from this, to stop blaming myself, to feel whole again, but it's so damn hard.

I squeeze my eyes shut, hoping to block out more tears but they break through. I bow my head and sob. Cindy silently sits there, allowing me the space to break down in peace. To absorb her words, the possible reasons for Christopher's death, and I feel as if my heart, my body, everything that is me is crumbling.

I jump when Cindy reaches forward to clasp her hand over mine.

"I know you did. But maybe Christopher couldn't grasp that, and that was not your fault. He was sick."

Or maybe I was too blind, too selfish, to see the pain in his eyes.

Did my happiness break Christopher's?

And just as Christopher did, I'm hiding my own pain from

the world—from my family and friends. I'm suffering in silence, and Jax is suffering too.

We understand each other.

But just like Christopher buried his sadness, I need to bury any thoughts of Jax and me.

22

JAX

"HEY, BOSS," Nolan says, stomping into the office with a goofy smile on his face. "Just stopping in to give you a heads-up that I'm heading out with Amelia."

I drop my phone onto the desk, and my forehead creases when I frown. "Where the fuck are you going with Amelia?"

Nolan appears confused that I'm questioning him. "She found a heat exchanger and wants me to go with her to pick it up."

Rising from the chair, I grab my phone and slide it into my pocket. "That's canceled."

Nolan scratches the uneven stubble on his chin. "What?"

He stares at me, wide-eyed, as I walk past him and yell, "Where is she?"

"In the parking lot," he calls out. "She's in the work truck, waiting for me."

"She's done waiting for you," I reply, not bothering to hear his response.

I haven't talked to Amelia since she snuck out of my bed two nights ago. It was for the best though. It helped me avoid a conversation I wasn't ready to have. Hell, I would have thought the entire thing was a drunken dream had my sheets not smelled like her.

For so many years, I've done a decent job of pushing Amelia away, and I need to fight like hell to keep doing so. Chris might be gone, but that doesn't mean Amelia isn't still his girl. She is. Not mine. She'll never be mine.

I stalk out of the brewery and walk to the old work truck. Chris and I bought the beaters specifically to haul large orders, products, and equipment.

Amelia is in the driver's seat, and she jerks in my direction when I open the passenger door and jump into the truck.

"Jesus." Her hand flies to her chest. "I need to pay better attention to my surroundings."

I slam the door shut. "Add communicating with your business partner to that list as well."

Amelia chews on her plump lower lip. "I've been told I communicate quite well, thank you."

"Why didn't you *communicate* that you found a heat exchanger and are taking a road trip with an employee then?"

"I did tell you."

"You most certainly did not." I'd remember her telling me she was going on a trip with Nolan.

"I emailed you last night." She waves her hand in the direction of the brewery. "Go check it, and you'll find I most certainly did."

"An email?" I scoff. "Text, call, or walk your ass into the office. Don't *email* me shit like that."

"Business partners email each other all the time."

Even though I shouldn't go there, I say, "Do business partners also sneak out of each other's bed at the ass crack of dawn?"

She grimaces before swiftly collecting herself. "Do they show up drunk at each other's house late at night?"

That shuts my ass up for a minute.

I scratch my jaw as she leaves me to soak in her comeback. "I told you I'd handle the heat exchanger."

"I found one faster."

"You found it. I'll pick it up." I shoot her a fake smile, and my tone turns mocking. "Good teamwork, partner."

She shakes her head. "I'm picking it up."

"*We're* picking it up then."

"It's a five-hour drive, ten-hour round trip." She glares at me without blinking. "No way can I be in this truck with you for that long."

"Ten hours?" I didn't even ask her details about the heat exchanger, where it was, or how much she'd paid. "You were going to take a ten-hour road trip with Nolan?"

She nods.

"What if you had to stop and sleep somewhere?" I check my watch. "It's nine in the morning. Are you going to drive all day and into the night?"

"Ten hours is nothing, *and* if we did get too tired, we could stop somewhere." She lifts her shoulders in a half-shrug, her response said so easily, as if stopping and sleeping with Nolan somewhere is no big deal.

I clench my jaw. "Oh, really?"

She theatrically groans. "Not in the same room, *obviously*."

"You'd rather take a road trip with Nolan than your business partner?"

"Nolan would be less annoying."

"You must not have spent much time with Nolan." I relax into my seat. "Now that that's settled, who's driving?"

"You want to come?" She unbuckles her seat belt. "You can drive then."

————

This isn't a road trip.

This is a hell trip.

The clouds are dark, and I'm waiting for the approaching downpour.

The leather seats are torn and squeak every time I move.

Amelia has hardly muttered a word to me since I switched spots with her, plugged the address into the GPS, and pulled out of the parking lot.

We're three hours into the drive, and we have done everything to prevent conversation between us. To do that, we've been having conversations with everyone else.

She called her mom, and when they got off the phone, I called mine.

Then, she called Ava.

I called my dad.

She called her dad.

Then, I called Toby to check on the brewery.

I'm waiting for her to call her damn mailman next.

"Do you ever think we were too happy?" Amelia asks.

The fuck kind of question is that?

I almost wish she had called her mailman now.

"Who wonders if they're too happy?" I stare straight ahead through the windshield and clench my hands tight around the steering wheel. "I don't know about you, but I haven't been happy in a minute, Amelia."

I'm hot and cold with her. If I find the perfect opportunity to push her away, I use it as a weapon. But after, I want to bring her back and nurse those wounds I created. It's just like when we were young. We'd torment the fuck out of each other but then make amends minutes later. She'd trip me, I'd get a bloody nose, so she'd get a napkin to help clean it up. I'd push her in the pool, she'd get pissed, but I'd make sure she had a fresh towel when she got out.

I don't take my eyes off the road. "Why are you asking me this?"

"I wonder if we were too happy and that made Chris unhappy."

"News flash, Amelia: Chris was happy until you broke up with him."

"I never broke up with him!" she shrieks. "I said we should wait to get married. That didn't mean it'd never happen."

"He sure thought that was what it meant."

"You don't know everything about my and Christopher's relationship, Jaxson, so shut your damn mouth."

"I'm not the one spewing out *were we too happy* bullshit." I grind my teeth, my jaw hurting. "Why would you even consider that?"

"Think about it." Her voice turns serious. "We came from good homes. Christopher didn't. His home was dysfunctional, and he was miserable, growing up."

"Yes, but then he moved in with me, and he was no longer in a toxic environment."

Sprinkles start tapping on the windshield, and I turn the wipers on.

"You can't run from your past," she states matter-of-factly, as if she were suddenly a professional on the topic.

"What are you trying to say? That Chris is gone because we came from good homes?" I stare at her out of the corner of my eye, keeping my attention on both her and the road as the rain worsens.

I thought we were past this.

Past this blame game.

Never did I ever throw my life's luxuries into Chris's face. I did everything in my power to make him comfortable and give him a better life. And not only that, but I've never been one who's happy-go-lucky, skipping toward the rainbows and shit like that.

So, for her to insinuate that pisses me off.

I draw in a sharp breath. "In case you haven't noticed, I'm not particularly sunshine and goddamn rainbows over here. So, no, I don't think I'm too happy. That means that it could have only been *your* happiness that made him unhappy. So, please, for the love of God, don't come at me with this bullshit."

"Just because the home he moved into was a happy one

doesn't mean there weren't underlying emotions," she says. "He could've been envious of what we had, or maybe he felt like he didn't belong or wasn't good enough. We'll never know why Chris died. But one thing is for sure: my asking to *delay* our wedding wasn't the sole culprit. He had other issues. His childhood, the abuse, the deaths of his father and brother, and feeling like he didn't have anyone to turn to. All of those contributed. Happiness isn't contagious like the flu, Jaxson."

"But depression is?"

"By the time he came to your home, he was already wired that way. He was withdrawn and isolated, and he had low self-esteem. That's harder to push away."

"You're right." My brain thinks back to all the times I had trouble understanding Chris.

Did he do the same with me?

But I thought if I was a good friend to him, it'd be all the help he needed.

I thought *my happiness* was contagious.

But Amelia is right. It isn't always.

I relax in my seat, and even though it's still downpouring, I feel like I see more clearly.

"Are you glad we kept it a secret?" I ask when I shouldn't.

She shivers as goose bumps cover her skin. *"Are you?"*

"I don't know."

Her lower lip trembles. "You don't know, or you don't want to be honest?"

"Does it sound bad that I'm glad we kept it a secret because he didn't have to experience the pain of knowing while he was here?"

I've never felt so wrong in my life. I should've let Nolan go with Amelia today. We could've avoided this conversation, like we've avoided each other for so long.

Was it unhealthy for us? Yes.

But for Amelia and me, it was for the better.

"Why does it feel like we're betraying him more now?" She doesn't glance in my direction as she says the words.

I clench my jaw. "Then, we need to stop."

She's right. Before, we kept a secret from him.

We didn't touch and damn sure didn't share a bed.

Even if we weren't intimate when Amelia was in bed, it was still betraying Chris's memory.

"We shouldn't even be in the same vehicle," she says, now almost frantic, as if the thought just hit her.

"Amelia, Chris left you his share of the brewery. He knew we'd be in the same vehicle."

I remember Chris's letter and how I shoved it into a dresser drawer.

Someday, when the time feels right, I'll rip it open and soak in every word.

It could have all the answers I'm looking for.

23

AMELIA

SIXTEEN YEARS OLD

JAX BRIDGES HAS CONSUMED my mind.

It's embarrassing, to say the least.

And unexpected.

Okay, maybe that last one not so much since I've been crushing on him for years.

I've stalked his social media profiles, narrowing my eyes at the girls who leave cute comments and hearts under his pictures, and pay close attention to his responses. None of them are too flirty, and so far, he hasn't posted any evidence of having a girlfriend.

A month has passed since our beach vacation, but we've stayed in contact. He texts good morning and good night every day, asks how my day went, and sends me funny memes. But we haven't seen each other since then. We're back in school, our parents are busy, and I'm nervous to ask them to see him. They'd know something was up and for sure assume Jax and I liked each other.

No way would my father allow Jax and me to be alone then

—which is all I think about anymore. I want Jax to touch me like he did on the beach, to kiss me, and for us to do more.

Now that our fathers are business partners at Down Home, we'll be in Blue Beech more, which increases my chances of seeing Jax. Like tonight, my mother has a work thing. When my dad said he was going to Down Home, I told him I didn't want to stay home alone. I immediately texted Jax, and he said he'd figure out a way to be there too.

He did, so now, we're hanging out at his father's old apartment above the bar while our dads are working downstairs. My heart skipped a beat when I walked in and Jax smiled at me. There's no guy I'm attracted to more than Jax. Sure, there are cute guys at school, but their personalities are that of stale bread, or they're obnoxious little pricks.

Jax's skin is still sun-kissed from our vacation, and his dark hair is in its unruly state. It doesn't look messy or like he rolled out of bed. It just looks like *Jax*.

My dad pointed to Jax and told him to keep his hands to himself and that he'd be back to check on us. I frowned at my dad's warning. If he scared Jax off from touching me tonight, he will be getting a crappy birthday present next week.

"Do you hang out here a lot?" I ask Jax, following him into the living room.

"With the guys sometimes." He kicks off his shoes, collapses onto the couch, grabs the remote, and turns on the TV.

I slide out of my sandals, take the end of the couch, and angle my body toward him. "Just the guys?"

Jax tosses the remote onto the coffee table, not bothering to change the channel from the news. "Sometimes, Essie tags along with River."

I twirl a strand of hair around my finger. "No other girls?"

He shoots me a lopsided grin. "Is that your way of asking if I bring other girls here, Amelia?"

"It sure is." I fight to keep my voice confident and steady. "I don't hook up with guys who have girlfriends."

Jax's eyes widen, and he shifts in his spot, adjusting his shorts. "No girlfriend."

Perfect.

I bite into my lip to stop myself from grinning like a madwoman. "Have you messed around with anyone since we ... you know?"

"Nope." He focuses his heavy gaze on me and runs his tongue over his lips. "Have you?"

A sudden giddiness hits me. "No way."

"I haven't even thought of another girl since the beach." He runs his hand through his thick hair, and I focus on that hand, remembering how amazing it felt when he touched me with it. "I'm stuck on you, Amelia."

This is not your regular Jax and Amelia.

We are no longer the kids who call each other names.

Somehow, our attitudes toward each other have changed.

Long gone is my urge to tell him to go away, now replaced with the need for him to stay. Even then, years ago, I probably didn't mean it. Because when he would try to push me away, I'd always follow behind him and talk shit. Jax and me arguing, us rivaling each other on everything, was almost our foreplay in a sense.

My breathing hitches, and Jax wears a confident smile as he reaches out to grab my elbow. I giggle when he gently tugs me onto his lap. My dress spills to each side of his knees as I straddle him. I wore the dress for this very reason. As I situate myself, I rub against his hard cock under his shorts, and I don't stop until it's nestled perfectly between my thighs. He groans when I slowly grind myself against him.

I shut my eyes, taking in how good it already feels. My mind flashes back to the beach and all that we did. Heat spreads through my body when he slowly eases his hands under my dress and rests them on my bare thighs. His touch is everything I've been anticipating over the months that have passed. I can't stop myself from rocking against him with an urge and need for more.

"Shit, Amelia," he hisses through clenched teeth and throws his head back.

Pleasure jolts through me at the reaction that I gave him, and I roll my hips back. I ignore the noise of the TV and the possible consequences of us being caught. I'm so wrapped up in his body that all I care about is him and me and the things that might happen.

He digs his fingers into my thighs to stop me. "If you keep doing that, I'll blow my load right here."

My smile is full of challenge. "Make me stop then."

He drops a kiss to my cheek. "How do you want me to make you stop, Amelia?"

I nod toward my waist. "You're the one with your hands up my dress."

His cock twitches beneath me, and God, do I wish his shorts weren't in the way, so I could feel him closer to me. I'm eager for more when he slides a hand up between my legs and brushes his thumb against the front of my panties. I whimper, settling my hands on his shoulders, and hold myself up to give him all the room he needs. My knees feel wobbly when he slips my panties to the side, holding them back with his thumb, and he leisurely drags the tip of his finger through my wetness.

He needs to speed it up.

Does he not remember that our parents could walk in at any moment?

"You were wet like this at the beach," he groans. "I remember how easy my cock slid through it. How good it felt."

I gasp when he slowly slides a finger inside me. I should be embarrassed over how wet I am, but Jax's heavy breathing tells me he likes it.

"It was so hot," he goes on, as if his words aren't already lighting me on fire.

He draws his free hand out of my skirt, stopping his finger

between my legs, and I clamp my thighs together to prevent him from withdrawing that finger. With his free hand, he drags it up my chest and around my neck, and then he bunches my hair in his fist.

"One day, I'm going to taste you." He pulls me into a deep kiss, and I savor the mixture of peppermint and root beer on his breath. "I'm going to kiss it just like this."

Our tongues meet, and I cup my hands around his face to hold him there as I kiss him with everything that I have. He spreads the fingers of his hand between my legs, nudging my thighs back open, and plunges a finger inside me ... maybe two because there's more pressure.

My head spins, and I'm nearly panting when I break away from him. "Do you have a condom this time?"

He nods, and I'm shocked at the seriousness on his face. "I put them in the bedroom before you got here."

I touch my lips, still feeling him, while grinning. "To the bedroom we go."

His fingers leave me as we rise from the couch. He doesn't try to hide his cock standing at full attention under his shorts as I hold out my hand to him—a silent confirmation that this is what I want.

His eyes shoot from his cock to me. "Are you sure?"

I rub my thighs together in anticipation, already missing his fingers there. "I've never been so sure of anything in my life."

It's almost like a dream as we walk down the hall to the guest bedroom. My heart heaves in my chest, excitement crawling through every inch of my skin. As soon as we hit the doorway, his mouth is back on mine, and he slams the door shut behind us. Pushing me against the door, he grips the hem of my dress and hastily drags it up my body before tossing it on the floor.

The ease and slowness in his movements have dissipated. His want and need for me take over. He unhooks my bra without any hassle and drops to his knees to drag my panties down my legs. I step out of them, and he backtracks a step. His eyes are trained on me, dark and intense, as I stand before him. Feeling insecure for the first time tonight, I hug my arms to my body, but I stop when he tells me to.

"I could look at you all day, Amelia," he says, running his finger along his bottom lip. "You standing in front of me, naked, will forever be burned into my brain."

We step forward at the same time, kissing again, and he guides me to the bed. I realize how soaked I am as I sit down, and I'm worried it'll get on the comforter. He stands before me, and I can't tear my eyes away as he pulls off his shirt. When his hand goes to his shorts, I stop him.

"Let me." I lick my lips, and I swear my mouth is as wet as the slit between my legs.

I yank down his shorts and boxer briefs, and his cock springs forth in front of my face. The light was limited the night at the beach, so I didn't get a good look at his cock then. I take it in, admiring the size, the swollen pink tip, and the veins on the side. Just like Jax said he'd kiss me between my legs, when I get bolder, more experienced, I want my mouth on him there.

His six-pack is no surprise to me since we've gone swimming together countless times, and the older we grow, the more his muscles become defined.

I drag myself backward onto the bed until my head is only inches from the black headboard, and Jax crawls over me, his cock rubbing against my thigh.

"Do you want to get under the covers?" he asks, his breathing sounding almost out of control.

I keep my head flat against the bed as I shake it from side to side. "This is fine."

His hands shake as he stretches over me to open the nightstand drawer. He's holding a condom when he returns, and I train my eyes on his every move as he rips it open and carefully slides it onto his cock, checking that it's secure when he's finished.

My breathing grows as erratic as his when he grips his cock, and I spread my legs wide, giving him room to make himself comfortable between them.

He stares at me, unblinking, like if he closes them, then this might not be real. He tilts his head forward, kisses my lips, then my forehead, then the tip of my nose.

"Are you okay?" He presses his lips to my forehead again to nudge loose strands of my hair away from my face. "You sure you want to do this?"

"I want this," I say with such certainty that you'd think I was reciting my birthday.

He presses his hand flat to my chest, somewhat cupping my boob, over my heart. "Your heart is racing."

"I'm just nervous …" I avert my gaze to the wall. "I've heard it hurts."

"If it does and you want me to stop, tell me. We don't have to do this."

I nod.

"Look at me and promise you'll tell me."

I meet his eyes. "I promise."

"Relax, babe. It's just me. Remember that." He keeps his hand over my heart, and there's a tenderness in his voice I've never heard before. "Open wider for me."

I do as I was told, and his hand leaves my chest to slowly stroke his cock a few times.

There's something about this moment with Jax.

My nerves aren't skyrocketing, like my friends have told me theirs were.

Mia said it was a terrible experience for her.

Ava said it was awkward.

But here with Jax, I feel content.

Comfortable.

Like my body knows it's in good hands with him.

"I'm going to slide in now," he says with so much patience in his voice.

He raises my legs so my knees are on each side of his body and guides his erection inside me.

I squeeze my eyes shut as pain rips through my entire body. I tense, my back going straight, and Jax doesn't move. He keeps his cock right there inside of me and gives my body time to adjust to his size.

He places a hand to each side of my face and bows his head to stare deeply at me. "Tell me when it's okay to move."

"I'm okay," I whisper while breathing heavily. "Keep going."

He nods, tenderly sliding out of me and pushing himself back in.

Then, he does it again three more times.

With each stroke, my body relaxes more.

"Can I go faster?" he asks, the words coming out between huffs, and he stares at me with intense desire.

"Yes."

I'm positive I hear him say, "Thank fuck," under his breath before he increases his speed.

He trails a hand up the back of my thigh before jerking it up around his waist and angles himself to hit a different spot inside me. It's the right spot because my back arches, and he halts. A cocky smile spreads along his lips before he continues fucking me.

And just like that, I've given the guy I thought I hated my virginity.

24

JAX

WHEN I SAY it's been a day, it's been a motherfucking day.

The weather chose to give the truck a car wash for the remainder of the drive.

Then, there was the nightmare of picking up the heat exchanger. The seller ignored our calls, so we sat in front of his shop, where a Closed sign was taped to the door.

"He literally said I had to pick up the exchanger today or he was selling it to the next person in line," Amelia said, chewing on her nails as we contemplated on whether to leave.

We'd come this far, so turning around without giving the guy a minute sounded like a bad idea. An hour later, the shop owner's brother called Amelia, telling her that the owner's wife had gone into early labor so he rushed her to the hospital. The brother agreed to meet us within the hour, so Amelia and I rolled through the drive-through for a quick bite while waiting for him.

Just like on the ride here, we had limited conversation. I'd never had such an uncomfortable ride before. Eventually, we started talking about the brewery, and Amelia blurted out question after question. I answered them nicely, not putting any sarcasm or animosity in my replies.

When the brother arrived, we inspected the heat exchanger, I told Amelia good job on her find, and we paid him. The brother opened the shop doors, allowing us to load it into the back of the truck, where there was thankfully a cover, and we were on our way.

It's overcast, the rain not letting up, and Mother Nature adds rushing winds that rock the truck. I lower my speed at the sight of standing water and hardly blink as lightning crackles around us.

Amelia's eyes are glued to the road, too, as our hazard lights flash. The same as the car in front of us because, otherwise, we wouldn't be able to make them out. I'm following them, not sure if I'm even driving in a straight line. It doesn't help that the truck is old and its headlights are junk.

I'm gripping the steering wheel when the yawns come and my eyes grow heavy.

"Amelia," I say without looking at her, "I think we need to stop."

"What do you mean, stop?"

"We either have to stop somewhere and sleep or sleep in the truck."

"We don't have to stop. I'll drive."

"You're not getting behind this wheel. With this weather and how long we've been on the road, neither of us should be driving. The last thing we need is one of us falling asleep."

I know my body and when it's on the brink of exhaustion, and all I've heard for the past thirty minutes is downpour and Amelia yawning.

"I know it's hard to see and all, but we're in the middle of nowhere," she points out.

"I'm aware of that. Why don't you check your phone and see if anything is around us?"

I don't see her, but I hear her grabbing her phone, and I assume she's looking.

"There's one place. Pink Elephant Motel." She blows out a stressed breath. "Just the name scares me."

I'm gripping the steering wheel so tight that my knuckles are turning white. "How far away?"

"It says the next exit."

"We're stopping."

———

I've witnessed Amelia be dramatic on numerous occasions—when I dunked her into the pool and got her hair wet, when her dad took her car keys away after she snuck out of the house with Ava and they drove around all night, and when she was bitten by a crab on the beach trip.

None of those were as dramatic as when we pull up to the Pink Elephant Motel. For someone who sleeps on her floor, you'd think she'd be fine with sleeping here for a night.

"Oh, hell no," she blurts. "I'd rather sleep in the truck."

I don't exactly blame her as we stare at the run-down pink motel. The place looks like it's been around since my great-great-great grandparents were alive. If it wasn't for the few beater cars in the lot and two guys rolling a shopping cart out of their room, I'd think they were closed.

"In the truck, huh?" I scratch my head, exhaustion hitting me, and motion toward the parking lot. "Out here?"

That shuts her mouth for a moment, and she does a scan of the dimly lit parking lot as the windshield wipers squeak with each movement.

"This was probably your plan all along. Take me to some haunted motel, so I'd die, and you wouldn't have to deal with me at the brewery any longer."

I unbuckle my seat belt. "I promise I won't let anything happen to you." I turn to look at her, hoping she can read the truth in my tired eyes. "I'm sure they have vacancies, but let me check."

She unsnaps her seat belt and snatches her purse. "I'll be going with you, sir. No way are you leaving me out here alone."

Amelia hops out of the car, and we sprint through the pouring rain into the motel's office. The only plus side of this musty-ass motel is that it's far enough that no one knows who Amelia and I are to each other. The only judgmental looks we'll receive are from those wondering why we're crazy enough to stay here.

25

AMELIA

THE MOTEL IS CREEPY.

Like Rob Zombie creepy.

Like *I will be skinned alive, and some guy will create a mask from my face* creepy.

Jax was right though. It was either we stop for the night, sleep in the truck, or attempt to drive, which would have been dangerous, given our exhaustion and the weather.

As we enter the office, I get a strong whiff of body odor and mold.

The frizzy-haired, middle-aged man behind the counter pauses his video game and sets the controller down. His name tag reads *Harry*.

"How many rooms do you need? The rate is sixty-five a night. If you want a week, we'll do one fifty."

Sixty-five a night? They should be paying us to stay here.

"Two," Jax says at the same time I say, "One."

No way am I sleeping in this serial-killer lair alone.

Sorry, Jax, but you're stuck with me tonight.

If Jax is shocked by my response, he doesn't show it.

Harry sneaks a grin at Jax. "Should I listen to the lady?"

Jax's gaze flicks to me, and I hope he sees the desperation on my face. "I guess one room then."

Relief hits me when Harry turns and grabs a rusty key. "That'll be sixty-five bucks."

I open my purse to pay, but Jax already has his wallet out, handing Harry the cash.

Harry drops the key in his hand. "Room twelve. It's to your right when you walk out. Checkout time is eleven. Drink machines are around the back corner."

"Thanks, man," Jax says with a nod.

As we walk out of the office, Jax's palm finds the base of my back. He rests it there, and my muscles loosen, as if there's a sense of safety with his touch.

We walk below the awning, checking room numbers, and stop at twelve. Paint is peeling from the door, and Jax wiggles the knob a few times to get the door to open.

The smell of harsh chemicals greets us when we walk in.

Hopefully, that means it was sanitized thoroughly.

"What was that about?" Jax asks, flipping a light on. "One room?"

"I'm not dying alone in here."

"No one is dying, Amelia."

"*But* if I do, then you do."

The door slams behind me, and as I do a once-over of the no-frills room, realization smacks me in the face. Harry didn't ask how many beds we wanted.

I take in the ancient TV, the half-peeled wallpaper, and carpet stains. "Uh … should we tell Harry that we need another room with two beds?"

"We can," Jax says, yawning and fighting exhaustion. "Or we can each take a side of the bed and crash." He tugs his shirt over his head, drops it on the end of the bed, and pushes his shorts off.

"Whoa." I hold a hand up. "What are you doing?"

Jax places the shorts on top of his shirt and stands in front of me, only wearing thin boxer briefs that show his well-endowed package. He towers over the bed, his body all defined muscle. His six-pack is there, but his body is different than when we were teens.

I take in all that's matured about Jax Bridges. The stronger jawline, the broader shoulders, the way he gives off so much more self-confidence. This is a man who knows he's attractive, who knows women drool over him, but that confidence doesn't come with arrogance. Jax doesn't need to prove he's hot, doesn't need to show he is, because he doesn't care what anyone thinks about him.

He clears his throat, breaking me away from admiring his body, and his eyebrow is raised as I slowly drag my eyes to meet his. I wait for the smart-ass comment, but it doesn't come. As if he doesn't have the energy to give me shit, he slides off his watch, sets it on the nightstand, followed by his phone and wallet, and slides into bed.

"I need to use the bathroom," I rush out, dashing in that direction.

"I took the side closer to the door, so I get murdered first," he faintly calls out as I flick the bathroom light on.

My body has been pleading for a shower for hours, but that turns into a quick no when I rip the shower curtain back. I can sleep in my grossness for a night. I use the bathroom, wash my hands, and trudge back into the bedroom.

Jax turned the bedside lamp on, and his back is rested against the headboard as he scrolls through his phone.

"Will you hit that light?" he asks when he sees me.

I nod and flip off the light. Even though I'm spent, sleeping in the same bed as Jax has me keyed up.

"I'm debating on sleeping with my shoes on," I tell him when I notice his are placed to the side of the bed.

He shrugs, not taking his eyes off his phone. "Suit yourself, but I promise, you've slept in worse. Remember that time we went on spring break and everyone chipped in on that place? It was worse than this."

"I forgot about that." I shake my head at the memory. "I was a stupid teenager who cared about having a good time with her friends, not worrying about hepatitis."

He sets his phone in his lap. "Sometimes, I miss being a stupid teenager."

"Same." I sit on the edge of the bed to slide my sandals off, not allowing my bare feet to touch the dirty carpet, and lower myself underneath the blanket. The sheets are cold, and I shiver while making sure I'm fully covered before awkwardly wiggling out of my shorts.

I shift to look at Jax, and his eyes penetrate mine. Even though I'm still wearing a tee and panties and I'm covered from him, I feel more exposed than ever. Jax's face hardens before he grimaces and looks away from me. He snatches the remote and turns the TV on.

The picture is staticky, and as he flips through channels, he discovers our options are limited. He settles on an old episode of *Cheers* and tosses the remote on the nightstand.

I make myself as comfortable as I can, pulling the blanket up my chest, and despise this weirdness between us. Since Christopher left me the brewery, all we've done with each other is give the silent treatment, throw out our resentment, or spill our secrets.

The pillow is uncomfortable as I lie back and stare at the ceiling. My breathing is shallow, and Jax keeps his gaze in the direction of the TV. But I can tell he's not watching.

My chest and limbs feel heavy, my body sore, and I blow out a breath before starting a conversation I shouldn't.

"What's your favorite memory with him?"

I've never seen Jax's entire body tense like it does now. He's silent, and I wonder if he'll answer me or act like he didn't hear my question.

He breathes through his nose, but I don't have the guts to peek at his face. I can tell by the change in his breathing that he'd rather talk about anything other than this.

"What?" he croaks out after what seems like forever.

"Your favorite memory of Christopher." My voice cracks. "What is it?"

"I guess it was ..." He stops, as if he's running them through his mind to find the perfect one, and he chuckles, a good memory hitting him. "The night of high school graduation ... Mia's party. We were sitting by the pool. Chris looked at me and said, 'Thank you.' I wasn't sure exactly what he was thanking me for, but I told him it wasn't necessary and that friends were there for each other. He said ..." He stops speaking, and then emotion tears through his voice. "He said he hadn't thought he'd even make it through senior year, let alone graduate. He said that he'd always been told he was stupid, but at that moment, when he was handed his diploma, he knew that wasn't true."

Jax throws his arm over his face, and his words come out more muffled this time. "I don't know if it'd be considered the happiest moment, but it's my favorite. It was as if he finally realized that he was a fucking human being and everything his piece-of-shit parents said was wrong."

Christopher was insecure in that way and always questioned if he was doing the right thing. He didn't trust many people, and at times, he wasn't the best at making conversation. But he tried, and I was so proud of him every time he forced himself out of his comfort zone. And I could see the pleasure on his face when he did. So, I smile at Jax's memory, loving that Christopher knew that he was a good man and that he mattered, but then that smile collapses as the reality train knocks into me. Christopher said all those things, so why did he decide to leave us?

Jax turns his head, glancing at me sideways, and his face appears pained. "What's yours?"

"The night he told me he loved me. He said he never thought

he'd love anyone because he hadn't known what love was. But I helped him discover that."

Since talking with my therapist, I've asked myself if Christopher loved me too much.

Was I a crutch for him to walk through life and he didn't know what to do without me?

"What's your worst memory of him?" I ask.

"The fuck?" Jax brings himself up to glare down at me, gritting his teeth, and his voice turns harsher with each word. "We know our worst memory. It's him dying."

I gulp. "Other than that."

"Other than that doesn't exactly matter, does it?"

My heart turns frantic inside my chest, as if it's warning me not to go there, telling me to keep everything bottled up inside, as I have been. But the desire, the need, to tell someone burns through that warning.

Maybe if I tell Jax, he'll understand.

He cut himself open and bared himself to me, albeit when he was drunk, and is acting as if he doesn't remember, but still, he did it. It was as if he couldn't imprison his truths any longer.

My eyes are moist, my stomach sinking, as I prepare to give him something neither one of us can ever take back. Just like when he sat in my foyer, on the floor, and said he wished I'd loved him, these words will be burned in his brain for a lifetime.

I blow out a stressed breath as rain pelts the windows. "Christopher started changing, or maybe I hadn't known much about him until we moved in together. He hardly slept, was irritable, and sometimes, he'd come up with the craziest stories. He'd turn from the sweetest man alive to someone constantly worried that I'd leave him. One morning, I walked in on him snorting something. I immediately accused him of it being some hard drug, but he shook his head, laughed, and said, 'Baby, it's just my depression medicine.' When I asked why he was snorting it, he said it was a one-time thing because he'd forgotten to take it for a few days and it'd hit him faster." My face twists in agony ... in regret ... in wishing I'd been smarter. "I was stupid to believe him, but I just didn't want to believe he was lying to me."

And then, I tell him in detail about the day my entire world shattered.

26

AMELIA

SIX MONTHS AGO

THE DOOR to the bedroom is halfway open. Our bed is unmade and empty, and boxes that were on the top shelf of my closet since I moved in are thrown across the room—pictures and papers and cards spread along the floor.

What the ...

I call Christopher's name for what seems like the hundredth time.

I take a step forward and nudge the door open.

Something is different.

Something isn't right.

The room is void of anyone and all the furniture is in place.

There's a thump as I open the door wider, and I move around it to see what's on the other side.

I scream when I see Christopher hanging, a belt noosed around his neck with the other end knotted around his over-the-door pull-up bar.

Tears fall down my cheeks, and my hand shakes so hard that I feel like I have no control over it. His hand is cold—*lifeless*—as I take it and check his pulse.

Nothing.

Christopher no longer has a beating heart.

I scream his name, as if my voice has the power to bring him back to life.

Could give me back the man that I love.

"Please," I cry out, my knees wanting to buckle but I do everything in my power to stay standing. "Christopher, please wake up!"

I jump up, trying to reach him, to pull him down, but I'm too short.

It's as if someone were choking me, as if I can't breathe myself, and I scramble across the room when I see Christopher's phone on his nightstand. I call 911 while dashing into the kitchen for a stool and scissors. The operator tells me someone is on their way, and I call my mom with my phone.

How I'm moving, how I'm speaking, I have no idea.

My body is on autopilot.

All I do is scream Christopher's name over and over while my mom begs me to tell her what happened. She says she's on her way, and I cry out that it's too late. We're all too late.

My sobs hit my body, assaulting it, as I return to my bedroom. I stand on the stool, struggling to balance myself, to keep hold of the scissors. I drop the scissors and curse myself, hating myself, as I bend down to grab them.

Then, I drop them again on my second try.

"Please," I cry out, heartbreak aching through me so heavy that I'm barely able to produce words. I feel like I'm dipping in and out of consciousness, and the only thing my body knows how to do is save the man I love.

All I want to do is cut him down and save him.

To have him in my arms, so I can tell him everything is okay.

It'll haunt me for the rest of my life—to see him like this. I want to run out of the room and hide, but I can't leave him.

I clutch the scissors in my hand and attempt to cut through

the leather belt, being as careful as I can not to hurt him in the process.

It's hard, so hard.

My hands are shaking.

My arm muscles ache.

And I want to collapse on the floor and die every time his body bumps into me.

"Come back to me!" I wail, my tears blocking my view of him, and my shoulders shake so hard, making it even more difficult for me to cut him down.

I'm pushed away by paramedics, one of them grabbing my waist and hauling me back as I try to fight against them. As I kick and scream and beg them to save him.

I'll never forget watching them cut him down. The way my mother holds me back, how I collapse into my father's arms.

Even though I know it'll kill me more, I ask to sit with him for a moment. The paramedics stare at me as if I'm a crazy person, and maybe I am, but I don't care. I trace his jawline, tell him that I love him and that everything will be okay. Then, I apologize for not being enough for him.

I gulp in heavy tears as I say good-bye.

My mother is sobbing. My father is holding back fresh tears —no doubt an attempt to stay strong for me. My father drags me out of my townhome and places me in the backseat of his car.

I've lost Chris.

He's gone.

The burden of his death sits at my feet.

I see it in people's faces and overhear it in their whispers.

They believe Christopher killed himself because of me.

Why else would a young man with such a bright future want to end his life?

Because of the woman, is the immediate response.

For a while, everything seems to happen in a blur.

I stay at my parents' for three months. My father cleaned my bedroom, and my mother packed my bags, so I wouldn't have to return to my townhome. My parents are overbearing, needing to check on me as if I might do the same, as if Christopher's suicidal thoughts rubbed off on me like a stain and they don't want me to be the next loved one they'll have to say good-bye to.

I go home even though they told me it was too early.

I go home, step into my bedroom, and fall apart.

I suffer in silence, kind of like Christopher did, and ask myself what I did wrong.

What did I miss?

What made him want to end his life instead of coming to me for help?

27

JAX

CHILLS RUN down my spine as I digest Amelia's words.

I knew she was the one who had found Chris, but I never heard the entire story. I never asked because that would be a reminder that my best friend was gone. The less I thought about that, the better.

The woman lying next to me isn't the Amelia I've known for years.

She's broken, tired, and misunderstood.

She'll never recover from that.

I loved Chris like a brother, but right now, I wish I could scream at him. He knew it'd be Amelia walking into that bedroom, knew it would destroy her, but he did it anyway. He scarred her for the rest of her life.

Every inch of my body aches to comfort Amelia as she sobs next to me. I want to drag out her pain and transfer it to me.

Give it all to me. I can handle it.

When I can't take it any longer, I pull her into my arms and cradle her to my chest.

"God, Amelia," I whisper through her cries, caressing her hair. "I'm so sorry."

Her tears hit my bare skin as she whimpers. Shame sweeps

through me when I lower my hand and trace her spine with the tip of my thumb to comfort her.

I'm unsure who makes the first move or how it begins, but our lips meet. Our kiss starts slow, timid, both of us wavering on whether to cross that line. When neither of us pulls away, we deepen our kiss. Amelia lifts herself, providing me with better access to her mouth, and her chest slides against mine.

We devour each other.

We need this.

So damn bad.

Our souls and broken hearts are thirsting for each other.

This won't heal us—that's for sure—but maybe, just maybe, it'll help us forget momentarily.

I flip her onto her back, pulling away, and with the limited light available, I drink in the sight of Amelia. She's changed so much since the last time we were in this position. Just like I told her the night we each lost our virginity, her naked body has forever been singed into my memory.

I hover over her, sinking my elbows into the bed on each side of her body, my pulse beating in my neck. Even though I was tired earlier, I'm now fully alert, as if I were energized after sleeping for a week straight.

Her hair spills over the edges of the pillow. She draws my tongue into her mouth as we kiss. I pull her shirt off, exposing her, and then push down the cups of her bra. Breaking our kiss, I stare down at her chest. Her hard pink nipples are begging to be sucked, and I capture one in my mouth. Her back arches as I suck on it, twirling my tongue around the tip.

"Jax," she says my name in a long moan, making it sound as if it's an entire sentence.

I suck on her other nipple before shoving my face into her neck, and goose bumps are on her skin as I lick the spot below her ear. When she whispers my name again, I shift so that I'm staring down at her.

"Thank you," she whispers, reaching up to run her fingers along my jawline.

I shudder at her touch, and my cock stirs.

"Let me make you feel good," I say, tugging on her lower lip with my teeth. "Let me touch you where you deserve to be touched."

I want to touch and taste every inch of her.

Even though it's wrong.

And I'll burn in hell for it.

"Do it," she pants. "Make me feel good, Jax."

And that's exactly what I do.

I trail kisses between her breasts, down her stomach, and I lower my body until my face is directly over her pussy. I want her more than ever—more than when we were at the beach or when I entered her for the first time when we were teens.

"Spread those legs wide, baby," I say, keeping eye contact with her. I grin as she parts her thighs, giving me ample room to make myself comfortable between them. I pat her legs in praise. "Yeah, just like that."

The room feels hot. My pulse feels as if it could come out of my body. I slow my movements to savor this. Hooking my thumbs along the strings of her panties, I drag them down her legs. I collect them at the end of her feet and hold them up. I shock myself as I lick the wet spot on her panties and then set them next to my pillow, knowing she'll kick my ass if I toss them onto the filthy floor.

Her legs shake when I drag her knees up and use my hand to open the folds between her thighs. I fall back, taking in the perfection of her pussy, and desire floods every thought in my mind.

"So beautiful." I maintain our eye contact, even when her eyes are slowly drifting shut, as I lower my head. "So damn beautiful." I place a soft kiss on her clit.

Those beautiful eyes of hers slam shut when I dip my tongue

between her folds, sliding it up and down before curling it around her clit.

"Jesus Christ," she hisses when I suck on her clit, putting just the right amount of pressure on it, and slide two fingers inside her.

I pause to grin up at her, a pleased smile on my face, even though she can't see me.

Then, I eat her pussy like I've never eaten anything before.

Like I'm a man who was starved for months and has been handed the one treat I craved the entire time.

She tastes incredible.

My new favorite meal.

And my mind wanders back to the night when I told her that, one day, I'd kiss her here. That one day is now, in this old motel room, in secret.

Her moans fill the room. They're angelic, music to my ears, a sound I want to put on replay. I pleasure her pussy harder when her hand plunges into my hair, pulling at my strands as she starts shoving herself closer to my mouth.

My greedy little Amelia.

She loves my tongue just as much as I love the taste of her.

This will forever ruin us.

It doesn't take long until her legs shake and she's falling apart beneath me. I've never heard my name cried out so loud. I give her another thrust of my fingers and two final licks before my mouth finds hers again and I shove my tongue inside.

"Taste yourself," I hiss into her mouth. "Taste what I just tasted. Taste yourself, baby."

She plunges her tongue into my mouth, savoring every inch of it, and reaches down to stroke my throbbing cock over my boxers. She loses my mouth when I throw my head back in pleasure from just her caressing my damn dick.

She teases me like I teased her and doesn't take me out, just jacks me off through the cotton fabric. My back straightens when she slips her hand beneath the band and frees my cock. Her soft, delicate hand wrapping around my bare cock sends every nerve in my body into overdrive, and I thrust into her hand, wishing to God I were inside her.

My mouth returns to her, and I kiss her hard, as if taking possession of her. My heart rages inside my chest, needing more, begging for more of her.

"Give me more, Jax," Amelia says, her tone between a whine and a whimper. She holds my cock, moving my hardness closer to her core.

"Are you sure?" I ask, jerking my hips forward, not wanting her to stop touching me.

"I need it." This time, she tries to move my cock so fast that I have to stop her, in fear she'll break the damn thing.

There's no doubt, from her frantic movements to her shaking limbs to her breathless voice, that she wants this.

My head spins as I assist her in guiding my cock to her entrance, and then I slowly ease inside her. The hairs on the back of my neck stand as Amelia's pussy clamps around me, as if it never wants my cock to leave.

I feel like I'm on top of the world as I slide in and out of her sweet warmth.

The old bed creaks with my every thrust.

She clings to my shoulders as I quicken my pace.

Faster.

Harder.

Deeper.

I shift myself between strokes to hit different spots in her pussy, finding the right one to make her fall apart again.

Her nails dig into my arm, breaking into my skin, making me feel more alive.

"Yes," I groan, nuzzling my nose into her neck. I whisper in her ear, "Scratch me. Wound me. Give me your pain."

She gasps and claws at me harder.

All my focus is on Amelia—her breathing, her pants, feeling her pussy tighten around my cock. When she's close, I throw her legs over my shoulders and pound in and out of her. She bucks her hips forward, meeting me thrust for thrust, moan for moan. Our thighs smacking together.

She buries her head into my sweaty neck, her pussy constricting around my cock, and cries out her release. Her eyes are heavy-lidded when she looks up at me post-orgasm. Her thighs are shaking. My arms are shaking.

"I'm close, baby," I grind out, my cock thickening inside her.

"Yes," she says, rolling her hips. "Let me make you feel good now."

When I hit my brink, my muscles tighten, and I pull out and release onto her stomach.

She doesn't complain or comment; she only rubs it into her skin, as if my cum is her favorite lotion. I collapse onto my back, and we both go quiet, catching our breaths.

Everything has just changed.

And who knows what the repercussions will be?

28

AMELIA

THE RAIN HAS SETTLED on our drive home—thank God. We're almost to the Blue Beech town lines—where our reality awaits—when I finally ask the question that's been on my mind since I woke up this morning.

"How wrong is what we did?"

Conversation between Jax and me has been limited since we left the motel. We stopped for a much-needed coffee and breakfast, but this is the first time us having sex has surfaced.

I know what we did would be considered wrong in anyone's eyes. People would shake their heads in disapproval and call us choice words if they found out what Jax and I did in that motel room.

But I'm not ridden with as much shame as I should be. Because for the first time since Christopher's death—and maybe even before his death—I enjoyed a good night's sleep. I didn't wake up fatigued, drained, and feeling as if I hadn't slept in weeks. In that rickety bed, in that seedy motel, post-orgasm with Jax was where I slept like a baby.

"On a scale from one to ten, probably a ten," Jax answers without paying me a glance. "Which is why we don't have to talk about it. We gave each other something we'd both needed. We can accept it and move on."

I fold my hands on my lap, unclear on how I feel about his response, and stare out the window. "Just our little secret."

Jax clears his throat. "We seem to be racking those secrets up, huh?"

"Sure seems like it," I grumble.

"Do you want to keep it a secret, Amelia?"

My gaze darts in his direction. "What?"

His eyes are sincere as they meet mine. "Chris is no longer here, so who are we keeping it a secret from?"

My stomach tightens at his words, my breakfast threatening to make its way up.

"Would it be that bad?" His question sends chills up my spine.

"Maybe not as bad for *you*, but people would tear me apart." I motion toward him. "You'd just be the best friend who did something wrong. I'd be the whore."

"Fuck anyone who would call you that," Jax hisses. "They don't know shit."

"*There's Amelia, the girl who made her fiancé commit suicide and is now sleeping with his best friend. The best friend who blamed her for his death, who called her names for years, and who competed with everything she did.*" I shake my head. "*Dumb whore, that Amelia.*"

"Don't call yourself that."

"Why not?" I half-shrug. "You've called me a whore before."

Jax holds up a finger. "A.) I've never called you a whore." He flips another finger up. "B.) It's easier to be a dick to your best friend's girl than to admit you want her."

———

"Do you want me to drop you off at home?" Jax asks as we drive into town.

"My car is at the brewery," I reply.

"You can get it later."

That's a predicament I didn't think of until now.

The first issue was the road trip with Jax and then us having sex, and we still haven't figured out what to do with the whole *will we keep it a secret* uncertainty.

My car is at the brewery.

The brewery truck is gone.

Toby and Nolan know Jax and I left in it together a day ago.

Please don't let them be gossipers.

Toby? I don't see him opening his mouth.

Nolan? I don't know him well enough. He's young, and sometimes, young guys can have stupid mouths.

"Don't worry about them," Jax says, as if he'd read my mind. "I'll drop you off at home, take the truck back, and then you can take the day off to get some rest."

"I don't rest at my house." I sigh. "So, sitting at home isn't exactly relaxing."

It's no party, hanging out in your laundry room, let me tell ya.

"Do you want to rest at my apartment?"

I bite into my lower lip and refuse to look at Jax.

His tone turns stern. "Do you want to go there, Amelia?"

I do, but I'm scared.

"Amelia." His voice is more demanding.

"I don't know," I rush out, throwing my arm in the air. "But what I do know is, I don't want to be alone in my house right now. And there's nowhere I'd rather be—nothing that would help me sleep, or relax, or whatever—than with you."

I slam my hand over my mouth, wishing I hadn't said all that.

Sure, Jax and I have said things to each other lately that shouldn't have been shared. But never like this. It's during moments of weakness—when he's been drinking, when we're alone in a motel room, or when we're kissing when we shouldn't be.

Jax makes a U-turn. "My place it is then."

The short drive is quiet, and he helps me out of the truck when we reach his apartment. When we walk in, I follow Jax into his bedroom. From the way Jax walks, to the way his voice has a slight drag to it, to the dark circles under his eyes, it's clear he didn't sleep as well as I did last night. I guess only one of us sleeps well with guilt.

He opens a drawer, tosses me clean clothes, and points to the bathroom. "Do you want to shower?"

I nod.

"It's all yours. I'll go next."

"Thank you." My cheeks blush, and I shyly tip my head down before scurrying to the bathroom.

He doesn't ask to join me.

I don't ask him to either.

We need a minute to process last night and what it means for us.

When I climb into the shower, my legs are sore.

But the good kind of sore.

The *Jax gave me all the pleasure I needed* type of sore.

I tremble as I run my hand along my thighs, remembering Jax's tongue and touch. I wash my stomach, wash away the evidence of Jax being there, and tip my head back, allowing the water to rain over me.

And for what seems like the first time in a long time, I smile.

I smile, and some of my loneliness drains along with the water.

29

JAX

I'M A PIECE-OF-SHIT FRIEND.

Ask anyone right now, and they'd confirm it.

I'm selfish. Disloyal. A disrespectful prick to my best friend's memory.

"You're the only person who can touch me and doesn't make my skin crawl," Amelia says when I join her in my bed, fresh out of the shower.

I inhale my bodywash on her skin and my shampoo in her hair.

"Same." I fall on my back and throw my arm over my face.

Amelia turns on her side, resting her elbow on the pillow, and stares down at me. "Should we feel guilty? Not even for us being together right now, but for the past too?"

This seems like a conversation we could have a million times over and still not figure out the correct answer to.

I slide my arm from my face, my eyes on her. "We never did anything while you and Chris were together."

"Never." She slams her eyes shut. "That's what I'll keep telling myself."

I wonder how long we can go on like this—with the ghost of Chris, the guilt, the secrets, the fear of when people will find out.

It'll either make us stronger or drown us. One thing I know for sure is, Amelia and I need to be as discreet as possible for now. Whether the motel was a one-time thing or whether we continue to do this, it has to stay between us.

Until we know where our heads are, where are hearts are, we have to keep our relationship—or whatever this is—hidden.

I reach out and twist a strand of her wet hair around my finger. "You being with him was our problem all along, Millie." I blow out a breath. "And I'm scared it'll always be our problem."

Her eyelashes flutter as she stares at me. "Are we destined to always be each other's *the one who got away*?"

I stroke my thumb along her jaw. "That's what I'm afraid of."

"Why didn't you fight for me, Jax?"

"I never thought losing you was an option." I shut my eyes. "Until it was too late."

30

JAX

SEVENTEEN YEARS OLD

THE SCHOOL'S social outcast was assigned as my Chemistry partner.

I'd known Chris Simpson since elementary school, but we never talked much. We hung out with different crowds. Well, I hung out with different crowds, and Chris was a loner.

But as the semester went on, we started a friendship. I discovered Chris wasn't the weird kid he'd been labeled. He just had a shitty home life, even shittier parents, and wore dirty clothes to school more times than I could count. But if you threw all that away, he was a nice guy.

One day, I ask my mom to pack an extra lunch for him. I've never seen a kid so excited over a Lunchable in my life. So, I keep doing it and then start inviting him over for dinner. My mom feeds him and packs him bags of food to take home, just in case he gets hungry.

At first, Chris is shy, hesitant on any helping hand, but the more I invite him over to hang out, the more he opens up to me and my parents. I take him under my wing, introduce him to my friends, and invite him to all our school outings. My mother starts caring for him like he was her own—buying him clothes, shoes, and other basic needs—and he stays at my house more than his own.

But when I get back from our beach vacation, I find Chris's life had gotten worse. The first time he came to school with a black eye, he played it off and said he'd gotten in a fight with a kid while I was gone. The second time, I tell my father. And the third time, it's three days after Amelia and I had sex. Chris shows up at my house with two black eyes, a busted lip, and broken ribs—all from his piece-of-shit stepfather.

I've never seen my father want to kill someone. He charges over to Chris's house and gives Chris's stepfather two black eyes, a busted lip, and broken ribs, all while Chris's mom screams that she's suing the shit out of our family. Chris holds his crying little brother, Corey, in his arms as all this goes down.

Then, my dad looks at Chris and tells him to pack his things. Corey, cries and asks why he's leaving. Corey begs him not to leave, but Chris does and moves in with us.

My father calls child services, explaining how no child is safe in their home, and Corey is put into the system.

His bruises fade, and as the newest member of the family, he is going to a barbecue with us. It'll be the first time I'll see Amelia after the night in the apartment, and even though we've texted some, I'm not sure where we stand.

I want her to be my girlfriend.

And I'm not going to pussyfoot around and ask over the phone.

It'll be in person.

When we arrive at the barbecue, Chris's eyes light up when he spots Amelia. No joke, the dude grins from ear to ear—something I've never seen him do before.

Since Chris, my parents, and our friends are around, I play it cool with Amelia.

I'll wait until I can get her alone.

Except that never happens.

When Amelia comes to talk to me, Chris is there.

And he doesn't leave.

Amelia and I don't have much of a chance to talk.

On the way home, Chris looks at me and says, "If you give me Amelia's number, I'll be the happiest man alive." He shakes his head. "I've never been around someone who gives off that ... happiness, you know? I want her to be my girl."

For the first time in our friendship, my friend is happy.

He deserves to be happy in the fucked up life he was given.

And as much as it kills me, I let my friend have the girl.

31

AMELIA

A TEAR FALLS down my cheek as Jax explains why he didn't intervene with Christopher and me.

An array of emotions floods through me.

Jax was selfless for Chris, but not for giving us a chance.

But at this point, anything is too late now.

We can't change the past or take anything back.

Jax let me go, and we need to accept that.

"I thought you didn't care," I tell him. "That what we'd done was over and you weren't looking for a relationship."

Jax shakes his head, a pained expression on his face. "You and Chris hit it off … and it hurt. I was a confused teenage boy, and that's my biggest regret to this day. It's not wanting you while you were with my best friend or touching you after his death. My biggest regret is letting you go, Amelia."

32

JAX

I WOULDN'T SAY I've never cooked for a girl.

Senior year, I snuck Ericka Smith over when my parents were out of town, and wanting to be the smooth teenager I was, I made her Bagel Bites. They were on the burned side, but Ericka said it was the thought that counted. But other than that, I'm more of a takeout or *we can go to dinner* kind of guy.

Which is why I don't know why my Bagel Bites–burning ass thought I could whip something glorious up for Amelia—let alone a goddamn surf and turf of a filet and sea scallops. But it's the first night she's coming over to actually hang out rather than just go straight it bed. I want it to be … special?

We've been sneaking around since the motel, *but* we haven't revisited everything that was shared that night. We act like we don't know each other all day, and then when the sky turns black, Amelia makes her appearance, slipping into my bed. We deserve an Olympic medal in the sport of discretion.

They say the best ideas come out at night, but so do the best secrets.

We maintain a professional relationship at the brewery. Not that it's hard since she travels from store to restaurant to bar, convincing potential clients to become a Down Home craft beer carrier. And thanks to that, the brewery has been busier than ever. It's captivating, watching the old Amelia slowly return.

Hiding a relationship with a woman wasn't on my life's bingo card, but, hey, here we are. Sleeping with my deceased best-friend's girl isn't something I saw in the cards either. So, for right now, we'll stay in the shadows. It's either have Amelia in secret or don't have her at all. And I'll take all I can get at this point.

Our relationship exists only in the confinement of my apartment. We can only touch between these walls. But eventually, we'll have to decide to either break things off or make our relationship public.

Amelia walks into my apartment, a black hoodie over her head, and scrunches up her nose. "Geesh, I take it, dinner by Chef Jax isn't going well?"

I left the door open to air out the place.

I glare at the charred steaks before shoving them into the trash. "Change of dinner plans. We're going to my grandma's."

She jerks her hood down to stare at me in horror. "What?"

"We're going to my grandma's." I motion toward the kitchen. "Meal failed. My grams invited us over for dinner."

"You mean, she invited *you* over for dinner."

"Myself and a plus-one." I wiggle my finger in her direction. "You, Millie baby, are my plus-one."

She raises a brow. "Does your grandmother know I'm your plus-one?"

"She does."

Her shoulders tense. "I thought we were keeping us private for now?"

"Grandma Lane won't tweet about it, I promise," I say, referring to my mother's mom.

She rolls her eyes at me. "It'll be weird."

"Not weirder than eating that food I attempted to make."

Right in the middle of me texting Amelia, asking what she

wanted from takeout, my grandma called for a meal update. She'd written down a grocery list, the recipe, and directions for making our dinner. I told her it was a total fail, that the steaks resembled a leather belt and the scallop texture was way off. She said she'd made a roast, and she invited my date and me to join her for dinner.

Ask anyone in Blue Beech. Grandma Lane is one of the best comfort-food cooks in town—her roast being a fan favorite.

I stroll around the kitchen island to stand in front of Amelia. "It'll just be the three of us." I tug on the two strings around her hoodie, playfully tightening it around her face. "My grams could use the company."

———

My grandmother has lived in the same house for nearly four decades. It's in the most prestigious neighborhood in Blue Beech —large brick homes with substantial unused space, trimmed hedges, and neighbors who give you the stink eye when you light fireworks in the middle of the street.

Got grounded for a week for that one.

Amelia is the one who had dared me to do it.

It took a good twenty minutes and more pleas to convince Amelia to come. The final push—and winning argument—was telling her my poor grandma was sitting at the dining room table, all alone, with a cold roast.

"Hi, Nancy," Amelia says when she walks into my grandmother's house. "It was last minute, or I wouldn't have come empty-handed."

My grandmother swoops her up into a tight hug. Had I not given my grandma a heads-up that it'd be Amelia with me, the greeting would've gone differently. Not because my grandmother doesn't like Amelia—she's loved Amelia ever since she tattled on me for breaking her crystal bowl when we were ten— but because most people wouldn't expect us to be together. It would've only made Amelia more uncomfortable had she witnessed my grandmother's initial shock.

"Oh, sweetie," my grandmother says as she pulls away, waving off her comment. "Don't you worry about that. We have plenty."

She hustles us into the dining room, where the table is fully set—as if this were a dinner party and not a meal for three on a Thursday.

And as usual, her roast is never one to disappoint.

My grandmother keeps most of the conversation flowing. She asks Amelia how she's been, throws out a thousand questions about the brewery, and says how proud she is to have such great entrepreneurs in our family.

After we've devoured the deliciousness that is Grandma Lane's dinner—roast, bread rolls, egg noodles, and roasted veggies—Amelia and I clean up.

As Amelia loads the last dish in the dishwasher, I edge behind her, wrapping my arms around her waist, and kiss her cheek. "Told you it'd be worth coming."

She swats me away, her gaze pinging around the kitchen, like she expects the dude from *What Would You Do?* to come out. "No touching or kissing at your grandma's! What if she walks in? She'll think it's weird."

"Amelia, baby, do you not know my family's history? We're a shitshow."

People once called the Lane family—aka my mom's side—the Kennedys of Blue Beech. My grandfather was their beloved mayor … and then all shit went to hell when his infidelities were exposed. My grandfather had a secret child, and my grandmother divorced him. My mom, underage at the time, kept sneaking into my father's bar, and my aunt Cassidy married a felon. The Lane family turned out to be not as perfect as people had believed.

And not even three minutes after Amelia swatted me away, my grandmother comes in. Staring longingly at us, she holds up the remote and asks, "How about you stay for a movie before you go?"

My grandmother doesn't act like she's in her early seventies, nor does she look like it. But she is a woman who lives alone, as she never remarried, and even though she tries to stay active in the community, there isn't enough charity work to stop you from returning to an empty home sometimes. But she refuses to sell her house—even after my parents offered to build her a wing off their house, and my Uncle Rex said he'd kick River out of their guesthouse and give it to her. But she says no.

Amelia genuinely smiles at her, and her tone turns upbeat as she says, "Of course we will."

Four hours later, I'm attention-deep into a Hallmark movie marathon. First one was about an asshole falling for his child's teacher, and she made him a ray of goddamn sunshine. Gotta be honest, not my fave. The second was a small-town romance—per what my grandmother called it—where a woman returned to town to help the family farm. She'd left her boyfriend, a gazillionaire, in the city, but the ex-boyfriend, a dude who smiled and talked about his horses too much, came back into the picture. And get this shocking twist: they fell in love with each other.

"A second chance at love." My grandmother's face shines as she stares at me from her chair. "They loved each other as kids and came together later. It's always possible."

———

I'm in bed, watching Amelia wiggle into a work dress, and I'm resting my arms under my head. "You going to my mom's birthday tonight?"

Amelia nudges her bedhead hair from her face. "Do you want me to?"

"Of course I want you to."

Her adorable nose twitches. "Will it be awkward?"

Yes. But it'll be amazing, having you there.

I drop my arms. "Come here."

She tiptoes toward me, stopping at the edge of the mattress, and I grab her waist. She gasps when I drag her back onto the bed, positioning her under me, and bow my head to her shoulder.

Shivers run over her body when I nudge my nose against her ear and whisper, "I don't know about weird, but it'll be hard, keeping my hands to myself."

It's true. Any chance I get to be with Amelia, I take it. We watch movies, eat meals together, and have sex.

She runs her fingers through my hair. "You can touch me all you want after."

When we first started sneaking around, I was worried it'd be weird, but nope. Every touch, kiss, and moan we share feels nothing but natural, like our bodies have been doing it for years and it's where we belong.

I kiss her arm. "What about touching you all I want now?"

I take her dress off, and I'm inside of her, making her moan my name minutes later.

———

There are two types of people in this world: those who enjoy surprise birthday parties and those who don't.

My dad? Me? Hell no.

My mother? She loves them.

Especially when they're for her.

I arrive at Uncle Rex and Aunt Carolina's fifteen minutes before my mom's scheduled arrival. Their house was chosen because the large square footage, open concept, and massive backyard make it perfect for parties. Their house is the shit and isn't one you'd imagine finding in a small town like ours. It's modern, nearly all solar, and it fits them to a T. They drive electric cars and are what Chris called tree huggers. My uncle builds video games for a living and is one of the smartest people I know.

That trait was passed on to River and Essie when they were young. River was hacking into websites before we hit high school, and then he taught Essie, who is just as dangerous. I always joke that Essie became a lawyer to help her brother stay out of trouble if he ever hacked into the wrong thing.

When Amelia walks in with Ava and Callie, she looks fucking sinful, and my eyes are hungry as I watch her every move. Anytime I see her—whether she's wearing a form-fitting dress that flaunts her every curve with her dark curls cascading down her chest or my baggy sweatpants and shirts that nearly swallow her body—she takes my breath away. I've seen Amelia at her worst and at her best, and every time, I always find her beautiful.

Amelia is perfection, but I just need to help bring her back to happiness—like the way she's leading me back to mine.

She gives her parents a hug, her dad a kiss on the cheek, and then Ava, Callie, and Amelia head in my direction, where I'm standing with the guys and Essie.

I scratch my cheek, trying to play it as cool as I can. "Hey, ladies." I slip a quick glance to her. "How have you been, Amelia?"

It might be wrong and obvious for me to ask only her how she's doing, but I can't *not* say anything to her. I have to bite my tongue not to say too much—not to tell her how beautiful she looks tonight.

Essie, the pain-in-the-ass cousin that she is, cocks her head to the side and says, "Don't you guys work together? You probably saw each other like, what, twenty times this week?"

Twenty times?

Essie always exaggerates everything.

Amelia freezes, her eyes shooting to mine.

I quickly gather myself. "Uh, yeah … but we do our own things within the company."

"I mainly work with clients, take orders, and do the work outside the brewery," Amelia adds. "Jax controls the day-to-day operations and beer brewing."

"Sounds like you two make a great team then, huh?" River says, a smile tugging on his lips.

Amelia steps to my side, and I can't stop myself from reaching down and brushing my hand against hers. It seems almost juvenile—a simple touch of the hand but it lights my body on fire.

"Everyone, quiet!" Aunt Carolina yells. "She's here!"

Conversations cease. I use everyone's attention turning to the door to my advantage and give Amelia's hand a squeeze before my mother walks in with my father and younger sister, Keelie. Amelia stares down at our hands, her lips parting and cheeks blushing.

Acting like we're nothing kills me.

My mother pretends to be surprised, but there's no way she didn't know. The driveway and street are lined with cars, and my father told her they were going to dinner.

My mom thanks people for coming, hugging them, and then makes her way to me. By now, Amelia has scurried off to talk to her parents.

"Thanks for coming, sweetie," my mom says, as if I've ever missed a birthday of hers, and she pulls me into a tight hug.

My father comes to her side, greeting me, and we make small talk about the brewery.

I fight to keep myself from staring at Amelia while we celebrate another year of my mother's life. When I pay her a glance, she looks away, and I wonder if she's been staring at me the same as I have been with her.

God, how I want to wrap my arms around her, be her man, and be how she was with Chris at parties.

They never had to play pretend. No, he got Amelia in public and in private. And it hurts that I can't have the same.

I do smile as I watch Amelia laugh and enjoy herself because for so long, she avoided our get-togethers. No birthday parties, no barbeques, no dinners. She bailed on all of them.

After an hour of small-talking with people, I walk outside, in need of fresh air. People are scattered along the yard, laughing, talking, and drinking—mostly Down Home craft beer, courtesy of the brewery. Taking a seat in a chair by the pool, I stretch out my legs and groan as I glance up to the sky, stare up at the stars, and wonder where Amelia and I are headed—as if those stars will give me a damn answer.

It's times like this that make me question if we're doing the right thing or setting ourselves up for heartbreak.

"Thank you."

I turn to find Silas taking the chair next to me. He makes himself comfortable, setting his beer and plate with a half-eaten slice of birthday cake—compliments of Callie—on the concrete.

"Thank you, Jax," he says again before I get the chance to ask what he's thanking me for. "The brewery is helping Amelia." He strokes his jaw. "I know you weren't happy about the situation because you and Chris had started the brewery from the ground up and it's your baby, but I appreciate you giving her a chance." He blows out a long breath as he half-slumps in the chair. "I wasn't sure what would bring my daughter out of her grief, and it seems it's the brewery ..." Bending down, he grabs his beer and points it in my direction. "And you."

I doubt he'd be thanking me if he knew all the dirty things I've been doing with his daughter.

His words send a warmth through my chest.

"It seems it's the brewery and you."

Silas clears his throat. "I liked Chris, but I don't like what he did to my daughter. Call it selfish, whatever, but she can't be hurt again. I'm not sure her heart can take much more."

It seems as if Silas is no longer talking to me, more to himself, as he's now staring at the pool. As if he needs to tell someone what's on his mind but he's worried to share it with his wife and daughter.

I like Silas. I don't think he's been my biggest fan since I gave his daughter hell, and when we were young, our moms claimed I'd someday marry his daughter, but he's never been a straight dick to me. This might be the first one-on-one conversation we've ever shared.

I nod. "I was worried at first, you know, but she's been a huge asset. We have so many clients that I've started looking for extra help."

He chuckles. "She is her mother's daughter, and if there's something they know how to do, it's sell liquor."

"Amelia could sell ice to an Eskimo."

When he turns back to me, I see the heavy worry in his eyes. "I'll pay you to stop asking to buy her out."

I wince.

"She needs the brewery just as much as you do. If it makes my daughter happy, then I'll pay the price."

"Half the brewery is Amelia's for as long as she wants it."

"Thank you." And with that, he doesn't say another word.

———

The next person to join me is my Keelie.

"Hey, big brother." She enthusiastically plops down in Silas's abandoned chair, a beer in her hand, and grins at me.

I confiscate her beer, causing her smile to collapse, and she groans.

"You're not twenty-one yet, you pain in the ass."

Keelie is the poster child for college coed. She joined a sorority the first chance she got and spends more time partying than studying. You wouldn't know that from her GPA. With her short skirt, crop tops, and blonde hair, like my mother's, she's the child who gave my father gray hair. Our older sister, Molly, is quieter, an attorney, and I saw her somewhere on her phone, talking about pleas or some shit.

"And you're not supposed to be eye-fucking Amelia." Keelie

snatches the beer back from me. "Looks like we're both doing shit we're not supposed to. Cheers to that." She takes a long draw of the beer.

"I'm not eye-fucking anyone."

"True. It's not just *anyone*. It's Amelia." She lowers her voice. "Chris's Amelia."

I grind my teeth. "Amelia doesn't belong to anyone."

She's not his.

She's not mine.

Amelia is Amelia, and I want her to be my partner.

My everything.

Hell, she already is my everything.

I want to be *her* everything.

Keelie eases closer to me, and the lightheartedness in her tone dissipates. "You know I didn't mean it like that, Jax."

"I'm so sick of hearing people say that."

"I just … don't know what to think about it."

"Then, don't think about it."

Keelie was only nine when Chris moved in with us, and I'm pretty sure she crushed on him for a few years, given I found a notebook with *I love Chris Simpson* written in glitter gel pen while helping her pack for college.

She taps her nails against the beer can. "I want you to be happy, and if she makes you happy, then go be happy with her."

"It's more complicated than that."

"Do you love her?"

I glance away. I'm not having this conversation with my little sister.

"You do."

I scrub my hand over my face. "I don't know what I feel anymore."

"You'd better figure it out before you lose her a second time."

I narrow my eyes at her.

"Just saying." She shrugs and chugs the rest of her beer. "You only live life once, big brother."

"Why am I taking Dr. Phil advice from someone who was most likely bonging beers in some dirty-ass frat house last night?"

She stands and taps the tip of my nose. "Because those who've never been in love give the best love advice, obvi."

33

AMELIA

MY PHONE BEEPS with a text from Jax.

> Jax: Can it be time for us to go?

Since I already know exactly where he is, my eyes immediately find him across the room. He's sitting with the guys, nodding as Easton talks, but his attention is on his phone. Slowly lifting his head, as if he feels my gaze burning into him, he winks at me.

I text him back.

> Me: How do we go? We can't just leave together.

> Jax: Why not? Say you want to go home and meet me outside.

> Me: I rode here with Ava. How will people think I'm getting home? On foot?

I yawn dramatically and stretch my arms in the air. "Is anyone ready to go?"

"It's not even nine o'clock," Ava says.

So much for Ava being my ride.

I ignore her when another text comes through.

> Jax: Why do you have to tell them how you're getting home?

I give him a pointed look, and he smirks.

> Me: I can't leave without telling my parents good-bye.

And then they will question who I'm leaving with.

It's a struggle, finding ways to sneak into Jax's apartment every night. He usually picks me up from mine, or I park in the Down Home Pub parking lot and slip my way to the back, so no one notices my car there.

I tap my chin, thinking of a master plan, as Callie talks about her cousin Trey coming into town. Ava makes a comment about how hot Trey is, to which Callie rolls her eyes.

I've only met Trey a few times since he lives in New York, but Ava isn't lying when she says he's hot. He's older— like, he has sixteen years on us—but you wouldn't think that. Trey is the secret child Jax's grandfather had with Callie's mother's sister. When Trey turned eighteen, he left Blue Beech, but he comes home to visit sometimes.

"Is he still single?" Ava asks.

"I think so," Callie says, narrowing her eyes at Ava. "But not single for you."

Mia grabs her Prada bag from the back of her chair and hitches it over her shoulder. "Yeah, I'm tired too. I had a long day and have an early morning." She shoots me a glance while standing. "I can take you home."

Thank you, Mia.

I nod and quickly text Jax.

> **Me: Mia is taking me home.**

Jax tells the guys good-bye—some of them fist-bumping or bro-hugging him or just waving—and then he makes his way to his parents and sisters.

The three of us say good-bye to our parents, and Jax walks out the door before I do.

> **Jax: I'll meet you at your place and then take you to mine.**

The air is sticky when we walk outside, and I don't expect Mia to immediately say, "If you want to go with Jax, I'll be your cover."

I stop mid-step.

She shakes her head. "I won't tell anyone, but the two of you couldn't be more obvious to those who pay attention."

It makes sense. Mia observes more than she talks. She's always been that way.

"I, uh …" I struggle for my next words.

Do I deny it?

Admit it?

Jax and I never discussed what we'd say if someone found out.

"You don't have to explain anything to me," Mia says, waving her hand in the air. "If you want to talk about it, I'm here. But no pressure."

My muscles relax. "Thank you."

We keep walking as I text Jax again, and my heart beats wildly with every step I take.

> **Me: Scratch that. If you're still here, she's going to fake take me home, and I can go with you.**

> **Jax: Flashing my lights.**

We spot his truck as Jax flashes his headlights three times.

"Jax is still here," I tell her as we stop at her car.

Her headlights are the ones blinking this time as she unlocks her Mercedes.

"Good night, Amelia," she says, opening the door. "Enjoy your night."

"Night, Mia."

She forces a smile before ducking into her car.

I trek across the street to Jax's truck, scan my surroundings, jump inside, and slam the door shut. I inhale the scent of his evergreen air freshener and barely detect the grin on Jax's face before he shoves his hand into my hair and yanks me to him. He kisses me. At first, it's slow and gentle and soft. But it quickly changes, turning frenzied, and we unleash all the control we had to use to stay away from each other tonight.

"I've wanted to do that since you stepped into the house tonight," he says, nipping at my bottom lip. "Do you know how hard it was, keeping my hands off you?"

"I absolutely do because I had to do the same." Grinning, I reach down and slide my hand over his jeans.

Just as much as he wanted to touch me, that same passion was inside me. He looks delicious tonight. From his wild hair to his black button-down shirt—I love a man who dresses up for his mother's birthday—to the smirk on his face anytime I passed him. My entire body was on fire with need for him.

He levels his eyes on me and says, "Amelia," in warning when I cup him through his pants and his cock immediately hardens. With a groan, he rests his hand over mine, stopping me. "We can't here."

"Your windows are tinted," I say, my voice desperate and salacious. All my inhibitions are gone when it comes to this man.

He holds our hands in place. "Yes, but there are people walking in and out. We're too afraid to even let them see us talk to each other. You want them to see us doing that?"

I shut one eye, my shoulders drooping, like a bummed teenager. "Eh, good point."

He leaves our hands coupled as he settles them onto my lap. "Sit like a good girl and keep your hands to yourself."

He awkwardly maneuvers himself, using his left hand to shift the truck into drive, as if it'll kill him to move his hand from mine.

I study him as he drives, taking in his contoured jawline, his long lashes, and his full eyebrows, but my eye-fucking is stopped when he slides his hand off mine to ease it under my dress.

Instinctively, I spread my legs, giving him room to do whatever he wants. "How am I supposed to *sit like a good girl* with your hand up my skirt?"

Jax doesn't reply. Instead, he multitasks, focusing on the road while also whispering, "Push your dress up your thighs. Yeah, just like that, baby. Now, move your panties to the side and slide closer, so I can play with you." Then, he uses his entire palm to cup my pussy.

I whimper, grinding my hips forward, and the truck feels as if it's a hundred degrees.

"I am going to fuck you so good when we get to my place," he says, pushing a finger inside me.

I dig my nails into his arm. "Why do you get to have all the fun?"

"Baby, if you start touching me, I'll either crash this car or pull over and fuck you on the side of the road."

As soon as we walk into his apartment, Jax slams the door and is on me.

I'm shoved against the door, his mouth assaulting mine, and our hands fight to get the other naked as we make out. Everything that we held in during the party is releasing—our secret unchained now that we've reached our haven.

Our sanctuary, where we can be ourselves, give in to ourselves and be free.

When his tongue slips into my mouth, I suck on the end of it. The action turns me on just as much as him.

"Do that somewhere else," he groans into my mouth.

I gasp, pulling away. "Like where?"

"Lower." His voice is husky. No bullshit. All business.

"Like here?" I suck on his neck, long and hard, hoping to mark him, that he'll be sporting a hickey there in the morning.

"Lower."

"Here?" I take off his shirt, feeling his heart racing, and suck on his nipple.

"Lower."

I skim my tongue down his stomach, sinking to my knees, and stop at his jeans. "Here?"

"Lower, Amelia." His tone turns more demanding.

I peek up at him, seeing his face darkening with need, and unbuckle his jeans before jerking them down. Then, I place a single kiss to his erection over his boxers.

"On my cock," he says, out of patience, sinking his hand into my hair. "That's where I want your mouth."

I open my mouth at the same time he jerks my head forward and glides his dick inside.

"Yeah, right there, baby. That's where lower is."

My head bobs, and Jax's groans and praises consume the room as I suck him in and out of my mouth.

This is only the third time I've given Jax a blow job.

That might seem lame, given that he eats me out on the regular, but blow jobs have never been my thing. And Jax always follows my lead. He never pushes my head or hands somewhere I might not want them.

The first time, I was scared to disappoint Jax because even

though I'd tried countless times with Christopher, I could never successfully deep-throat him. But Jax does it differently with me. He helps me as I suck his dick. He guides me, positions himself in my mouth until I'm comfortable enough to allow him to fuck my face.

"You suck me so good," Jax says.

I jerk him off in sync with my mouth, play with his balls, and Jax controls my movements with his hand on the back of my head.

"I'm coming," he groans out his warning, thrusting into my mouth deeper. "I'm coming."

I suck him harder, an invitation to come in my mouth, and when he does, I swallow down the taste of him.

"Jesus, fuck," he hisses through his clenched teeth. "That was …" His body shakes as he catches his breath.

I fall back on my butt, wiping my mouth, and he shakes his head while looking down at me.

"Up, Amelia," he says, his demanding voice returning. "I need to have my mouth between your legs."

My knees grow weak, and I struggle to get up, so Jax helps me. I wrap my legs around his waist, and his hand dives underneath my skirt, cupping my ass as he takes the few strides to the kitchen. Every item—the fruit bowl, papers, a water bottle— glides off the island as he settles me onto it and sprawls me out.

The granite is cold against my ass, but I ignore it. My mind is on better things, like Jax fisting my dress to my sides, telling me to hold it there, before he stations himself between my legs, his mouth right at my core.

I blush, the same way I do every time his face is down there. I can barely control my breathing, and my gaze is pinned on him. I rest my legs on his shoulders, sliding against his already-sweaty skin, and he pulls me as close as he can to his mouth.

My back arches as he starts dipping his tongue in and out of me. He licks me, sucks on my clit, tells me how good I taste, and sticks more fingers inside me than I've ever had before.

"Such a good girl for taking so many fingers in your pussy," he tells me. "Such a good girl for letting me prep you for my cock."

His words, his tongue, his fingers, just *him* in general set me on fire. I don't make it as long as he did with my mouth wrapped around his cock. In no time, I cry out his name so loud that I'm worried the people in the bar underneath us will hear. My legs fall slack against him, and I know there's no way I'll be able to walk for the next hour.

My head falls against the island as I catch my breath, my heart swelling with emotion as Jax rains kisses along my thighs.

I pant his name as he picks me up.

"Wrap your legs around me, Amelia."

I position my legs around his hips the same way I did on our way to the kitchen, and he carries me to the bedroom.

He tosses me on the bed and yanks me to the edge of it by my ankles, and I wiggle underneath him in excitement as he rolls a condom on.

He's catching his breath, staring down at me, while taking deep swallows.

Then, he slams into me.

I moan out his name, my back arching off the bed, and it feels so good.

Then, slowly, so damn slowly, he draws back.

Then slams back into me harder.

He keeps up that pace.

Hard, then slow. Hard, then slow.

I settle myself onto my elbows to see our connection—to see what we're both taking so much pleasure in—and I realize why Jax can't take his eyes away from me.

"That's ... that's so hot," I say in a half-whimper, half-moan, playing with my clit.

"It's hot as fuck," Jax groans, his focus on him sliding into me. "And it feels so fucking good." He slows his pace. "I love looking at us, at my cock in your pussy, at your juices on it. I love watching us right before I come. I never want to stop doing this." His voice grows raspier with each word.

"Me neither," I whisper, unsure if he even hears me over our moans, grunts, and the sound of our thighs slapping together. "Me neither."

He pumps inside me.

He possesses me.

"Tell me we'll never stop." His voice is strained, telling me he's close, and he slams his eyes shut. "That we'll do this forever."

I nod, relentlessly meeting him thrust for thrust, coming apart with another orgasm. "Forever."

"For-fucking-ever, Amelia," he hisses before withdrawing, rolling off the condom and releasing on my stomach. "All mine forever."

I love it when Jax marks me.

It's as if he enjoys seeing his pleasure on me.

And so do I.

———

I hug Jax from behind as he stands in front of the toaster, pulling out a waffle. "I love when you attempt to cook for me."

He turns to press a kiss to my lips. "Whoa. Frozen or not, this is still considered cooking for you."

"Time to call your grandma for a good meal again."

"Yeah, go ahead and call her at midnight and tell her we need a post-sex snack."

It's midnight.

Nowhere near breakfast time.

But we were hungry, and I said, "Let's have waffles."

So, we're having waffles.

I hop up and sit on the edge of the counter—the same spot where he ate me out, where I cleaned after, thank you—and watch him. "Mia knows."

He lays a waffle onto a plate. "That doesn't worry me."

"Why?"

"Because Mia is good at keeping secrets."

I raise a brow. "Why do you say that?"

He hands me a plate of waffles, kisses me another time, and pours syrup onto them. "Because she still hasn't told anyone that she fucked Trey—among other things. If there's anyone you can trust with a secret, it's Mia."

"What?" I almost drop my plate on my way to sit on the other side of the island. "Callie's cousin Trey?"

"Mmhmm."

"How do you know this?"

He grins. "I know everything."

I shove his shoulder.

"People share more than they should with bartenders."

"Does anyone else know?" I grab a fork, cut into my waffle, and take a bite.

"I don't think so." He collects his plate and plops down on the stool next to me. "Mia probably doesn't even know that I know."

"Trey told you?"

"Trey told me."

"How? When? Where? I need details."

He shrugs. "I was at Down Home one night, and I told him to move back home. He was drunk and said he hated this town. I said it wasn't that bad. To which he replied that it was hard for him to come back when he hated half the people here and had fucked Mia Barnes."

I gasp. "I've heard some shocking shit, but that most definitely makes the top ten."

Mia and Trey don't like each other. Trey has always had choice names for Mia, most of them stemming from her being wealthy and assumedly stuck up—only because she keeps to herself. Basically, Trey is just a jerk to her.

"I think it was when she was at NYU," Jax adds.

"Wow, I wish I could ask her all the details."

"Good luck in getting those, and don't say I told you. And speaking of people who know about us ..." He pauses. "Keelie does too."

"Ugh, not your sister." I throw my head back in dread. "She loved Christopher."

"She likes you too."

I chew on my nail.

Jax sets his fork down, and his voice turns serious. "How long are we going to do this, Amelia?"

"Do what?"

"Hide."

34

JAX

AMELIA STARES AT ME, unblinking, while conjuring up the perfect answer to my question. "I ... I don't know."

Asking that question was dumb.

We were having a good night.

But sometimes, you have to ask the shit that hurts.

And my brat sister's words are in my mind.

"You'd better figure it out before you lose her a second time."

"Are we just waiting it out ... to eventually break apart when we fizzle out, or are we really going to try this?" I swivel in my stool to capture every emotion that flashes across her face.

She's quiet.

I swallow. "Amelia, tell me what you're thinking."

"I don't know," she whispers, and the room falls quiet. "We need more time."

"That's fine."

"Let's give it a month."

I nod. "A month, and we'll see where we're at."

A month.

Thirty days for us to decide where our hearts are and where they will go.

Thirty days to find out if this is only sex ... or something real.

35

AMELIA

I'VE NEVER BEEN on what I'd consider a real date.

That might sound bad, coming from a twenty-six-year-old woman, but it's the truth. That's not to say Chris and I didn't go to dinner or do things together. It was just rare for us to go beyond our comfort zone. And he never planned anything himself. It was always my doing.

Did I feel like I was missing out sometimes? Yes.

But I'd committed myself to being with him, and I loved him.

When I heard my friends talk about dates, there were times I'd feel a deep yearning inside of me to have that—to have a man plan and surprise me with an entire night out.

Yesterday, Jax walked into his bedroom, drying off his hair post-shower, and told me to pack a bag, that we were going out of town. He said he wanted to take me on a real date, and if we couldn't do it in Blue Beech, we'd do it somewhere else.

I kept my cool, but inside, I was jumping up and down like a kid who'd been told they were going to Disney World.

Mia helped me pack ... and let me borrow the sexiest little black dress I'd ever seen in my life. It also probably cost as much as I made in a month.

I got a manicure, a fresh wax, and it seemed like I was having a much-needed self-care day.

And Jax doesn't disappoint.

He books a suite in the ritziest hotel in the city, four hours outside of Blue Beech. He reserves a table on a river dinner cruise, and our last stop is the crepe stand. Every time I go into the city, I get a crepe. He remembers that s'mores are my favorite, and we devour the sweetness while walking back to the hotel.

We're a regular couple, doing regular things.

This might sound lame, but it just feels … *good*.

"This is more than just sex for you, right?" Jax asks when I step out of the hotel bathroom, wearing the comfiest robe—hell, the comfiest thing—I've ever worn.

Underneath is the lace lingerie set Mia insisted I bring.

He's sitting on the edge of the bed, his black shirt half-unbuttoned, with his legs planted wide. His shoulders are slumped forward.

I stop. "What do you mean?"

"I'm asking if whatever is going on between us is mainly focused on sex." Vulnerability is in his eyes. "Because it's not just sex for me, Amelia. The thirty days we said we'd wait to find out where our relationship goes is creeping up on us, and every day, I look at the calendar and wonder if I'm closer to keeping you or losing you."

"Jax," I whisper, inching toward him.

"You remember the night I came over drunk and said I wished I had been the one you fell in love with? It wasn't drunk rambling. It was *the truth*."

I suck in a breath, feeling as if my lungs might collapse. Each step closer to him feels so heavy.

He keeps talking, like if he stops, then it'll never come out. "This isn't me saying we need to talk about marriage and kids or those types of things, but I love you, Amelia. And I want you to love me—for us to start on the road where we become each other's somebody."

"We're already there. *I* am already there."

This has never been about just sex with Jax. It will never be about just sex with him. I've known this man my entire life, and our relationship has shifted countless times. I trusted Jax with my virginity for a reason, and I trusted him the night he told me I was going to his apartment after he learned I had been sleeping in my laundry room. In the end, even during the times he'd blamed me for Christopher's death, I knew if I needed something, if I was in trouble, he'd throw all that disdain out and help me.

So many years ago, when we were teens, I'd been nervous to trust him.

Now, I'm ready to hand him my heart because I know I can trust him with it.

He doesn't move as I sink onto the mattress next to him. I climb around him, my chest to his back, and wrap my arms around him—well, halfway around him since I can't reach that far.

His breathing relaxes as I rest my chin on his shoulder and say into his ear, "When it's been thirty days, I will be here. I will be *with you*. You don't have to worry about today, tomorrow, a month, or even a year from now. You are that somebody for me, Jax."

I gasp when he maneuvers us so quickly that I'm unsure of how it happened. I'm on my back, the comfortable mattress adjusting to my body, and Jax stares down at me.

His face has relaxed, and he keeps firm eye contact with me as he runs his fingers down my arm. "I love you, Amelia."

"And I love you, Jaxson."

I don't know where we're going from here, but I know deep in my soul that this man loves me.

And tonight, we hand over everything we are to the other.

"We said the brewery was off-limits for sex," I say, laughing as Jax kisses my neck.

"Hmm ..." He circles his tongue around my earlobe, and I shiver. "Maybe we should revisit that little rule, huh?"

The thing about the whole *office sex* rule is that we're not in the office together much. So, it's been easy to keep that rule.

I'm perched on the edge of the desk, and Jax is settled between my legs. He shoves his hand beneath my dress and traces patterns on my bare thigh.

I buck my hips forward—a silent plea for more. "You might be right."

He draws his head back, his eyes shooting to the door at the sound of knocks. The knocker doesn't wait for a response, and the door flies open. Nolan appears in the doorway. Jax immediately removes his hand from under my dress and pulls it down.

"Oh no," I squeak, my hand flying to my mouth as I keep my back to Nolan.

Nolan makes no comment about me being nearly being spread eagle on the desk, as if it's not the most important subject on his mind, and he keeps peering over his shoulder.

"Nolan, get the fuck—" Jax starts to say.

"Boss, we have a problem," Nolan rushes out.

"What the fuck?" Jax hisses, his head jerking back as two people appear behind Nolan.

I peek over my shoulder and gasp.

36

AMELIA

JAX HELPS me off the desk.

Why now?

Out of all times.

I want the floor to swallow me whole as I shift to stare at two people I swore to hate until the day I died.

Two people I've never been formally introduced to or said a word to, but still, I despise them.

Sandra and Mick Ruins.

Christopher's mother and stepfather.

This is my third time seeing Sandra in person. The first time was when Christopher and I were at the movies and the two were there. She called out his name, but he ignored them. The second was just his mother at his funeral. Mick didn't show because he is the biggest piece of shit out of the two of them.

I want to scream at them to get out, but I'm struggling to find words.

This is bad.

Real bad.

The first people to see Jax and me in a compromising position are the last people I wanted to.

Sandra and Mick exchange looks at the sight of Jax and me—no doubt vicious wheels turning in their heads.

"Well, I'll be darned," Mick says, slapping his thigh. "The best friend and fiancée?" He chomps on the toothpick in his mouth. "Now, that's some messed up shit, and that's saying a lot, coming from me."

Sandra snickers.

Nolan shuffles to the corner of the room and shoves his hands into his pockets, watching the impending shitshow.

Mick motions toward Jax and me. "I bet you two were fuckin' the entire time." He bumps his shoulder against Sandra's, and I swear to God, the demon laughs. "Probably why Chris killed himself."

"Excuse me?" My heart sinks into my chest as I step around the desk and stare at them venomously.

Jax creeps to my side, as if he's my bodyguard. "What in the living fuck are you doing here?"

"What do you mean, what are we doing here?" Mick raises his arms in greeting. "We own half this place."

"You don't own shit, except a one-way ticket to hell." Jax points to the doorway. "Now, leave."

"That's where you're wrong." Mick steps forward, his stature as if he really does own the place. "We talked to an attorney." His teeth are smoke-stained when he grins from ear to ear. "That attorney told us that since Chris never married or had any dependents, his side of the business goes to us."

Jax shakes his head. "Your attorney is wrong."

"Chris owned half of this business." Sandra inches forward to stand next to Mick. "That half is now ours."

I always knew Sandra was a damn lunatic, but this confirms it.
This chick is batshit crazy.

"Christopher left his half to me," I tell them, gnawing at my lower lip to stop myself from telling them how repulsive they are.

"You stupid lying bitch," Mick shouts, staring at me with

such anger that if Jax wasn't next to me, I'd either prepare to run or kick him in the balls.

This man is a predator to his core.

This man is the one who physically, mentally, and emotionally abused Christopher—who not only left bruises on his body, but every inch of him inside as well.

He is the guiltiest culprit and one of the main reasons why Christopher took his life.

He did the most damage.

I keep my voice as strong as I can. "He did." I straighten my shoulders, proud of myself for not giving away the nausea in my stomach. "I can email you the attorney's information Christopher consulted for his will. Nothing is yours. Now, leave."

Sandra cackles. "No way am I letting this whore have anything of my son's." Her bloodshot eyes skim over to Jax. "Look at her, spreading her legs for you now that Chris is gone."

I dart my hand out to catch Jax's arm when he advances toward the monsters in front of us. "Like I said, he had a will. It doesn't matter how you feel."

"A will can easily be forged," Mick says. "Chris would never leave anything to a whore who is screwing his best friend."

"Call her a whore again, and I'm breaking your jaw," Jax hisses, his gaze pinned to Mick, and his arms are shaking in anger. "That's my final warning."

"Why are you defending her?" Sandra asks. "She's the reason Chris is dead."

I whimper, my knees buckling, and I'm relieved that I'm gripping Jax's arm, or I'd no doubt collapse to the floor.

"Everyone says it," Sandra goes on, smoothing her hand over her greasy hair. "Don't they, Mick?"

Mick repeatedly nods. "Sure do. What kind of woman leaves a man for his business partner? Now, my wife is here suffering 'cause he killed himself over it. We want what's ours."

"That's right," Sandra sneers. "It's all this rich bitch's fault that my son hung himself."

They've hit the last link of Jax's patience, and my arm drops to my side as he advances toward them.

"It's not her fault Chris is gone," Jax screams, the walls shaking at his roar, and he thrusts his finger toward Sandra. "It's yours." His finger swings to Mick. "And yours." His stance widens, covering more of my body, as if he'll stop anyone who comes my way. "Amelia gave him a longer life, a happier life, but you two killed him. You ruined him from the goddamn start." He jerks his arm out toward me. "Maybe if you loved your son the way Amelia did, he'd still be here. Now, leave because you don't deserve one goddamn thing from him."

Jax sticking up for me says so much.

He doesn't blame me.

He needed a reason to hate me, to stay away from me.

"Leave," Jax demands. "Or I'm calling the police to escort you out."

I'm running low on breaths, my hands sliding up and down my arms, and Nolan joins my side, his arm wrapping around my shoulders.

"The cops are already on their way," Toby says, joining us in the office.

I glare at Sandra when panic crosses her face. I'm sure it won't be her first run-in with the police and certainly not the last either.

But how could she think she deserves anything from Christopher?

I don't want the brewery for the money. It means so much more to me than that. Mick and Sandra only see it as dollar signs.

Christopher told me he hated his mother more times than I could count. He'd comment that he wished he had parents like mine, like Jax's, and didn't understand why God had destined him to them.

I take Sandra in, her skinny body and sagging face, and wonder how she could let someone hurt her child. I want to lunge at her, scratch her eyes out, and tell her she ruined him. They're the ones who deserve to be dead. Not him.

And I thank God that, even for the short time he was here, he experienced love from me and my family, Jax and his family. It was probably the only love he'd ever felt in his life.

37

JAX

THERE'S ONLY BEEN two times in my life when I've wanted to murder someone, and both times, Mick has been on the receiving end.

I'm shocked I didn't punch Mick within the first five minutes he started spewing off lies and insulting Amelia. I held back for the sake of Amelia, so Mick couldn't sue me, and because I didn't want to look like a lunatic in front of my employees. I have so much pent-up aggression toward him that I'm not sure I could stop if the time came where I could finally get my hands on him.

Toby called the cops as soon as Mick and Sandra barreled into the brewery, stupidly assuming they owned the place, so the cops were pulling in at the same time Toby informed us of his call.

The two assholes in front of me don't get the chance to scurry off like the cockroaches they are.

Mick's and Sandra's entire demeanors change when the cops walk in.

Considering they're sketchy as fuck, that's not a shocker.

From their weight and the sores on their faces, I'd guess they fight over who gets the last hit of meth on the regular.

Ava's father, Gage, and my uncle Kyle are the officers who arrive. Uncle Kyle's eyes narrow at Mick.

Sandra called the cops when my father beat the shit out of Mick, and it was Kyle who showed up. He didn't arrest his brother-in-law, and when he asked why the children had bruises, they stopped their demands for my father to go to jail.

They agreed to leave with no hassle or running of the mouths, except for Mick throwing out, "You'll be hearing from our lawyer."

As if Amelia refused to allow them to see her cry, she bursts into tears as soon as they disappear from our view while Gage and Uncle Kyle walk them out. Her body shakes as I pull her to me and hold her to my chest. Anguish zips through me at her having to hear Mick's and Sandra's accusations.

I bow my head to kiss the top of hers, and as much as I want to shove the thoughts away, I remember every vile word that I spewed at her since Chris's death. I'm no better than Sandra and Mick. How could I ever think I was any different? I'd given her the same shit they just did. I'd blamed her the same way they did.

We separate when my uncle and Gage return to finish the police report.

"I'll take you home," I say to her, and her, "Okay," is hardly audible.

It's in this moment I make the decision.

It's time to read Chris's letter.

38

AMELIA

THERE'S NEVER BEEN a silence so loud as when Jax and I get into his truck. I rode with him to work today, so it is either he takes me home, I ask Kyle or Gage, or I call someone for a ride.

I'm glad it's Jax because my heart sinks at the thought of being alone after Mick's and Sandra's insults.

How could they be so cruel?

Scratch that.

I shouldn't be shocked.

They're abusers.

I could hardly face Nolan and Toby when Jax told them he was taking me home and to call him if Mick and Sandra returned. By the worry in their eyes when the cops walked in, I have a feeling they'll be more careful about their visits.

"Are you good to go home?" Jax asks. "I need to take care of a few things."

I simply nod, despising his question in every way possible.

There's a shift in him. It's not *my Jax* who asked this.

I don't remember the last time he didn't just drive me straight to his home.

Even though he comforted me during my breakdown after

Mick and Sandra left, he's distant now. His eyes haven't met mine. He's hardly spoken a word.

"You're not planning on doing anything dumb, are you?" I ask when he pulls in front of my townhome. It appears almost haunting since all I've done lately is grab clothes and scurry out.

"No," he replies.

It's like Mick and Sandra's visit has Jax pushing me away, but I'm sure seeing them affected him, too. And I don't look back as I walk into my house.

———

Want to know a way to make your head spin?

Pace your tiny box of a laundry room while waiting to see if the man you most definitely shouldn't be falling in love with might be up to questionable activity. Jax had the look of a determined man when he dropped me off, so wherever he was going, he knew precisely what'd happen.

Two hours have passed since he dropped me off with a simple, "I'll talk to you soon," and a kiss to my forehead.

I pause my pacing when my phone vibrates in my hand, and I press my hand to my chest when I read Jax's text.

Jax: I'm outside.

Good. I won't need to go to the ATM for bail money.

I nearly trip as I rush to the front door and whip it open.

As per what seems to be usual with Jax, I find him standing in the doorway, heavy rain showering him. Water drips from his lips, from his arms, from his pants. His shoulders are slumped as he ignores the rain, allowing the thick droplets to pierce him, as if he's accepting it as a punishment.

"Jesus, Jax," I shriek. "Get in here."

He doesn't move.

Literally taking matters into my own hands, I capture his

hand in mine. It's freezing, almost numbing, and I easily tug him inside.

Jax kicks the door shut with the back of his sneaker and shakes his head, water flinging in every direction. I study him as he silently stands, drenched, in front of me. His tormented eyes meet mine, and all I see is pain in them.

He stares at me for what feels like forever, his gaze never tearing away from mine, as if he wants to prepare me for whatever torture is coming my way.

A shiver runs the length of my spine, and sheer panic shoots through me.

What happened in those couple of hours?

Did he hurt someone?

Did someone hurt him?

I'm afraid of his response, but I ask, "Jax, what's going on?"

"He knew," he screams, his voice as loud as the storm outside. "He fucking knew!"

"What?" I stammer.

"Chris knew about us."

He rips something from his pocket, and I immediately recognize it.

Christopher's letter.

"Read it." He shoves the envelope in my direction, like it'll catch fire if he holds it any longer. "Fucking read it, Amelia."

There's agony, pure suffering, on Jax's face, and what's in that letter terrifies me. Whatever is inside will destroy what's left of me, and selfishly, I'm not willing to let it.

I'd rather sleep in my bedroom for the rest of eternity than read it.

I've witnessed Jax sulk, I saw him weep at Chris's funeral, but I've never seen him this vulnerable.

"He knew about us."

He desperately attempts to hand over the letter again, but I scramble back a step, holding my hand out to stop him.

I don't take it.

I won't take it.

He strides to me and pushes me against the wall, crowding into my space. Our noses brush against each other. Our mouths are so close that we're inhaling each other's sharp breaths. I quiver at his touch, tears falling down my cheeks, as Jax strokes my jaw. I shut my eyes, my heart slowing, and my shoulders relax.

I can't lose him too.

Jax presses a gentle kiss to my lips, and I know this is his good-bye.

"We're done, Amelia."

I blink, processing the weight of his words, and he steps back.

"What?" A weak sob leaves me, and I grip his sleeve to stop him. "Why?"

He doesn't have the balls to even look at me. "This was a mistake."

"Mistake?" I shove his chest, and he backtracks closer to the door. "Why was it a mistake, Jaxson?"

"You want to know why?" His voice weakens. "Read the goddamn letter."

"Jaxson," I cry out.

"May we rot in this hell of guilt forever."

He drops the letter, and it falls to the floor in what seems like slow motion.

My walls vibrate when he slams the door shut behind him, and my knees give out. I sink to the floor, cover my face with my hands, and scream.

I scream out my pain, wishing it'd make every inch of hurt stabbed inside of me break free.

What did I do wrong to deserve this?

I thought I was a good person. A good girlfriend. A good friend.

I do charity work. Pay my taxes on time. Have never broken

one of those kindness chains through the coffee drive-through. Feed the freaking squirrels in my yard.

I've always strived to be a decent person, but it feels like I'm suffering worse than those who aren't.

Putting every ounce of energy I have left inside me, which isn't much, I use my foot to slide the letter to me. I blow out a series of breaths before opening it.

Christopher's handwriting is sloppy, and some of the ink is smudged—although I'm not sure if it's from him or from the paper getting wet from the rain.

Jax,

I want to start this letter by saying I'm sorry. I don't know when you'll read this, if you'll ever read it, but everything I'm writing beyond this point won't sound like the friend you've known for years.

First, I want to thank you for all you've done for me as a friend. One might say you gave me a few more years since I didn't think I'd make it past twenty. It was nice, feeling normalcy for a change.

But anyway, remember when my brother died?

It was the worst day of my life.

Like always, you were there for me.

Your mom helped with the funeral arrangements.

The second worst day of my life was the day of his funeral.

Not only did I have to bury my brother, but I also found out my best friend was a liar.

That the woman I planned to marry was also a liar.

It was the day of the funeral when I asked to borrow a dress shirt since mine no longer fit. You told me to stop at the apartment and grab one from your closet. I did, but while doing that, something caught my eye. It was a box, and I'm sure when you're finished with this letter, you'll know what box I'm talkin' about.

You were supposed to hate my girl, not fuck her.

I found the notes, the pictures, all of it.

Gotta say, it broke my heart, man.

You sat there at the funeral with me, all the while knowing you were keeping that secret. Later, when Amelia wasn't home, I snooped through her stuff. She also had a box of mementos, some with you and some with me, and then I found her high school diary.

I sat on the floor, weeping while reading how my best friend and girl had touched each other, kissed each other, FUCKED each other. And not one of you bothered to ever tell me.

Then, my mind started racing. Did you never tell me because you were fucking my girl behind my back?

It hurts for a girl to betray you, man. It hurts real bad. But your best friend? That's a knife to the fucking heart.

I don't know how much longer I'll be alive, but before I go, I want you to know that I know you betrayed me. I want you to know that's one of the reasons I'm dead too. I don't know if you'll care because then you might get my girl.

I trust you to take good care of the brewery.

Just like I trust Amelia will too.

And this time, let me trust you not to touch my girl.

Godspeed.
Chris

A sob catches in my throat as I run to the bathroom and puke.

Wiping my mouth, I go to my bedroom without glancing anywhere but at the bed, and I grab the letter he left me.

39

JAX

GUILT IS a wicked wound to the heart.

I'm a disgrace of a friend.

When I slide into my truck, I recollect my last times with Chris. I don't remember him acting differently. I slam my fist against the steering wheel, and it blares into the night.

Why didn't he come to me?

Confront us?

I don't understand.

He never gave us the opportunity to explain ourselves.

I would've welcomed any punishment for lying—an ass whipping, losing our friendship, anything if it meant he'd still be here.

After I dropped off Amelia at her townhome earlier, it took me an hour to gain the guts to read the letter. I read it once. Then twice. Then three times.

Then, I dashed to my closet and found the box I'd forgotten about.

Hell, I didn't think I'd even put the box up there. My mom must've done it when she helped me move in.

The box had *Times with Amelia and Friends* written across it in my sloppy handwriting. Who knew why I put Amelia's name on there instead of someone else's or just *Friends*? I opened it to find pictures—some of them in good shape, some of them faded, and some ripped into pieces. The only torn pictures were ones of Amelia and me.

I choked out a groan and picked up a sliver of the picture we took the night we lost our virginities. It was a simple picture of us watching TV, and I had my mom go to Walgreens to print off physical copies along with other photos. And my lovesick teenage dumbass self scribbled on the back of it, *The night we lost our virginities. Best night of my life.*

I also saved stupid messages and notes we'd left on each other's beds, growing up. All of those were ripped to shreds. He destroyed every trace of Amelia and me.

"Fuck," I screamed, throwing the box across the room, its contents scattering everywhere.

I drive to my place but instead of going into the apartment, I walk into Down Home Pub. I break through the crowd, finding a deserted stool, and slump onto it like a drunk on the brink of being cut off.

"I slept with her," I say as soon as my dad approaches me, tossing a bar rag over his shoulder. "I slept with Amelia." I drop my forehead against the sticky bar.

My father sighs. "I know."

I lift my head. "How?"

"Her car was here all the time." He starts counting the obvious reasons off on his fingers. "You hurried her into your apartment countless times." He shakes his head. "It's no wonder you were always caught sneaking out as a kid." Grabbing the water gun, he fills a glass and slides it to me. "Kyle told me about Mick and Sandra showing up at the brewery."

I glare at the water and then at him. "This conversation warrants a substance stronger than water, don't you think?"

"Alcohol and heartache don't mix well, son." He signals to Frankie when a customer attempts to wave him over.

"As someone who has united them aplenty, I rebuke that

statement." I zero in on the top-shelf liquor. "Give me the strongest you have."

"That won't fix the problem."

"It'll erase the problem."

"Temporarily, and then tomorrow, you'll wake up with the same mess while also dealing with a hangover." His eyes are stern. "Fix it."

I slap my hand to my chest. "What do you mean, fix it? I didn't do anything."

"Not only are you my kid, but I've also bartended half my life. I read people well."

"Chris left me a letter."

"What'd it say?"

"That he knew Amelia and I had sex—"

My father draws in a hiss between his teeth. "Jesus Christ, Jax—"

I hold up my hands, my palms facing him. "It was before they were together. We never touched when they started dating."

A frown creases his forehead. "But you never told him?"

"What was the point?" I run my finger along the rim of my water glass. "All it would have done was hurt him. Amelia and I were sixteen, kids who wanted to lose their virginities. We didn't want it to be a big deal."

"And now, you and Amelia have … rekindled?"

"Rekindled?" I shake my head. "Have you been watching Hallmark with Grandma again?"

He shrugs. "It's the only channel she'll watch."

I rub my chin. "I don't know what to do."

The longer my father listens, the more concern floods his face. "Do you have feelings for Amelia, or is it just physical?"

I stare at him sullenly. "I'm in love with her."

"Then, you have a tough decision to make."

———

I drive back to Amelia's.

The windshield wipers squeak as I stare up at her townhome to find all the lights are out. This time, I stay in my car before texting her.

> Me: I'm outside.

My text vibrates in my hand at her reply.

> Amelia: I'm not home.

> Me: Where are you?

> Amelia: My parents'.

> Me: I'm coming over.

> Amelia: I don't think that's a good idea.

> Me: It's the only idea I have left.

Amelia's parents live only a few miles from her, and I lower my speed as I turn into their private drive. Amelia is standing on the porch of their two-story brick home. The dim light shining from the front door sconce doesn't show much more than her silhouette, but I'd know that body from anywhere.

I kill my headlights, grab a hoodie from the backseat, and pull it over my head. With the hood up, I step out of the car, jog forward, and join her on the porch, keeping us at a distance.

"Hey," she whispers.

Her cheeks are blotchy, and her face is red. Her eyes are probably just as red and full of pain, but I can't break myself to look into them.

"Hi." I lower my hood as the wind whips around us.

She slowly releases a stressed breath. "Why are you here, Jax?"

That's a good question.

And I don't exactly know how to narrow all my reasons down.

"Did you read Chris's letter?" I finally ask.

She crosses her arms. "I did."

"Then, you understand why."

"Why what? You need to be clearer."

"Why you and I can't see each other anymore." The words burn my throat as they exit my mouth. "Why this has to end."

"What was it all for then?" Her voice cracks. "Why string me along?"

I slam my eyes shut. "I didn't string you along."

"Bullshit," she hiss. "You're the one who kept coming around." She erases the distance between us and pokes her finger into my chest. "The one showing up *on my doorstep,* asking"—she mocks my voice—"*Amelia, where are you sleeping tonight? Oh, your laundry room? Come to my bed then.*"

Her finger stabs at me again, and I accept any anger she wants to throw at me.

The anger in her voice morphs into sadness. "Why, Jax?! Why would you do that to me … after everything I'd already been through?"

She's right.

I wasn't fair to her.

I did the wrong thing, and now, we're both paying for it.

"I …" My words falter until I can't hold myself back any longer. "Because I fucking love you!" Unable to stop myself, I reach out and skate my fingers along the soft skin of her cheek. "I love you, Amelia." I scoot closer to her, and our mouths nearly touch, but neither of us crosses that line. "I know it's wrong, a disgrace to my friend, and I'm sorry. I messed up, and we're both paying for it now."

Tears slip down Amelia's cheeks, stopping at the blockade of my hand on her face. "You don't have to end things. We can figure this out."

I stare at her and know what I'm about to say will break us

both. "I have to do this. I'm so sorry, Amelia—I really am—but I owe it to Chris. I regret not keeping you when I had the chance. But knowing now that he knew about us … the two people in the world who meant more to him than anything …" I hold back my own unshed tears. "God, Amelia. Can you imagine how he felt when he opened that box? And on the day of his brother's funeral. I'm the worst fucking friend. I killed him. I fucking killed him!"

I blow out a breath, completely losing it. "I could never betray him all over again. I love you, and I know that I will always love you, but I can't do this." And just to drive the point home, I stare into her beautiful, heartbroken eyes. "I won't do it."

Without saying anything more, I turn and walk away from the only woman I've ever loved.

40

AMELIA

I'M NOT one to speak ill of the dead, but right now, I'm angry with Christopher.

I am one to speak ill of the living though, and right now, I despise Jaxson.

They left me, not caring about any damage they'd leave behind.

After I read Christopher's letter to Jax, I called my father.

Because sometimes, a girl needs her dad to assure her that everything will be okay. Sometimes, we need to be with the one man in the world who we know will handle us with the utmost gentleness and care. Which is why I was at my parents' house when Jax texted me.

I wait on the porch, a thick sweater wrapped around me, until Jax's headlights disappear into the night.

I walk into the living room to find my dad on the couch, nursing a glass of orange juice. It's funny, watching him drink such juvenile drinks as if they hold alcohol.

My father glances at me with worry as I sit on the chair by him.

He opens his mouth, but I beat him to it. "Do you remember what was in the boxes that were thrown around my bedroom when you cleaned it up ..." I pause to brace myself. "When you cleaned it up after Christopher killed himself?"

I rarely say those words in reference to what he did. The same with the word *suicide*. I tend to stick with *when we lost Christopher* or *when Christopher left us*.

He rests his drink on the coffee table, and his eyes flash with comfort. "Pictures of you and your friends, notebooks, yearbooks, stuff along those lines. Why?"

I drag my knees to my chest. "My diary was in one of those boxes, and Christopher read it."

My heart thrums in my chest, and I take a deep breath before telling my father everything.

My father gathers me in his arms as I sob and kisses the top of my head. "I lost a girlfriend in high school," he says when I'm finished, his voice soft-spoken.

I draw back and blink away tears to stare at him. "What?"

My father isn't a sharer. He keeps his emotions to a minimum and hardly mentions his teenage years. I once asked him if he'd even attended high school since he never talked about it. He paled, and my mother told me not to ask that again.

He swallows and grows unusually quiet for a moment before going on, "Her brother was my best friend, so we were sneaking around. He was drunk when he found out, and it ended in them both dying in a car accident." There's a sadness in his voice that I recognize. "The circumstances aren't the same, but I understand how hard it is, pointing the guilty finger at yourself in a situation like this. I struggled for years, and like you and Jax, I lived as if I wasn't deserving of happiness. I hate seeing you hurt like this. It breaks my heart, seeing you experience so much of the pain I felt. And I might still be in that sorrow had your mother not dragged me out of it. Give yourself time. Give Jax time. You don't have to be together in the end, but you need to find happiness."

And for what seems like the first time, other than when my younger sister was born, my father's eyes well with tears.

He blows out a breath. "Now, come on. I paid off a cook at Shirley's Diner for their hot chocolate recipe. I think tonight calls for one."

———

I stare at the envelope with my name written on it.

This small object scares me, and my heart races as if I were watching a scary movie and waiting for the murderer to jump out. I know it's coming, but I don't know when or how.

I have to do this.

It needs to be done.

Sitting on my bed in the room I grew up in, a framed photo of Christopher and me on my nightstand, I rip the envelope open.

Amelia,

I want to start this letter off by apologizing for the pain I've caused. I'm not sure how I caused it yet, but I know, no matter what, you will be the most wrecked from losing me.

So many times, I lay next to you in bed and wonder how I deserve you. The answer is, I don't. I was the loner, the practically homeless and poor kid living with his friend's parents, but you still love me. You love me when I thought I'd never be loved.

But you also don't know all of me. I hide so much, in fear that I'll be too much for you to handle.

Three years ago, I talked to a doctor and was prescribed medication. I was proud of myself for how I was handling my sadness while hiding it from everyone.

Then, Corey died.

I don't know why it hit me so hard, but all I could

think about was him begging me not to leave with Jax and Maliki and me selfishly walking away from him. He had been going through the same hell as me, and it'd probably gotten worse after I left.

My brother didn't have an Amelia, a Jax, a Sierra, or a Maliki. All he had were the people who'd done nothing but hurt him. I had been happy while he was suffering.

So, I stopped taking my medicine. You noticed the change in me. I saw it, and I feared it, but I couldn't fix it.

I went and saw my mother yesterday. I don't know why. She hasn't changed and made sure to tell me that you'd never love me for me, for the trash that I was. Later that same day, when I came home, you asked to postpone our wedding.

It was as if she'd spoken the truth.

I've thought about dying since I was six years old. I don't know why either. It's just always been there, like a monster lurking in the shadows. When I shave, sometimes, I look at the blade and consider slitting my wrists. There are times I'm driving, and I wonder if I should drive off a bridge. It's always there, in the back of my mind, teasing me, like Mick did all those years.

I could tell you. I should tell you. You'd do everything that you could to help me, but no one can help me. Not even the prettiest girl I've ever set eyes on, the one who has given me years of happiness I never thought I'd get and the one who isn't ready to marry me.

I don't blame you either.

A man who wants to kill himself isn't a man anyone should marry.

And I am a man who wants to kill himself, and I don't know how much longer I can keep that monster in the shadows.

I love you.

Christopher

I cover my nose and mouth to choke back tears, and my hand holding the letter falls limp, the piece of paper hanging loosely, not feeling as heavy as the words scribbled along its lines.

Christopher's letter confuses me. There are parts that make so much sense as I think back on our relationship. The change in behavior I thought was due to stress and his past. When he went to a therapist, he said it felt good to talk it out, and that was it. I asked him if he wanted to talk with me, but the more distant he became, the less he shared with me. It was almost like he became a stranger.

The part I don't understand is, why Jax and not me?

Where was the anger and the accusations that were in Jax's letter?

Jax and I had done the same thing, so why did he point all the blame at Jax?

I want to call Jax, crawl into his bed, and have him hold me. I need his comfort now more than ever, but that's no longer an option. I'm stuck in this bedroom, crying over two men who did nothing but break me.

———

I wake up with Christopher's letter in my hand.

Then, I walk into the kitchen, hug my mother, and tell my parents, "I think it's time for me to go home."

They drive me home and hug me good-bye. My mother asks

if I want them to come in and spend some time with me. I thank them but say I need a minute to myself.

I walk into my home with a sense of dread, but I know it has to be done.

And with a deep breath, I enter my bedroom.

I walk in and I force myself not to run out.

41

JAX

FUCKING up once with the girl you're in love with is unfortunate.

Fucking up a second time proves you're a dumbass.

And I, ladies and gentlemen, am a fucking dumbass.

Three weeks have passed since I read Chris's letter and broke things off with Amelia. I never asked for the letter back, and we haven't spoken since I walked away, leaving her crying on the porch.

Not seeing or talking to her has been my personal inferno, but I deserve it.

I'm in the office, sitting in the pleather chair, and grit my teeth when I see an email with the subject line: ANOTHER DAMN EMAIL.

I glare at the computer screen like it's my worst enemy when I click on it to read it.

Jaxson Bridges,

Per my last email, I need the turnaround time for the Coffee Cream Ale. I have several clients asking. Please promptly reply, so I can do my job.

Not best,
Amelia Malone

I *promptly* hit the reply button.

Amelia,
  I have attached a PDF with turnaround times for all flavored ales.
  Save it, so we don't have to circle back to this.
  J

We're acting the same way we did when we were kids.

But instead of hateful letters, it's emails.

And our vocabulary has improved.

To my surprise, the brewery is running smoothly. It's as if we're silent partners, which works for me because it's less of a reminder of all that's happened and all that I've lost.

———

Amelia rubbed off on me.

I hate sleeping in my bed now.

I *do* sometimes, yes, but it's miserable.

It smells like her, even after I ripped the sheets off and bought new ones. It's like her aroma is pumping through the ventilation system. Every morning I wake up and reach out, expecting her warm body to be there, but it's empty. And when I walk into my kitchen, I think about all the times we ate there … and I ate her out there. Damn memories everywhere.

I've made it my personal goal to crash anywhere but in my own apartment now.

The brewery's office: 0 out of 10. That floor is worse than Amelia's laundry room.

My old bedroom at my parents': 6 out of 10. The bed is comfortable, but my mom asks too many questions.

Easton's living room: 8 out of 10. The couch is decent, but I'm woken up with a Barbie in my face and sticky lip gloss on my lips, courtesy of Jasmine.

Tonight, it's River's turn to be my Airbnb.

Sure, I could crash with Darcy or some random chick, but being around another woman makes my stomach weak. Even if I tried to get over Amelia by screwing another woman, I doubt my dick would get hard. It apparently only desires Amelia now.

"There's the dumbest guy I know," River says when I walk into the guesthouse on his parents' property.

Along with the infinity pool and impressive home, they also have two guesthouses—one for each child. I think it's Carolina's way of having them at home for as long as she can. And River is fine with it because free rent and all.

I flip him off and furrow my brows. "I'm not in the mood."

The night after I broke things off with Amelia, I got shitfaced and told River everything—Amelia and me being together, the letter, me ending things with her.

River drops his video game controller onto the coffee table. "Have you talked to her yet?"

I toss my overnight bag onto the bamboo flooring. "Have you learned to mind your business yet?"

"Where's the fun in that?" He chuckles. "Do you want my advice?"

I grab one of our orange ales from his fridge and plop down on the couch. "Hard pass on taking advice from a guy named after a body of water."

This time, it's him flipping me off.

He snaps his fingers, as if a thought suddenly hit him. "Don't forget my and Essie's birthday party this weekend. We're doing something simple at Down Home."

"Will Amelia be there?" is my immediate response.

"She's your *business partner*. Why would you care if she's there?"

"Our conversations consist of emails." I pop open the can. "I think you know why I care, asshole."

"Just act like you did when you guys disliked each other." He strokes his smooth jaw and smirks. "Unless you don't dislike her."

"I'll send you a fruit basket for your birthday. Don't expect me to be there."

———

I'm leaving the brewery, working on a Saturday because I don't have shit else to do, when my phone rings.

I dig the phone from my pocket to find my dad's name flashing on the screen.

"Hey, Dad," I answer.

"I need you to cover at the pub for a few hours," he says on the other end.

I grimace. It's Essie and River's birthday party tonight.

I'd rather take a baseball bat to the kneecap than work tonight.

"I wish I could, but I can't tonight."

"I'm sure you planned to be at the pub for River's birthday anyway," he goes on as if I hadn't said no. "Keelie got into a car accident up at the university—"

"What?" I interrupt. "Is she okay?"

"Yeah, yeah. Everything's fine. She's just shaken up, and her car is totaled. Your mom is away on her girls' trip. All you have to do is cover for a few hours, and when I get back, I'll let you off the hook."

How can I say no?

"All right," I grumble. "I'll be there."

42

AMELIA

I SLEPT IN MY BEDROOM.

Not my bed, but on the floor.

But, hey, progress is progress.

The one plus side of having Jax for the small amount of time that I did was, he helped me deal with heartache. And now, I'm using it for him.

I spent three sessions with my therapist talking about Chris's letters.

And speaking of letters, asking Jax if he wants his back has been on my to-do list. I just can't seem to check it off.

And tonight, in my effort to heal, I'm at Down Home Pub, celebrating Essie's birthday. I declined the invite, worried about seeing Jax, but Essie insisted he wasn't coming. Even though I'm making progress with other things, I'm not ready to face the Jax issue yet.

Men leave me. I guess it's good to learn this early in life.

No longer will Amelia Malone trust a man.

Hell hath no fury like a woman who continually gets her heart broken.

So, here I am, sitting at a sticky pub table, with a fruity cocktail in my hand, compliments of Frankie.

"I could kick Jax's ass," Essie says after ordering another round of drinks and instructing the waitress to put it on River's tab.

I wince at Jax's name, and Essie continues her rant. "He's crashing with River for God knows what reason, and every time I see him, I want to dunk him in the pool. Cousin or not, he deserves a good almost drowning."

"You are terrible," Ava says, shaking her head. "*But* I'm game on the whole *dunking him* idea." She wipes French fry salt off her hands. "Just make sure you record it."

"You and Jax really ..." Callie asks me while innocently chews on the tip of her straw, and her cheeks blush. When no one finishes her sentence, she throws her hand out. "You know!"

Essie produces a red-lipped grin and settles her elbow on the table. "We know what?"

"She's asking if they did this." Ava grabs a straw wrapper, forms an *O* with it, and then sticks a straw through the hole. "Yes, they most definitely did that."

I do a circular motion at the table. "I'm never drinking Skinnygirl Margaritas with y'all again."

That's how they found out about Jax and me. Come to think of it, he and I should've had a quick chat—over email—to confirm who could know about us. Granted, I don't know how much of that agreement would've stuck with that much tequila and sugar flowing through my system.

"Can I ask one more teensy-weensy question?" Ava asks, squinting an eye. As a girl who hardly spends time out of the ER, she's a lightweight, and fruity drink number two is already doing a number on her.

"No," I say with as much seriousness as I can muster while holding back laughter.

This is nice, being with them again, feeling somewhat normal.

"Sex with Jax"—Ava beams—"was it good?"

"Gross. That's my cousin," Essie says, flicking a cherry stem at her.

"What?" Ava shrugs and goes back to sipping on her drink. "He's hot. Not my type since he's had a thing for Amelia forever, but he's still hot."

Mia shakes her head at Ava. "Sometimes, I question how we come from the same bloodline." Mia straightens her thick black hair that's parted in the middle and peers in my direction. "You love him, don't you?"

Instead of replying, I chug the remainder of my drink.

"Pretty sure that's a yes," Callie says from the stool next to me.

"And speak of the devil," Essie yelps, looking over my shoulder and scowling.

I twist in my stool and grimace when my gaze falls on, yes, *the devil*. Jax is talking to his father in the corner. He absorbs my attention as I coldly stare at him, that even though I despise him, I can't hate the sight of him. I squeeze my thighs together to stop the tingling between my legs, wishing I didn't have this reaction to him.

Maliki slaps Jax's shoulder before walking away. Jax steps behind the bar, calls out something to Frankie, and approaches a group of women sporting bachelorette sashes.

I whip around and lean across the table to hiss, "You said he wasn't coming," to a confused Essie.

She throws up her arms in innocence. "River said he wasn't. Go yell at him."

Callie taps her pink nails against the table. "I think he's working."

"Probably covering a shift, like I'm always doing at the hospital," Ava says before raising her glass in Jax's direction. "Welcome to my life, Jax-hole."

I fix my stare on Jax, observing his every move and feeling every bit like Joe from *You*, and wait for him to cast a glance in my direction. But he keeps his attention on his job, as if he knows I'm in the crowd.

Ava bumps her shoulder into mine. "Stop staring."

"That's easier said than done," I grumble.

When Essie gets up for a restroom break, I hijack her stool, so I have a third row seat to the Jax bartending show.

He never looks at me.

We really are back to the old Jax and Amelia.

———

The longer I watch the woman sporting a *Maid of Dishonor* sash flirt with Jax, the more I drink.

She's been up his ass all night, as if she wants him to be her plus-one to the impending nuptials—whispering sweet nothings into his ear and leaning over the bar to show off what's under her low-cut shirt.

And still, no glance in my direction from him.

Nothing.

My attention is stolen from Jax and Dishonor when a man's voice asks if he can take Ava's neglected seat. She and Callie ditched me to dance, leaving me to my Jax creeping.

I nod. "It's all yours."

The guy doesn't drag the stool away, like I assumed he would. He plants himself on the stool and holds out his hand. "Grant." He jerks his head toward the table where Rex and the guys are hanging out. "I'm friends with Rex. We went to school together."

I do a quick scan of Grant—attractive, on the slender side, patterned collared shirt—and then shake his hand. "Ah, that makes sense."

He straightens his clear-rimmed designer glasses. "What does?"

"You are a poster child for Silicon Valley."

"Oh God." He chuckles. "Am I that obvious?"

"Very." I genuinely smile at him.

And for the next hour, my conversation with Grant diverts me from my Jax stalking.

———

I've never casually chatted with a guy in a bar before.

And it's not as bad as my friends have described it.

Or maybe that's because they get the typical dudes who think buying you a drink is an admission ticket into your panties.

I got lucky with Grant. He seems … normal.

His sense of humor is top-notch, he can hold a conversation, and he hasn't uttered a sexual innuendo once.

That doesn't mean my friends haven't kept their insinuations to themselves. Essie nearly ran into a waitress to give me a thumbs-up when she passed us for yet another restroom break.

Grant stops the waitress to take our drink order, and I order *just one more* fruity cocktail. Ava, Callie, and Mia return to our table, and we're in deep conversation with Grant when I sense someone behind me.

It's not just *someone.*

I know who it is.

By the smell of whiskey and the brewery.

By the weight of his chest pressing into my back.

By his thick breathing.

The table falls silent.

"Calm down on the drinks, Amelia," Jax hisses into my ear, and goose bumps spread up my arms. "A drunk girl glaring at the bartender and every girl he talks to isn't a good look."

My gaze shoots forward to find the bar has lost a Jax and gained a Maliki.

A chill runs the length of my spine, and fury pours through my heart. As if fucking with my head and ruining my night was his sole intention and now that he's won, he walks away.

All the commotion around me fades.

No sound.

No people.

Only me, Jax, and the thumping of my heart, raging to dump

itself out of my chest—to drop at this asshole's feet and show him the damage he's done.

"Uh-oh," Ava mutters when I slide off my stool.

Jax charges past Rex's table, and I follow him, weaving around people I wish weren't here. We dash through the employee door, down the narrow hall, and outside. It's not until the door slams shut behind us that he faces me.

Like so many times I wish it weren't, Jax's face is unreadable.

But his heavy breathing and the way his chest moves in and out, as if it's working on overdrive, give some of him away.

Showing that he isn't as invulnerable as he thinks.

"So, now, you want to act like I don't exist?" I scream at him. "And then when I finally start to enjoy myself, you decide to ruin it?"

Jax bares his teeth. "Trust me, Amelia, I know you exist, and so does every guy in that goddamn bar." He thrusts his finger in the direction of the building with the last six words.

I narrow my eyes at him. "That's real cute, coming from you, Mr. I Entertain Bachelorettes Like It's My Second Job. Screw you, Jax."

"Screw me?" He takes a step toward me. "I think you have, and it was the best time of your life."

"You wish." I turn my back to him. *Come on, heart. Do what you need to do.* That's when my heart does a U-turn, and a sinister smile is on my lips when I face him again. "But I do think it's time for someone else, Jaxson."

Jax winces, as if I'd slapped him in the face, and his face reddens.

Good.

"What did you just say?" He spits each word out of his mouth, as if they disgust him.

"You heard me. You're a coward, Jax."

"Amelia," he warns, coming closer.

I start talking so casually, as if I were singing a slow and taunting lullaby. "A coward who doesn't care about anyone but himself. Well, guess what. I'm done wasting my time with a coward who can't even deal with his own emotions."

Jax slams his hand against his chest. "That's bullshit, Amelia. You know why I walked away."

"Yes, because you're too dense to show your true feelings, *coward*." I wave him away, feeling icky with myself for it, but if Jax wants to push me away as if I were nothing, then I shall do the same. "I'll go back into that bar, where guys know I exist and won't leave me heartbroken on a porch in the middle of the night. I'll find me a man who isn't a coward."

"Coward?" His eyes blaze into mine.

"Yes, a coward!"

"I'll show you coward."

He grabs my waist, jerking me into him, and kisses me.

He kisses me hard and deep and rough and relentlessly.

Jax kisses me as if he wants to prove he's not a coward in any way, shape, or form.

As if he wants to sink himself back into me as though he'd never left.

We consume each other, our kisses so frantic that we sometimes don't even hit each other's mouth.

My body is on fire, need swirling through me, when he walks me backward toward the stairs that lead to his apartment.

"Take it back," he hisses into my mouth. "Take. It. Fucking. Back."

"No," I breathe out. "I. Fucking. Won't."

He moves up the steps while dipping his hand underneath my dress. He's multitasking—leading me, kissing me, and ripping at my panties, as if he doesn't care how they come off, just that he needs them to.

When he realizes he can't do both at the same time, he stops mid-stair, out of view from anyone.

"Unbuckle me, Amelia," he rasps against my mouth. "Take my cock out, and it'll be all yours."

I should tell him no, not here, but I don't. I can't walk away from this because my body is pleading for everything this man is. My thighs are shaking, and my panties are soaked and ready for whatever he'll give me tonight. Even knowing that this might result in more pain, my body still aches for Jax the same way my heart does.

We separate, and my hands are frantic as I unzip his pants, dropping them just low enough to free his erection. A vein throbs through the middle, the head swollen, and I bite into my lip, remembering all the times it's made me come alive.

He strokes himself. "Does this make you think I'm a coward? The way I make you ache for me?"

I swallow.

"Does it?" He releases a rough laugh, his voice thick and emotionally charged. "And now that my cock is out, smart-mouthed Amelia is gone?" He jerks me closer to him so we're on the same step and shoves his hand underneath my panties, succeeding in tearing them this time.

"Coward, my ass," is all he says before he tilts up his waist, levels his cock with my core, and slams me down onto his erection.

I throw my head back and moan, ecstasy shooting through me, and it's as if our bodies have missed each other and immediately know what to do.

"Feel how hard this dick is for you?" Jax groans as I slam down on him.

I moan.

"All for you, Amelia."

"Yes. All for me."

He stretches out his legs and leans back. "You fuck me so good, baby. Ride me so good."

He fucks me. He praises me.

Him reaching under my dress and playing with my clit is my undoing.

Needing to see us, I bunch up the fabric of my dress and hold it up, watching his wet cock slide in and out of me.

"Yes, I love how you love to watch us," he says with a grunt.

He grips my waist, controlling my movement while pumping me up and down on his cock. Sex has never felt so good, so deep, so wild.

"You have no idea how much I've dreamed about having your pussy again." He licks down my neck and sucks hard on my skin. "I know it's not right, but, *fuuuck*, it's so good."

We fuck hard.

And rough.

As if he wants to fuck his need for me, his lust, out of us.

And when we've both cried out our releases, he rests his forehead against mine and says, "You need to leave."

43

JAX

AMELIA HAULS herself off my lap, not giving a shit if it's uncomfortable as she pulls my cock out of her.

Spoiler alert: it is.

I've never seen such a murderous glare on her face before as she shoves her dress back down.

"Like I said," she snarls, "a fucking coward."

I stand, tucking my cock into my pants before she decides to assault that next, and buckle myself. "Me, a coward? Says the girl who can't even sleep in her own bed."

Tears are in her eyes, and I know it's killing her to not look away from me.

"You should've left me alone," she cries.

"I tried," I grit out. "And you should've done the same with me."

She scoffs. "I wasn't the one showing up at your door, asking where you were sleeping, was I, Jax?" She shoves my chest. "I wasn't the one demanding you take work trips with me. That was you. I was good in my little world."

"Bullshit." I accept another shove from her. "You were miserable in your little detached world."

"As soon as our time is up, the brewery is all yours."

I stare at her indifferently. "Thank fuck."

"Was this your plan all along?"

"Maybe it was," I lie.

———

I follow Amelia down the stairs, and I watch her open the back entrance to the pub and disappear through the door. Then, I trudge back to the steps and slump down, feeling every bit of the coward she said I was.

I intended to keep my distance from her tonight, but intentions rarely follow through. I loved that she watched my every move as I worked, but my stomach twisted when that ended. Her attention had moved to someone else, some preppy-ass-looking dude, and it took everything in me not to raise my soda gun and spray the shit out of both of them as they talked and laughed.

When my dad returned to the bar, I shooed bachelorette chick away and went straight to Amelia, and the best way to get her attention was to provoke her.

And that just fucked us up more.

I grab her ripped panties, slide them into my pocket, and stomp up to my apartment—feeling like the miserable bastard that I am.

44

AMELIA

JUST WHEN I'D sworn that Jax was no longer my problem, he became a bigger one. I should've ignored his rude comment and stayed with Grant. That would've pissed him off more.

He knew he'd gain a reaction from me.

Knew what he was doing.

And I played right into his ridiculous game.

And now, I'm standing in the back hallway of the bar, waving Frankie over and asking her to get Essie for me. No way in hell am I facing anyone out there. I'm sure there were plenty of people who caught Jax's furious face, his angry strides, and the murderous glare on my face as I chased after him.

Essie rushes toward me and drags me into her arms, and I sob into her shoulder, feeling bad as my mascara smears her cashmere sweater.

"I promise, I will be doing more damage to my cousin than just a simple dunking." She soothingly rubs her hand up and down my back.

When I lean back and rest against a wall, I ignore the Down Home employees eyeing us, but, hey, I'm the owner's daughter. It's not like they can kick me out.

If I want to have an emotional breakdown back here, let me.

Essie texts Ava, instructing her to grab my purse, get her car, and meet us in the back.

My stomach twists into a ball of nerves at the thought of returning to where I was and possibly facing Jax. But he's *one* face. If I choose to exit through the main entrance, it's more faces and more gossiping. All I have to do is not pay a glance to the staircase he just fucked me senseless on, and all will be good.

And that's what I do.

I don't steal a look to see if he's there.

I slap my forehead when I squeeze into the passenger seat of Ava's Honda while Essie takes the back.

How could I have been so dumb?

I'd love to slap my vagina, too, pissed at it for aching for Jax, but that would only cause my friends to think I've lost my mind more, and my lady regions are also sore from Jax's hard thrusts.

Ava drives to Essie's, where Callie and Mia meet us, and we enter Essie's *guesthouse*, which resembles a cottage you'd find in a fairy tale. I'm shaking as I walk to the bathroom and clean myself up. Essie lends me a pair of silk pajamas while I profusely apologize for ruining her birthday.

Essie shakes her head and plops down next to me. "Girl, I'd much rather be in here, hanging out with you guys, than with my brother's friends anyway."

We watch movies, and then I trek to the guest room, remembering my and Jax's last words.

"Was this your plan all along?"

"Maybe it was."

Then, I silently cry myself to sleep.

The world hates me.

Swear to freaking God, it hates me.

As if a hangover and morning of regret aren't enough, when I walk out of Essie's for fresh air, I come face-to-face with Jax as he exits River's. Oh, and my hair is a rat's nest made in heaven.

What did I do in my past life to deserve this?

I halt in step, him doing the same, while I give him a once-over, taking in his vacant, tired eyes and solemn face. He's changed, freshly showered, but even that can't mask his internal misery that's beginning to display externally.

"What are you doing here?"

"I slept in River's guesthouse." He rubs the back of his neck. "What are you doing here?"

"I slept at Essie's." I blink rapidly, urging my sleepy eyes to stay open.

He kicks his Chucks against the concrete. "Do you want a ride home?"

I'm quiet.

He might look as if he's been through the wringer, but I don't forget what he did last night.

For that, for not even giving me a simple apology, I will have limited sympathy for him.

"It's on the way." He runs his hand through his hair before tugging on the collar of his black tee. "Get in my damn car, Amelia. It's too early to go back and forth with you."

Everyone in the house is asleep, so I'd have to either wake someone up or wait until they wake up on their own.

"Fine," I say, feigning annoyance, as if he's forcing me to leave with him. "Let me grab my purse."

I pass Callie, who is stretched out on the couch, and Ava, who's on the love seat next to her, and then I tiptoe past Essie's bedroom, where she and Mia are sleeping. Embarrassingly, I stop in the bathroom for a quick check of my reflection. I run my hand through my hair—a failed attempt to tame its wildness—before stealing one of Essie's hair ties. It's when I'm shoving my hair up in a messy bun that I notice the bruise-like mark on my neck.

That motherfucker gave me a hickey.

Jax is standing outside Essie's door, his hands shoved into his pockets.

"Why are you sleeping at River's?" I ask as we creep up the paved walkway alongside each other, walking toward his Land Rover. "Essie said you've been crashing here."

He lifts his shoulder in a half-shrug, offering me nothing.

Him opening my door, leaving me space to slide inside, and shutting it behind me surprise me.

When he joins me in the Land Rover, I can't hold myself back from asking, "Why are we on this roller coaster, Jaxson?"

Hopefully, he'll answer this question.

"I don't know," he grumbles, shifting the SUV into drive.

Jax isn't putting us through hell for shits and giggles.

He's not playing with my heart for fun.

The man is warring with himself, guilt eating at him.

And I'm the easiest person for him to push away and also the easiest person for him to lash out on.

The ride goes quiet, neither one of us giving the other any more explanations.

It isn't until he's edging onto the curb of my townhome and I'm unbuckling my seat belt that he says, "This has to stop."

I nod in agreement, bowing my head. "This has to stop." My throat burns. "Are you, uh … with someone?"

You should've asked that before riding his dick last night, dummy.

He jerks back, as if that's the biggest insult I've ever given him. "That'd be a negative."

"No way Jax Bridges has been celibate for that long."

His eyes are red, and he rubs them with the lower part of his palm. "I haven't touched or thought about another woman. So, no, there's no one else because it's always been you."

Here it comes, this roller coaster starting again.

"Always been me?" I huff. "You've had your share of hookups for years."

His gaze flicks to me, the grim expression on his face darkening. "I'm sorry, Amelia, but has it always been me for you?"

This time, it's me jerking back at the insult.

"Did *I* date someone for years?" His voice suddenly reeks of repulsion. "Did I say yes to marrying someone else? Yes, I fucked a few girls here and there, but it was still always *you*. Can you say the same?"

"There you go," I say, eyeing him warily. "Pushing me away more."

He groans, dropping his head against the headrest. "We've always been this way, pushing each other away, since my balls dropped."

"Don't say things that will make me laugh."

He lowers his head, meeting my eyes again, and my entire body trembles when he reaches out and caresses my neck. Using the pad of his thumb, he strokes small circles in a particular spot, over and over, and I relax into his touch. My breathing turns uneasy, and I'm not sure how long we sit there, parked, as he touches me for what feels like the last time.

"If only this could stay here forever, like you will in my heart," he says, his voice as soothing as his touch, and he pulls away. "Good-bye, Amelia."

I replace his hand with mine, realizing he was talking about my hickey. Without a response, I grip the door handle and step out of the car.

"And, Amelia?"

I cast a glance at him over my shoulder, not turning around.

"Were you lying about selling me your share of the brewery?"

I slowly shake my head.

"Be a woman of your word."

There's no need for me to reply, so I don't.

But I swear, right before I shut the door, I hear him desperately say, "Please, don't," under his breath before I slam the door.

45

JAX

THEY SAY it takes courage to admit when you're wrong.

And I've tried to muster up that courage for Amelia for weeks now.

I've wanted to tell her I lied when I said, "Maybe I was," after she asked if breaking her heart was my plan to gain full control of the brewery. I want to take back when I told her to be a woman of her word.

But then Amelia, sweet Amelia, proved she was exactly that.

"What the hell do you mean, she agreed to sell?" I shout at Marshall Haney.

"The ninety days ends soon. She wants to start the paperwork, so everything is ready when the time comes." Marshall scrunches his bushy eyebrows together. "Isn't that what you wanted?"

Marshall Haney, Dude Who Delivers Bad News at Law, called this morning and asked to schedule a meeting. In hopes of seeing Amelia, since she'd shown up last time I met with him, I scheduled his soonest available appointment.

Amelia has nine thousand percent become a silent business partner. No emails. Not even replies to me. No texts, even when

I send random questions. The pain-in-my-ass woman of her word acts as if I no longer exist.

I fucked up.

I did more than fuck up.

My father told me that verbatim.

My mother said it in kinder words.

But neither of them understands the torment of guilt festering inside me.

Guilt. That damn word.

It's as if it were a cuckoo clock on repeat, singing out every single hour, a heavy reminder of what Chris accused me of.

Then, last week, Amelia's father, Silas, paid me a visit at the brewery. I stood, positive he had come to kick my ass, but I'd accept it because I deserved to get my ass kicked for what I'd done. But that wasn't what he did.

He sat down across from me, and I returned to my chair.

Silas clasped his hands into his lap and asked to talk to me, not about his daughter, but as a friend who'd gone through a similar hell as I had.

Peculiarly, he was easy to speak with, and it helped.

Did it completely erase the guilt?

Fuck no.

But it helped me understand it better.

It was ... eye-opening? As corny as that sounds.

"Mr. Bridges?" Marshall asks, his voice cutting like a whip through my thoughts.

"Yeah, shoot, sorry." I shake my head. "Tell her I don't want it."

He stares at me, as if he'd just come out of a coma and I was the first person he saw. "Isn't that ... isn't that what you wanted?"

"Not anymore."

"I'll inform Amelia you've changed your mind ... unless you'd like to do it yourself?"

"I'll tell her myself."

She's cutting me off for good.

I start to brush past him when he says, "Oh, and one more thing, Jax."

I raise a brow.

He tugs an envelope from inside his blazer and holds it out for me. I leer at the envelope, seeing my name in familiar handwriting but in red ink this time.

Jesus, fuck. Not again.

My gaze flicks from the envelope and settles on Marshall. "What's this?"

He nudges the letter toward me, and flashbacks of when I did the same thing to Amelia in her entryway hit me. "It's for you."

I shake my head violently. "I don't want it."

"My job is to give it to you. What you do with it is none of my concern."

"Why now? Why didn't you give me this before?"

"Chris asked me to wait."

Not only does it seem like Amelia's life mission is to give me hell, but it seems like it's Chris's death mission as well— torturing me from the grave.

I take the envelope from Marshall.

He thanks me for coming and asks me to keep him updated on the future of Down Home Brewery.

I leave his office and get into my car. This time, I don't wait to open the envelope. I rip it open, dig out the folded paper, and toss the envelope onto the passenger floorboard.

Then, I read Chris's second letter.

The writing is neater, not sloppy, and there are no smudge marks this time.

Jax,
I want to start this letter with an apology. Sorry for the first one, man. I wrote it months ago and told

Marshall that even if I begged for it back, not to give it to me. I didn't want to throw it away, to take back what I'd written because at the time, it was how I felt. I won't lie, bro, and say those thoughts still don't creep up on me sometimes. But I'm sure you feel betrayed by me as well.

You're probably wondering why I didn't confront you. I wanted to. Hell, did I want to. I wrote that letter the day after Corey's death and took it to Marshall. He was my father's attorney, the one who'd broken the news to my mother that my father had left me everything.

The first time I planned to confront you was when I returned to the brewery following Corey's death, fresh after finding out about you and Amelia. I walked in, and you hugged me and then handed me a business plan for a new ale—one named Corey in memory of him, with all contributions going into a college fund for his one-year-old son.

The second time was my birthday. Amelia and your family threw me a surprise party. I didn't want to do it in front of your parents, so I sat back on the couch and watched you. I watched you watch her and realized I'd been blind as fuck to not see it earlier.

You were in love with my girl.

It was as clear as day.

You didn't stay away from her because of some stupid childhood rivalry that didn't make any sense. You stayed away because you wanted to be with her. And from reading Amelia's diary, she had feelings for you then too.

I was already deep in my suicidal thoughts, but instead of wishing you the worst upon my death, I want to do the opposite. But I don't want it to be easy, like I'm allowing Amelia to just fall into your lap. As bad as it sounds, I want you to suffer some for your secret, not for loving my girl.

So, you see, I'd wanted to die before I found out about you and Amelia, so don't put all the blame on yourself.

But if you are stupid and lose her, I want you to have this.

If she came to Marshall to sell her share, to change her mind, you need to stop her. Because, Jax, no matter how many plans I had to confront you, there was never a good time because you're a great dude.

You've been nothing but a good friend to me, even in times when I couldn't reciprocate.

I left Amelia the brewery for a reason.

Even though I was so furious with you for what you'd done, after I sat and thought about it, I knew you were the only one who I would trust with her heart again.

I don't want to live anymore.

But I want Amelia to.

Take care of her for me.

You're the only man I know who will.

May we meet again soon.

Chris

I drop the letter in my lap and cry my eyes out in the parking lot.

46

AMELIA

"YOU'RE NOT SELLING THE BREWERY," Jax says nearly in one breath as soon as I answer the door.

I cross my arms. "I am, and the first thing I'm doing with the check is hiring a doorman to stop you from showing up at my home, uninvited." I wave him off. "You got what you wanted. Bye now."

I wasn't sure when Marshall would tell Jax I'd decided to sell my share of the brewery. I'd battled with myself on what to do, but in the end, I'd decided my heart was just as valuable as memories of Christopher. I have plenty of memories with him—his letter, photos, mementos.

I wanted to keep the brewery so bad, but not at the expense of my heart.

Jax stares up at me in … expectancy? Like he could show up, tell me what to do, and I'd be all okay with it?

I think not, heartbreaker.

With his arm, he blocks me from shutting the door in his face. "Amelia, I made a mistake."

"*Mistakes*," I correct, kicking a foot out. "Plural. Meaning many of them."

Just like the past few times I've seen Jax, he isn't a man

who'd win the Happiest Man Alive award. He still towers over me, his face puffy—almost as if he's been crying—and brimming with desperation.

"I'm sorry," he says.

"Keep your apologies. I don't want them."

"Amelia—"

I stop him from moving past me into the townhome. "Leave, Jax!" I thrust my finger out toward the sidewalk, not caring if neighbors overhear me. "Get off my doorstep. Stay off it. And leave me alone."

"I won't buy it."

I stare at him indifferently and shrug. "It won't be hard, finding another buyer."

He tsks me. "Sweet Amelia, per our business agreement—the contract you also inherited with the brewery—all owners must be approved by both you and me. Spoiler alert: I'm not approving shit."

"In that case, as soon as you leave, I'll hire Essie to find me a loophole."

"*Please.*"

Never in the decades that I've known Jax has he ever pleaded like this. Not even when I stole his favorite Pokémon card or that time when I dared him to skinny-dip. I swiped his swim trunks and made him beg me to tell him where they were as he stood in front of me, his hands cupping between his legs.

Jax Bridges is not someone who begs.

"You made me feel whole again, Jax," I say, and his body jerks at the change in my tone. "I thought I was finding love again … and then you broke my heart. And instead of saying, *I'm sorry, Amelia. I'm too broken for you*, you said you did it to convince me to sell you my share of the brewery."

He jumps when I clap my hands.

"Guess what. It worked." I clap my hands again—three times. "Yay for you. I'll find the absolute worst buyer I can."

"Listen to me—"

I hold my hand up and speak over him. "Like I asked you to do at my parents', or after you fucked me outside on a stairway and then said, 'K, thanks, bye? Is that what you want to talk to me about, Jax? You've had weeks to talk to me but never did." I stop to blow out a series of breaths. "You didn't even give me my panties back, asshole."

A quick flash of a smile hits his lips at the last sentence. "Technically, they were ripped, and you wouldn't have been able to even put them back on anyway."

Yep. He totally kept them.

"That's not the point." I shake my head. "You dismissing me after that is the point. Your push and pull—"

"And you haven't pushed and pulled with me? All our lives, that's what we've done."

"We're not kids anymore, Jax." I repeat the same motion of pointing to the sidewalk. "You said what you needed to say, but your silence said more."

"We were both hurting."

"Hurt people don't always have to hurt people."

"I'm sorry," he says in a low voice. "I'm sorry. Please. Please accept my apology."

I cross my arms again. "I'll accept it, but it doesn't change anything, Jaxson."

"But I want it to change everything."

"Leave."

"I will make this up to you, Amelia. I will. I'll prove that you can trust me with your heart again."

"All you need to prove to me is that you'll stay away. You want to help me? Stay out of my way and buy the brewery from me. That's how you can make it up to me."

I slam the door in his face.

———

The next morning, I walk outside to find my tires slashed.

Any sane person would accuse the guy who begged on their doorstep for forgiveness, but Jax would never do something like that. Which means it was someone else.

I call the non-emergency line to file a police report, and ten minutes later, a cruiser pulls into the space next to mine. Kyle and Gage step out, donning their police uniforms, both middle-aged men who look nothing like their age. Ava wanted to kill me all the times I told her that her dad was a DILF.

Speaking of Ava, seconds later, her car comes swerving toward us, and her brakes squeak when she stops behind the cruiser.

"I was on the phone with my dad when the call came in," Ava explains as the three of them observe my car.

They don't get through many questions when a call comes through the radio.

"Vandalism call," the woman's voice says. "Down Home Brewery, off Kemper Avenue. Anyone close to take it?"

Gage clicks his radio. "Kyle and I are on our way."

Kyle closes his notepad and looks at me. "Your brewery, right? You can ride with us."

"No," I rush out. "I'll stay behind. You guys can take care of it."

"The brewery is your business too," Ava says like *duh.*

I haven't shared the news of my selling it to Jax. I'm not ready to hear the opinions on the matter yet.

"I'll ride with Ava," I tell them.

They nod, and we follow them to the brewery. I cover my mouth when we pull in. The front windows are busted, the exterior is spray-painted with neon colors—the words illegible—and the sign looks as if someone attempted to kick it in but didn't have the muscle to do so.

"This is weird," Ava says, parking her car.

"Way weird," I grumble, my skin crawling.

Even though I don't work here as much as Jax and the guys, I still feel violated. This is our business that we've worked so hard on, and then some asshole came to destroy it.

Jax's eyes are trained on me, as if there weren't two police officers and a rambling Ava at my side, as we approach him and Toby.

Toby is taking pictures of the damage with his phone.

"What happened?" I ask.

"I don't know." His gaze remains focused on me. "We checked the cameras, but the line had been cut. My guess is punk kids, probably trying to score alcohol for their next bonfire."

Kyle taps his finger against his cheek and stares at his nephew in concern. "Any chance it could be Mick and Sandra?"

Jax finally looks away from me to answer him. "Nah, we haven't heard from them again. Considering all their illegal activity, I'm sure they'll stay away. Their attorney contacted us, and I forwarded him to our lawyer. Since then, nothing."

"But what about Amelia's tires?" Ava asks. "The two have to be connected. Blue Beech isn't a place known for its high crime."

She's right. It's like *Mister Rogers' Neighborhood* half the time.

I motion with my finger slicing across my throat to get her to shush it.

Ava's eyes widen, and she mouths, *Sorry*, to me.

Jax's attention snaps back to me. "What happened to your tires?"

My face flushes. "Someone slashed them."

"What the fuck?" he roars, shocking everyone but me. "Why didn't you tell me?"

"Why would I tell you?"

"Because you're ..." His voice trails off as *everyone* awaits his answer.

I raise a brow. "Because I'm what?"

He changes the subject. "I called a contractor to look at the damage, and he'll be here tomorrow. Toby is boarding up the windows and keeping an eye on the brewery tonight." He looks at Ava. "I'll take Amelia home."

I can't help but smirk and correct him, "Ava will take me home."

Jax throws his arms up and shakes his head. "Fine. Then, I will follow you and Ava to your house. You're not staying there alone."

"I'll stay with Ava then." My attention swings to Ava. "You want to have a sleepover?"

"What is happening?" I hear Gage ask Kyle in the distance.

"My guess is, Jax likes Amelia, but she doesn't like him at the moment," Kyle replies with a chuckle.

"I work a double tonight." Ava chews on her lip, apology on her face. "But the loft is all yours, Amelia."

Like most of my friends, she's still at her parents', living in the loft above their garage.

"Looks like we're having a sleepover at Ava's," Jax says, feigning excitement.

"I think the fuck not," Gage shouts from behind Jax.

Jax lowers his voice, as if he's sick of our audience. "I'm only trying to protect you."

Ava, who apparently has the ears of a moth, chimes in again, "She can stay with her dad to keep her safe, or *my dad* is literally a cop who lives, like, five feet from my loft. She's covered in the safety department."

"Thanks for the town directory, but I don't give a shit about any of that," Jax tells Ava before tapping his watch. "And didn't you say you have to work? Get to the hospital and save lives. Amelia has to stay, so we can discuss a few things as *partners*."

"I am so happy I accepted all dares to spit in your cups when we were kids," Ava says to Jax before turning and giving me a *what do you want me to do* look.

"Go ahead," I grumble. "I'll get rid of him and call you when I make it to the loft."

Jax snorts.

She hugs me good-bye. Kyle and Gage ask all the questions cops need to know when your business has been trashed, and when they leave, I childishly kick Jax in the shin.

"What the fuck?" he hisses, bending over.

"Really?" I coldly glare at him. "You just made a scene as if I were a teenager being scolded."

"Eh, I think it's more of a toddler being scolded because that's the current age you're acting."

"I don't need you, Jax."

"Too bad because I need you."

47

JAX

AMELIA CAN LOOK like she wants to scratch my face off all she wants, but she's not hanging out at her house, in Ava's loft, or anywhere alone until we figure out who slashed her tires.

Ava's annoying ass was right.

The two have to be connected.

We chat with Toby for a while, who says he'll keep an eye on the place. I tell him it isn't necessary, that it is my job, but he says he needs the overtime pay anyway. Then, I call a tow truck company and have Amelia's car moved to a repair shop for new tires.

"Take me home," Amelia demands when we're in my car.

I keep my eyes on the minivan in front of me, the kids in the backseat sticking their tongues out at us. "Why not mine?"

"If you're so adamant on protecting me, which I couldn't care less about, we're doing it on my terms. Otherwise, go to your house, and I'll call you if I see any tire-slashers lingering around."

"Amelia." I blow out a ragged breath. "I'm not trying to be a dick. I want to protect you."

She scoffs. "From what?"

"Oh, I don't know. Chris's psychotic-ass family?"

280

"We don't even know if it was them."

"Whoever it was, I'm not taking the chance of them fucking with you again."

"You should've protected me when you were breaking my heart."

I grip the steering wheel, not wanting to go there because I need Amelia to not kick me out of her house. We'll save that chat for when she can't tuck and roll out of my car.

"Are you sure you don't want to stay at my place?" I ask. "Your laundry room floor kills my back."

"Sorry, Senior Citizen Jaxson, but no. And you don't need to worry about the comfort of the laundry room because you're sleeping on the front doorstep, where you love to hang out anyway."

My stomach grumbles as I ignore her comment. We both know that's not where I'll be laying my head down tonight. Not that I expect her to sleep with me, but I won't have the same sleeping arrangements as the random animals that come to her door at night because she feeds them.

Chris showed me pictures of her feeding a racoon once. She'd put Cheerios, peanuts, and a deli sandwich on a plate, as if it were a toddler, and left it out for the animal. Yeah, not about to get attacked by Rocky Racoon because he thinks I stole his ham sandwich.

And since my thoughts are on food, I turn in the opposite direction of her house. "I'm starving. Lunch at Shirley's it is."

She lets out a sharp laugh. "Oh, man. That starvation must've already hit your brain if you think that's happening."

Rather than answer her and get smacked with another insult, I stay quiet, and so does she until I turn the corner and veer into the diner's parking lot.

"Are you nuts?" she shrieks, causing my ears to ring.

I start unbuckling my seat belt, and her hand flies out, stopping me.

"Do you not remember the last time we were at Shirley's together?"

I nod, turning to look at her and hoping she detects my remorse. "I do, which is why I need to make it up to you." I force myself to put some pep in my voice. "And what better way to apologize for my stupid behavior than to feed you as well?"

She isn't having it. "Feed me an M&M's granola bar for all I care."

I carefully ease her hand off the seat belt and finish unbuckling it. "I've never seen those on the menu, but I'll be sure to ask."

"People will see us together." She wraps her hand around my wrist, her face pleading, as if stepping into that diner will condemn her to hell.

"I don't give a shit," I say with all the honesty in the world.

She icily stares at me. "Since when do you not care about that?"

"Since I became a man on a mission to get his girl back."

She winces at my response. "I was never *your girl*."

"Bullshit," I hiss, shifting to face her. "Who was in my bed every night for weeks, Amelia?"

She presses her lips together and doesn't answer.

"You. Who did you have an out-of-town date night with?"

Silence from her.

"Me." My voice speeds up, the same as my heart. "Who told me she loved me?"

Her eyes water, but there are no words.

"You."

"Stop, Jax," she says around a shaky breath.

I don't stop. I can't stop. "And who fucking told you he loved you back?"

"I said, stop it," she bites out.

"How much more do I need to go on?"

"Who did you fuck and then tell to leave?" she screams before stabbing her hand into her chest. "Me, Jax! Me!"

That shuts my ass up real quick.

I reverse out of the parking lot, both of our breathing ragged, and drive to her townhome.

———

Amelia stays in the living room, working on her computer, and keeps her distance from me the rest of the day. The only time she *reluctantly* talks to me is when I have my buddy, who owns a security company, come to the house and install the best alarm system on the market.

It's late, and we just finished our How to Work Your New Alarm 101 when there's a knock on the door.

Amelia turns away from me and rushes to the door, her bare feet pitter-pattering along the tiles.

"Whoa," I say, stopping her before she gets there, as if Mick is on the other side with a chain saw. "I'll get it."

Ignoring me, she swings the door open. The same teenage boy who saw me being an asshole to Amelia at the diner is holding up a takeout bag with Shirley's logo on it.

His eyes bulge as his gaze pings back and forth between Amelia and me.

Oh, he definitely recognizes us.

"Uh ..." he mutters, holding up the bag. "Shirley's delivery."

Amelia opens her purse that's hanging from the hook across from the door, dragging out her wallet, but I quickly snag a hundred-dollar bill from my wallet and exchange the food for the cash.

"Really?" I ask when she tells the teenager bye and shuts the door.

"What?" She shrugs. "I've been craving Shirley's since we left."

"We could've easily gone in."

"Jax, there's nothing *easy* between us right now."

That's the understatement of the goddamn year.

Amelia strolls into the living room, flashes of her bare back showing under her crop top doing crazy things to me, and plops down on the living room floor. I have some faith that she doesn't want to castrate me in my sleep when she holds up a sandwich.

"Burger. Pepper jack cheese. No pickle."

"Thanks."

Like most of the day, we eat in silence. The Animal Planet channel is playing on the TV, but I don't watch it.

"You still do that?"

Amelia cocks her head, a ketchup packet in her hand. "Do what?"

I chuckle. "Take the onion out of the onion ring?"

"Sure do." She picks one up. "You know I hate onions."

"Yes, but you love onion rings."

"I love the onion ring batter," she corrects, and her shoulders straighten, as if something dawned on her. "I should invent an onion ring batter chip ... or cookie. Yeah, most definitely a cookie." She slides a long onion from a ring and settles it onto a napkin, as if it were the nastiest thing in the world.

I shake my head. "I think you should stick with the brewery, baby."

She levels her eyes on me. "The brewery won't be mine for long."

"That's where you're wrong." I point a French fry at her. "You thought I was a dick, trying to run you off. Just wait until you even attempt to bring someone else around."

"Why are you making this difficult?"

"Why are *you* making this difficult?"

"My forgiveness no longer comes easy, Jax."

———

When the clock strikes midnight, as if it were her bedtime, Amelia stands from the couch. We've spent the past few hours watching an old-school vet save lives. At first, I was bored as fuck, but then I saw how content it made Amelia and got into it. It's actually not bad.

"You sure you don't want to change your mind and stay at my place?" I ask Amelia, standing and stretching my arms. "I hate that laundry room floor."

She releases her hair from its ponytail, and it drapes over her shoulders as it falls.

I hate how just that simple movement from her causes my dick to stir. I shift from one foot to the other, telling my cock to calm down.

"You can take the guest room," she says, jerking her head in that direction. "If someone tries to hurt me, I'll scream."

I can't stop myself from saying, "I remember when I used to make you scream."

She moves toward me, swinging her hips with every step, and stands on her tiptoes. My cock twitches in excitement. Her lips linger in front of mine, and I open my mouth, thanking the good Lord above for whatever just came over Amelia.

She does a double slap along my cheek, drops back onto her heels, and laughs. "Memories are all you'll have."

I swallow, rerunning what she just did in my head. I watch her stroll past the laundry room, and then she enters her bedroom, as if it's nothing.

Uh, what?

I follow and am immediately hit with the smell of her—a combination of citrus and apple blossoms.

My bedroom smelled like this each time she came over.

And then each time she left.

But that scent is gone now, and damn, do I miss it.

"Whoa," I say, standing in the doorway, watching her unclasp a necklace and set it on a nightstand. "You're sleeping in here now?"

Her cheeks flush as she nods.

I lean against the door. "Since when?"

"I started on the bedroom floor first a few weeks ago. One

night, it got so uncomfortable, so my on-half-a-melatonin brain moved me right on up to the bed. It was like the shove I needed." She motions toward the hallway. "The guest room, laundry room, porch, or wherever is all yours."

I don't back out of the room. Instead, I inch farther into it, keeping an eye out for any flying objects headed in my direction.

"What are you doing?" she hisses.

"You said *wherever* is all mine." I peer down at the carpet. "And, floor, I choose you."

She shrugs, tugging her tee off, so she's only wearing a thin sports bra, her nipples peeking through. "Fine."

She removes her ninety thousand pillows, and I grunt when one gets thrown at my head. Catching it, I smirk.

"Thanks, babe. I needed this." I whistle. "Now, how about a blanket?"

She flips the light off.

I undress to only my boxer briefs and apologize to my body for making it sleep on a floor. I dramatically fluff the pillow a few times, lie down on the floor, move, and fluff the pillow again. I am as loud as possible in an effort to get comfortable.

"Oh my God," she groans, flinging a blanket at me, and like the pillow, it also whacks me in the head.

———

I'm cold, half-asleep, and so uncomfortable when I hear Amelia gasp in her sleep. At first, I think she's dreaming—hopefully about me—but then she whimpers before crying out loud.

Something isn't right.

I throw the blanket off and practically dive into her bed. Sliding underneath the blankets, I find her tucked into the fetal position, sucking in deep breaths.

"I got you, baby," I say as she stretches out and allows me to pull her into my arms. "I got you."

Falling on my back, I take her with me, and without delay,

she snuggles into my side, resting her cheek and hand to my chest.

"My therapist says it's normal," she says, soft-spoken, into the darkness. "She said it helps that I stay in here and don't run out of the room."

I run a hand down her bare arm, and she shivers. "Does it work?"

"It does."

"I'm proud of you. This is big, Amelia."

She scoots in closer to me, a light whimper leaving her.

My hand slips up her shoulder and into her hair, massaging her scalp. "When was the first time you slept in here?"

"The night after you broke up with me."

My hand in her hair freezes. "And the bed?"

"The day you took me home from Essie's and I said I'd sell you the brewery. It's like with each shove, you pushed me back in here, I guess."

I squeeze my eyes shut, hating every reminder of all the times I've hurt her. "I miss you."

"I miss you too."

And just like in the motel room, when it wasn't supposed to happen, we kiss.

48

AMELIA

THIS IS *NOT* a chapter in my *let's see if Jax is being genuine and make him grovel* book.

In my book, there's no kissing.

No Jax's tongue darting into my mouth, dancing with mine.

No Jax shifting me onto my side, hiking my leg up around his waist, and slipping his hand beneath my sleep shorts.

No Jax pushing me onto my back, pulling down my bra, and sucking on my nipple.

No Jax gently playing with my clit, as if it's his favorite toy he must be careful with.

No Jax shoving not one, not two, but three skilled fingers inside me, groaning in my mouth about how much he loves how my pussy takes his fingers and dick.

No moans—ninety-five percent of them mine—radiating through the room.

No me begging him for more and him scooting down my body.

No him praising my pussy until I'm crying out his name to the ceiling.

None of that was in my plan, but sometimes, Jax Bridges starts kissing you, and all your plans get shot to hell.

My legs are shaking, and I open my eyes to find Jax on his knees between them, staring down at me, his boxer briefs down his thighs.

Did I pull those down? I honestly don't recall.

No. It was him. Because I demanded it.

The moonlight peeks through the blinds, giving me a tiny glimpse of him stroking himself while telling me how much he's missed being inside me, breaking down the details of how he'll fuck me nice and slow.

And just as he starts guiding himself into my entrance, I clamp my legs tight around him and say, "Wait."

He freezes, waiting for me to elaborate on my outburst.

My vagina is telling me I'm a stupid, stupid girl because it'd love nothing more than Jax's cock, but I have to stand my ground.

Well, half-stand my ground because his mouth was just between my legs.

"I changed my mind," I say with a shaky breath. "You can leave now."

A dose of his own medicine.

His hand drops from his cock, but it's so hard that it doesn't move. "What?"

"Get back on the floor and stroke your cock, Bridges."

He shakes his head, as if he didn't hear me correctly.

"I'm not having you screw me and then say, *Oh, good-bye.* Heck, I wouldn't even be surprised if you told me to leave my own home."

"Bullshit, Amelia. You know that wouldn't happen."

"Hmm …"

He moves from between my legs, crawls up the bed, kisses my shoulder, and collapses onto his back next to me. "Is this my punishment? Like you actually want to *torture*, torture me?"

"I'm just suddenly so tired." I fake a loud yawn. "And so is my vagina. She has a curfew."

"Can I at least stay in the bed?" I can't tell if he's whining or forcing back a laugh. "I'm not saying you have to get me off. My dick will sadly stay to himself. *But* can't a guy get a mattress for consoling you and then eating you until you fell apart underneath him? Not to say that I didn't enjoy either one of those things because I most certainly did."

"Fine, you can sleep in the bed." I fake annoyance.

He turns on his belly, lifting himself up on one elbow, and stares down at me. "And we can still spoon, right?"

I groan, swatting him away when he licks my cheek. "Ugh, fine, but you're pushing your luck."

He kisses my nose and pulls back to look at me. I can't see him that well, but it's as if I can feel his eyes searching mine, tender yet hesitant.

Then, he shifts to his side and whispers, "Turn and face me, Amelia."

I do as he asked.

He reaches out and runs his hand through my hair. Tears well in my eyes at his gentleness, at how he's touching me as if I'm the most important person in his life.

"And I can call you mine again, right?" he softly asks, brushing his hand over my cheek. His voice is thick with emotion.

But I can't give him that yet.

I can't be his again because the next time I allow someone to call me his, I have to be certain he'll stay.

My heart wrenches in my chest, and my throat burns with the need to tell him yes, but I can't.

"Go to sleep, Jaxson."

In a faint whisper, he says, "I love you."

I lie there, and it hits me.

He calmed me down during my panic attack in the bedroom.

And then we almost had sex in this bed, in the one I'd shared with Christopher, and I'm not freaking out.

My hurt is my storm.

And Jax seems to be my shelter.

49

JAX

STANDING IN THE DOORWAY, I admire Amelia—her sexy bedhead hair, plump lips, nipples showing through her thin sports bra … and I slightly drool.

That's my girl.

Well, who I want to be my girl, but she's not making it easy on me.

I place my hand on the nightstand and slip back underneath the sheets with her. I've missed her body heat since I dragged my sleepy ass out of bed when my phone rang in my pants pocket. I snuck into the living room, not wanting to wake her up, and tuned in to the information Uncle Kyle recited.

My elbow digs into my pillow as I stare down at her, tip my head down, and gently brush my lips against hers. She stirs, one eye opening and then the other, and I hope she doesn't kick me in the balls for waking her up like she's damn Sleeping Beauty.

I'm still trying to wrap my head around last night. I can't blame Amelia for her doubt toward me. My track record with her hasn't been the best these past few weeks. If she wants me to prove I'm not a flight risk, then that's what I'll do.

"Morning," I say in a hushed voice, drawing back.

"Morning," she whispers.

"It seems we can blame Sandra and Mick for the vandalism and tire-slashing after all." I love starting the day with pleasant news.

She groans. "Ugh, hearing those goblins' names first thing in the morning is like a bad omen for the rest of the day." She snatches one of her pillows and rests it over her face. "Wake me up tomorrow."

I chuckle. "Sorry, Millie, baby, but we have to be brewery bound. Toby shot good ole Mick."

"What?" she squeals, shoving the pillow off her face and swatting it away. "Is he dead?"

"Nah." I scrub a hand over my face. "Toby took out one of his kneecaps. Mick will live. He'll just wobble when he walks."

"That's unfortunate." Her cheeks redden. "Why did they even go back? Didn't they do enough damage?"

"Mick told the officers that he thought it was me in the office, not Toby."

She sucks in a breath. "So that means he went there to hurt you … like kill you?"

"Sure does, sweetheart." I'm particularly calm for a man who found out another guy had planned to shoot him last night. But it was Mick, and Mick is a fucking idiot. I'd welcome Mick to show up and try to kill me because I'd love to be the one to put him ten feet in the ground myself. I wouldn't aim for the kneecaps.

"That might be a worse omen to start your day with," I add.

"What happens now?"

"Mick and Sandra are in jail since she was the getaway driver. They found enough meth at their house to keep the town high enough for a month. My uncle said they'll most likely be locked up for a while."

———

Hours later, Amelia and I trudge into the townhome with heavy eyes and endless yawns.

She didn't exactly invite me inside, but she didn't stop me from stepping out of the car and following her either.

Even on the brink of exhaustion, I've held my tongue back all day.

We need to have the dreaded *what are we* talk.

The day has been long. We went to the brewery, had Amelia's tires replaced, and then stopped for dinner at Shirley's.

Yep, Amelia agreed.

It was her idea actually.

We walked in and got gawked at—unsurprisingly—but eventually, everyone's attention went elsewhere. There were whispers, yes, but what's a small town without low murmurs and heavy gossip?

I lean against the doorframe to Amelia's room as she rummages through a drawer, and I cross my arms while observing our surroundings—something I didn't do last night.

My breathing briefly stops at the realization that there's no sign of Chris. The picture of them on the nightstand, his clothes draped over the white chair in the corner, and his exercise equipment—all gone.

"You moved his stuff out." It's more of a statement rather than a question.

She nods, sitting on the edge of the bed and kicking off her sandals. "The stuff I haven't gone through yet is in the guest room."

"Did you do it by yourself?"

"My parents helped."

Look at my girl.

She's stronger than me.

I draw in a shallow breath, and a weight settles in my chest at her progress—allowing her heart to heal, sleeping in her bed, and closing her chapter with Chris. Not forgetting him, but just moving on to a new page.

I tug at the collar of my shirt, as if someone cranked up the heat, and my voice is strangled when I say, "Chris's death, it fucked me up."

She stills, staring at me, speechless.

Which is okay.

I need to get this out.

I step farther into the room, each step feeling heavier in my sneakers. "But that letter?" A thickness forms in my throat. "It did a number on me."

"Jax," she whispers, touching her throat, as if she wants to say more, but the words aren't coming.

Even though it's a short distance, the walk to her seems like hours before I reach the bed. I fall on my knees in front of her, as if I'm a man ready to unveil his deepest confessions.

And maybe that's what I'm doing.

I'm not a man who wears his heart on his sleeve.

No one would be able to win the What Is Jax Feeling game.

I can't rehearse love devotions, nor do I want to.

Whatever I profess to Amelia tonight will be raw and real.

Something no one has ever gotten from me.

Something that only Amelia will ever be able to tear out of me.

I tilt up my head, my eyes meeting hers.

Please see the truth in them.

For the love of God, please see that you're my heart.

"After reading his letter, every time I did anything, I'd think, *Chris can't do this any longer because of choices I made*," I say, staring up into her eyes. "I'd get into my car: *Chris can't drive anymore.* I'd go to Down Home Pub: *Chris can no longer enjoy a beer here.* I'd see you: *Chris can no longer be with Amelia.* And in my mind, I thought he would be able to if it wasn't for me."

"Jax," she whispers.

I rest my hands on her knees, no doubt the anguish on my face as transparent as water. "I made a mistake. I was just in so much pain—but that isn't an excuse, I know. I should've never said the things that I did, and I can promise you right now, that'll never happen again." My grip tightens on her knees. "I don't know if you have it in you to forgive me, and if you don't, I'll completely understand and respect that decision. But if you do, I beg that you give me that chance. The chance to make up for the hurt I caused you. To prove how much I love you. I don't believe in second chances, but this time—and only this time—I'm begging you to please give me that chance."

Tears well in her eyes.

I focus intently on her face, the need to witness her every reaction to my words. "I'm in love with you, Amelia. Hell, I didn't even know what love was before. And I want to say, hey, maybe that's why I fucked up, but it's not an excuse. I know what love is because it's how I feel when I walk into a room and see you, how it lights me up inside when I make you laugh, how you're the only woman I ever want to touch again, and how it's felt like I'm living life with a knife through my chest after losing you."

I've emptied all that I have, exposed every emotion, and I pray to the good man above that it's enough. My eyes mist, and my heart thunders against my chest, telling me it'll also leave me if I fucked this up and lost her.

I wait.

Wait for her to declare my future—whether I'll be one of those men who stays brokenhearted for the rest of his life or if I'll have the chance to devote my everything into being the man she needs, the man she deserves.

"Jaxson," she says, tears falling down her cheeks, and she reaches her hands out to stroke my hair. "How can I say no to that?"

That isn't enough.

It isn't enough to get my goddamn heart to calm down.

"Say it," I choke out. "I want to hear you say it."

She sobs, grabbing at my elbows in an attempt to pull me to my feet. Instead, I lean in closer to her, both my arms resting alongside her legs, and shift my chest forward until my face is mere inches from hers.

"I'm in love with you," she says, her voice soothing.

"With who, Amelia? Who are you in love with?"

Her hand slides from my hair down to the light scruff on my cheek. She strokes my face the same way she stroked my hair. "With you, Jaxson. I'm in love with you."

I smirk, give myself a mental pat on the back, and kiss her.

It's not quick and urgent and forbidden, like so many of our other kisses.

It's slow as we take a moment for our tongues to meet.

She whimpers, "I love you," again as I lower her onto the bed.

I rain kisses along her jawline before returning to her mouth to breathe, "Who do you love?" into it.

"Y-O-U," she says, her tongue tracing my lips.

I undress her, and she pulls my shirt over my head and unbuckles my jeans, freeing my cock from them. It jerks in her hand, but I ignore how hard it's aching for her.

Instead, I kiss every inch of her body in a leisurely pace as she writhes underneath me and says, "If you love me, you'll stop going so slow."

I love her, but that doesn't mean I listen.

My mouth pays the most attention to her nipples, sucking on each of them and twirling my tongue along the hard pebbles, but that changes as I slide down, settling my face between her legs. That's where I could spend forever and never get bored.

I slide my finger between the lips of her pussy, keeping that same slow pace, and with a surprising strength, she pushes me closer to her, aiming for my cock to be inside her pussy.

Then, I bend down, grab a condom from my pants pocket, and give her what she wants.

I slide my dick in, inch by inch.

My strokes are deep and precise and unhurried as I make

love to the woman I love. And when I know she's close, oh-so close, I ask her if she's my girl.

She looks into my eyes and says, "I think, in a way, I always have been."

———

"Jax Bridges is a poet, and I didn't know it."

"Baby, my love proclamation was far from a haiku, *but* I told you I'm a man of many skills," I say as we lie next to each other in bed.

She mindlessly strokes my chest. "You never asked if I read my letter from Chris."

I peer down at her. "Did you?"

She nods. "You don't want to know what it said?"

"No."

"Why?"

"I already placed enough blame on my shoulders. I don't know how much more I can hold before I collapse."

"He wasn't mad in his letter to me. Hurt? Yes. But angry? No."

I appreciate Chris saving her from that pain.

For placing it all on me.

I twirl a strand of her hair around my finger. "At least he didn't wait until the second letter to do that with you."

"Second letter?" She rises to stare at me with wide eyes. "You got a second letter?"

I nod.

"Can I know what it says?"

"He asked me to take care of you."

Her entire demeanor changes. "Is that why you're asking for forgiveness? To fulfill his wish for you to take care of me—whatever that means?"

"No. I could *take care of you* and not be with you, Amelia."

"Why did you wait so long to tell me this?"

"I needed to work on myself to be strong enough for you—to be the man you deserve. I talked to my mom, my dad, your goddamn father. I couldn't fix our relationship until I fixed myself. I refused to give you a broken man since broken men can do stupid shit that make them lose their girls."

50

AMELIA

"I DON'T MEAN to be mean, but you guys are really boring now that you like each other," Essie tells Jax and me from across the pub table.

River laughs, stretching his arm along the back of his stool and Ava's. "Leave them alone, my demon sister."

Essie flips him off.

"Geesh, why is your attitude the one I'd expect when your parents finally cut you off?" Jax asks.

She flips him off next, her nails a pale pink.

"Adrian Castillo is what's wrong with her," River replies as if he were Essie's spokesperson. "A new guy at the firm. Essie and he are vying for the same open position."

"First off, there's no competition because I am a better attorney," Essie quips.

"Adrian Castillo … the name sounds familiar," Easton says, knocking on the table, thinking.

"We roomed together in undergrad," River says.

"That's before you dropped out, right?" Mia asks from next to him, her posture nearly perfect on her stool.

River shrugs. "The college life wasn't for me." He grabs his glass of whiskey. "You don't need a degree to build video games when you've been doing it since you were three."

"Or when you have a dad who's the best developer and gets your foot in the door," Ava counters.

"Anyway," Essie says, as if she's the only one who can give her brother hell, "Adrian is an asshole, and soon, I might have to represent myself after I commit coworker homicide." She performs a sweeping gesture around the table. "One of you'd better send bail money too."

"Adrian is hot though," Ava says with a tipsy smile. "We met him a few years back at some frat party."

River drums his fingers along his glass. "The frat party I told you and my sister *not* to attend."

"You said you had a hot roommate," Ava argues. "We had to see for ourselves."

Jax points to Ava. "Never did I say, *Adrian, my roommate, is hot.*"

"He's right," Essie says, scrunching up her face. "He didn't, but we stupidly wanted to see if he was hot. Too bad he ended up being an asshole from hell."

"A *hot* asshole from hell though," Ava corrects.

Essie plucks the cherry out of Ava's glass and tosses it at her. "You're supposed to be Team Essie, traitor."

"We are Team Essie," Callie says.

"We're not rooting for him." Ava brightly smiles. "Call it *keeping a good eye on your competition.*"

"How is the brewery going?" Mia asks, ready to move on to another subject. "Is everything back in order?"

"We're good to go," Jax answers, referring to Mick and Sandra's vandalism.

They were simple fixes, and if a few busted windows and paint were all it took for those monsters to get themselves locked up, then it was worth it.

Obviously, I didn't sell my half of the brewery to Jax. Business has tripled since we stopped our *silent partners* charade and became Team JA, as Jax likes to call it. We've scouted out land for a second location, and last week, I sold my social media marketing client list, so I could focus solely on the brewery. It brings me happiness, and I get to work with Jax. Win-win.

Toby was promoted to manager, giving Jax and me the luxury of spending time together outside the brewery. At first, when we walked into Down Home, or a carnival, or a town event here, people would gawk at us like *we* were the night's entertainment. But it's gotten better. That, or I've improved on not caring.

And once a week, we meet up with our friends at Down Home to catch up.

I've climbed out of my corner of isolation into a world I once loved, and all with the help of the guy next to me … whose hand is slowly creeping up my skirt as the conversation moves to something else. I'm not sure what that something is since his hand up the skirt and all.

I smack his hand and hiss, "Stop it."

"Stop what?" A devious grin is on his face.

I roll my eyes and jerk my head toward my lap, where his hand remains.

He tips his head down and whispers, "I think it's time for us to leave," into my ear, and I can't stop myself from inching my thighs a little farther apart.

"I hate when you do that."

"Hate what? When I play with you?"

My heart speeds up in my chest. "Make me want to straddle you right here in this bar."

Jax's hand tightens around my thigh before it abruptly leaves. He stands, throws cash onto the table, and drags me off of my stool. "It's my and Amelia's bedtime."

River scoffs. "I figured either that was coming or Amelia was about to." River slides his thumb back and forth over his glass before giving us a cheers motion.

My face turns as red as the cherry Essie threw at Ava.

The rest of the table looks confused, so at least that's a plus.

"I think it's most definitely our bedtime then," I mutter.

Everyone shares quick good-byes, good nights, have funs right before Jax and I rush out of the back of the pub and up the stairs to his apartment.

Stairs that I once hated, but on a quiet night when the pub closed early, I told Jax he needed to fuck me there again. He stared at me as if I'd grown a horn out of my forehead, but I told him I needed a new memory there.

And that's exactly what he did.

Three times.

———

"I think this is the one," I say, peering over at Jax in an empty living room with a vaulted ceiling, superior natural lighting, and a white-stoned fireplace.

"New build, four bedrooms, the perfect home for a couple wanting to start a family," Jeanine, our realtor, rattles off with a *come on, buy it* smile.

I don't blame her. This is the sixth house we've looked at, and none have screamed *the home of Jax and Amelia* yet.

Until this one.

I sold my townhome and moved in with Jax. It wasn't like we weren't practically living together anyway. We just rotated beds every other day.

Jax is paying no mind to the home or Jeanine. His attention is on me. "If this is the one, then it's the one." He flashes a quick glance at Jeanine. "Write an offer."

Jeanine eagerly nods and throws her arms into the air. "Yay! I'll call the sellers' realtor now and let her know!"

She scurries off, and I inhale the strong smell of the man I love as he steps in front of me. I relax into his touch, the tension of house-hunting melting away when he wraps his arms around my waist.

"I'm happy you like it, baby." He presses a lingering kiss on my lips.

"But do *you* like it?"

"I like whatever you like." Another kiss.

"Really." I slap his shoulder. "I want this to be *our* home, Jax."

He returns to his place and nuzzles my neck. "Baby, you are my home."

"You know what I mean."

"No, that's exactly what I mean. It can be here, the apartment, or hell, even the Pink Elephant Motel."

I smile at the memory.

"When I am with you, I am content. I will lay my head down next to you anywhere."

He kisses my neck, and my body trembles in his hold.

If he doesn't stop touching me like this and saying these sweet things, we'll be forced to buy it when Jeanine walks in on us having sex.

"*Plus,*" he says, and his tone bleeds with tenderness, "you told me this morning we'd have babies soon. I'll buy you the whole damn block if you want it."

Not caring about Jeanine, I stand on my tiptoes and kiss the man, sliding some tongue in there as he grabs my ass and pulls me into him.

Our journey to happiness wasn't easy. It hurt, it stung, and some might even call it unconventional, given what brought our hearts together, but it only made us stronger.

Our parents were wrong.

We were never rivals.

We were just two kids fighting the spell of falling in love, who then grew up and couldn't fight it anymore.

epilogue

JAX

Chris,

I want to start this by saying, I miss you every single day.

It took me a while to understand why my best friend had decided to leave us, but I'm learning, and I'm sorry you went through feeling as if you were alone.

But you're making changes down here. We've raised $90,000 for Corey's son from his craft beer sales. And then we named a beer after you. It took a while, but we figured out a way to mix your two favorites into one. All proceeds will go toward the American Foundation for Suicide Prevention. You'll be helping those who are going through the hurt you had. Your beer will help save lives.

Can't wait until we meet again someday and share a beer, brother.

Jax

PS. She's in good hands, I promise.

I FINISH THE LETTER, place it back into the drawer where I keep the last one he left for me, and sigh. Then, I stand and slip the diamond engagement ring into my pocket.

Next time I return to this desk, I hope to be engaged.

also by charity ferrell

Blue Beech Series

(each book can be read as a standalone)

Just A Fling

Just One Night

Just Exes

Just Neighbors

Just Roommates

Just Friends

Only You Series: A Blue Beech Second Generation

(each book can be read as a standalone)

Only Rivals

Twisted Fox Series

(each book can be read as a standalone)

Stirred

Shaken

Straight Up

Chaser

Last Round

Marchetti Mafia Series

(each book can be read as a standalone)

Gorgeous Monster

Gorgeous Prince

Standalones

Bad For You

Beneath Our Faults

Beneath Our Loss

Pretty and Reckless

Thorns and Roses

Wild Thoughts

Risky Duet

Risky

Worth The Risk

about the author

Charity Ferrell is a USA Today and Wall Street Journal best-selling author of the Twisted Fox and Blue Beech series. She resides in Indianapolis, Indiana with her fiancé and two fur babies. She loves writing about broken people finding love while adding humor and heartbreak along with it. Angst is her happy place.

When she's not writing, she's making a Starbucks run, shopping online, or spending time with her family.

Visit my website here:
www.charityferrell.com

Made in the USA
Monee, IL
18 June 2023

36078494R00182